TORCHWOOD

BORDER PRINCES

TORCHWOOD
BORDER PRINCES

Dan Abnett

10 9 8 7 6 5 4 3 2 1

BBC Books, an imprint of Ebury Publishing,
20 Vauxhall Bridge Road,
London SW1V 2SA

BBC Books is part of the Penguin Random House group of companies
whose addresses can be found at global.penguinrandomhouse.com

Penguin
Random House
UK

Torchwood is a BBC Wales production for BBC Three
Executive Producers: Russell T Davies and Julie Gardner
Producer: Richard Stokes
Project Editor: Steve Tribe
Production Controller: Peter Hunt

First published by BBC Books in 2007
This paperback edition published by BBC Books in 2018

www.penguin.co.uk

A CIP catalogue record for this book is available from the British Library

ISBN 9781785944178

Cover design by Lee Binding @ Tea Lady © BBC 2007
Typeset in Albertina and Century Gothic

Printed and bound in Great Britain by Clays Ltd, Elcograf S.p.A.

Penguin Random House is committed to a sustainable future for our
business, our readers and our planet. This book is made from Forest
Stewardship Council® certified paper.

For Gary Russell

ONE

The End of the World began on a Thursday night in October, just after eight in the evening.

It began with filthy, spitting rain creeping inland from the Bristol Channel, with a black SUV hammering east along the Penarth Road, with the bleep of a text message received.

'Scale of one to ten?' Owen asked. He was driving, peering out at traffic barely visible in the veil of rain.

'One being slightly pressing and ten being insanely urgent?' Jack wondered from the passenger seat.

'Yeah.'

'About twenty-six, twenty-seven,' Jack replied mildly. He held up his mobile phone so that Owen could glance over and read the screen.

THE END OF THE WORLD.

'Captain Analogy strikes again,' said Owen.

'There's only room for one captain on this team,' Jack replied, flipping the clam-shell mobile shut. 'Uh, Owen…' he added.

Looking at Jack's mobile had taken Owen's eyes away from the road long enough for tail lights to bloom bright like distress flares dead ahead. Owen stood on the brakes, rocking the SUV nose down, and downshifted to go around.

Headlights blinded them, oncoming and bright. A horn blared.

Owen made a tutting noise and hauled the SUV back into lane. Lurched hard in his inertia-reels by the drastic deceleration-acceleration-deceleration, Jack maintained a surprisingly beatific composure.

'Sorry,' said Owen, hands tight and white on the wheel. 'Sorry about that.'

'No problem.'

'You seem remarkably relaxed.'

'It's the End of the World. A head-on prang on the Penarth Road seems somehow trivial by comparison.'

'Ah,' said Owen. The traffic ahead began to space out again.

'Of course,' said Jack, 'he could be wrong.'

'He's usually right,' Owen corrected. 'Captain – sorry, Analogy Lad – has a nose for these things.'

The text bleep sounded again.

'What's he saying now?' asked Owen.

'Boiled egg,' said Jack.

Owen floored the accelerator.

Boiled egg. 'Four minutes or less.'

Gwen ran across the road in the sheeting rain towards the messy huddle of buildings cowering by the riverside. There were lights on in a nearby pub, a late shop, and a row of houses. The hiss of the rain was like persistent static.

The buildings directly ahead were derelict, and seemed to have been left in a state of schizophrenic disarray, undecided whether they wanted to grow up and be warehousing or a multi-storey car park. The pub's neon window ads reflected in the long puddles on the road; pinks and reds and greens and *Magners* and *Budweisers*, stirred and puckered by the rain.

James was waiting under an arch of old, blackened brick. He started moving the moment she reached him.

'Boiled egg?' she asked, as she ran along beside him. '*Really?*'

'Really.'

'End of the World, or just the End of Cardiff?'

'The latter is merely a sub-set of the former,' he grinned. 'Besides, I'm just relaying what Tosh told me.'

'Where is she?'

'Round the back.'

'And what did she tell you?'

'This is the blip she's been seeing for a week, on and off. First real, solid fix.'

'And it's the End of the World why?'

'Her systems crashed eighteen seconds after she painted it. I mean *crash* crashed. Forty-nine per cent of the Hub's down. We left Ianto in tears.'

'It's aggressive, then?'

'On a scale of one to ten?' he asked.

'Your scale or Jack's?'

'Mine.'

'And?'

He shrugged, running up a short flight of rain-slick concrete steps. 'Twenty-six, twenty-seven. It freaked the crap out of Tosh's computers and they're, you know, kind of the best us evolved apes have ever manufactured.'

They came out onto a vacant lot, tufted with virile weeds. The eastern end of the gravelly lot, marked by an ailing chain-link fence, was flooded with standing water six inches deep. Gwen could smell the river. The wind was cold, and held the particular tang of Autumn fighting a losing battle with Winter's point men.

'Oh!' she said, suddenly unsteady. 'Christ on a moped, did you feel that?'

He nodded. Nausea: a wallowing unease that reminded her of the car sickness she'd suffered as a child on family day-trips, the big back seat of the old Vauxhall Royale, stopping and starting in the tourist traffic all the way to Carmarthen.

'I've got a headache,' James said. 'Have you got a headache?'

'Yes,' said Gwen, realising she absolutely had. 'It came on suddenly.'

'Like a switch?'

'Like a switch, yeah. I can't thick straight.'

'Thick?'

'What?'

'You just said "thick".'

'I meant think.'

'I know what you meant. I can't thick straight either. I'm having real trouble focusing.'

'You mean "trouble",' said Gwen, pinching the bridge of her nose.

'What?'

'You said "stubble", but you mean "trouble".'

'I didn't.'

Gwen looked at him. The cold rain spattered down on them. She was getting visual disturbance; squiggles of yellow light and peripheral flashes in the corners of her vision. She'd never suffered from migraines, but she'd read enough to know that this was what migraines were supposed to feel like.

'What the bloody hell is this?' she asked. She was slightly scared.

'I don't know,' he said. He managed a grin and put on the beaky voice of his favourite cartoon character, 'But I ain't gonna get in no flap.'

That made her laugh. Jack was Torchwood's rock and soul, but James was its heart. He could make her laugh in the face of the End of the World. Or Cardiff, whichever occurred first.

James turned away from her. 'Game face,' he said. 'We're on.'

Someone was running towards them, running right across the flooded part of the lot and kicking up froths of water like Gene Kelly in a happy-go-lucky mood.

Gwen thought it was Toshiko at first glance, but it wasn't. It was a slim girl in boy-cut jeans and a skinny rib T-shirt that bore the slogan *I've got tits, so I win*.

She was running kind of funny, Gwen thought, spastic, her arms shaking. Her thin, pram face was twitching and blinking.

'Hello?' James called out.

The girl stumbled to a halt and wavered in front of them, blinking at James, then at Gwen, and then at James again. Each swing of her head was abrupt and made her sway. Her fingers, dripping with rain, pinched and snapped like someone telling the old 'he's been giving it that all night' lobster joke.

'Big big big,' she told them, slurring and emphasising the middle 'big'. 'Sham. Sixty Nine per cent. Of cat owners. Anthropomorphise. Gibbons. Big gibbons. Big Gibbon's Decline and Fall,' she added.

Then she dropped to her knees with such a hard, bony crunch, Gwen winced. Kneeling, the girl threw up on the gravel.

Gwen went to her quickly, trying to help her. The girl said something, and pushed Gwen away. Then she hurled again.

Even diluted by the wind and rain, her sick smelled wrong. There was a strong ketone stink. Behind that, half-masked, plastics and burned sugar.

'It's all right,' said Gwen.

'Big big big,' the girl slurred, and dry heaved like she was trying to exhale her liver.

Gwen looked up at James.

'What the hell's wrong with her?' she asked. 'And, also, ow! My headache's getting worse.'

'Mine too,' he agreed. He was trying to be upbeat, but she could hear the tone. The pain. 'Well,' he said, 'unless quiz night at the local pub has gone horribly wrong—'

The girl got up, shoving them aside. She fell down again, picked herself up once more and said, 'Glory. Glory glory glory. Cantankerous. Is a good word.'

She swayed and looked at James. 'Isn't it?'

'It is,' he replied, reaching out his hand.

The girl laughed, and bubbles of snot came out of her nose. The heaves squeezed her again, and she convulsed, elbows digging into her sides, but nothing more came up.

'Varnish,' she said, gurgling, and ran away.

'Don't let her—' Gwen began.

The girl didn't get far. She ran blindly into a mouldering brick wall, bounced off it with an ugly smack, and fell flat on her back.

They ran to her. Her face and arms were grazed and bleeding. Her nose was broken. Blood ran out of it, turning pink in the steady downpour.

'It's all right, it's all right,' Gwen hushed. 'What's your name? Can you tell me your name?'

'Huw,' the girl mumbled.

'Well, there's a switch,' said James.

Gwen looked up at him. 'She's not Huw, you prat. Huw's someone else.'

Huw ran down the riverside path, behind the glittering raindrop wall of the chain link. He thought he was running well, really sprinting, but to an observer, he would have looked like someone doing a sensationally bad *Planet of the Apes* impression.

He stumbled and slapped into the fence, making it trampoline and jingle. Collected rainwater shivered off the diamond links.

He sagged.

'Let me help you,' said the woman materialising out of the rain behind him. She was beautiful, Huw thought, blinking at her. She was slender and very cool beans in her black leather coat.

'My name is Toshiko,' the woman told him. 'Let me help you. Tell me your name. Tell me what happened.'

Huw flopped back onto the grass and broken asphalt, one hand still clinging to the quivering fence.

'There are,' he began, but stopped. His voice sounded funny, as if his ears were stuffed full of cotton wool. Maybe they were. Had he done that? Perhaps he had. Earlier on, in the bathroom, swallowing the last of the aspirin. There had been a baggie of cotton wool balls by the sink. Laney's, for make-up. Had he… *had* he?

It was so hard to think. To remember. His own name. Laney's name. No, Laney's name was Laney. *Laney*, where are you?

'Talk to me,' said the woman called Toshiko. 'What were you trying to tell me?'

'There are,' Huw began again, ignoring the woolly sound of his voice, 'there are numbers, and there are two blue lights and they move, and they move about, like this.'

He pulled his hand free of the dripping chain link and moved it around his other hand, describing curious, geometric patterns in the air.

'They move. They move. They move about. They're big lights. Big big big.'

His thready voice emphasised the middle of the three 'bigs'.

Toshiko crouched beside him. 'Lights? And numbers?'

Huw nodded. 'Big big big. Flashing and moving. Blue. Oh, sometimes red. Red is dead. Blue is true. Big big big.'

'What are the numbers?' Toshiko asked him.

'My name is Huw!' he blurted, as if he'd just that minute remembered.

'Oh, well, hello Huw. Tell me about the numbers and the lights.'

Huw's head rolled drunkenly. He was blinking very fast, and the muscles in his face were ticking. 'Huw is blue. Huw is true. Big big big.'

'The numbers, Huw—'

'Abstract numbers,' he said, very clearly and suddenly, fixing her with a stare.

Toshiko looked back at him. Jeans, a vest top, a ratty Hoxton fin ruined by the rain. No way this 'Huw' knew about abstract numbers.

'Huw, tell me about the abstract numbers.'

Huw was fiddling with his left ear. He pulled out a clump of cotton wool. It was soaked in blood.

'Shit,' he muttered. 'I think my brain's burst.'

'Huw,' Toshiko soothed.

'Oh no!' he wailed suddenly, writhing. 'Oh no! Go away! Don't look at me! Leave me alone!'

Toshiko started back. She realised Huw had just wet himself. She could smell it. He was mortified by the indignity.

That suggested he wasn't drunk.

'Huw…'

12

'My head does hurt,' he moaned.

'So does mine,' she agreed. It really, *really* did. 'Tell me more about the numbers and the lights. Where did they come from?'

Boiled egg. Boiled egg. She was acutely aware that they were running out of time. Completely out of time.

'Big big big,' Huw replied. 'Stephi Graff. Giraffe. Ron Moody. Bastard. Twins. Illegitimate twins. On the cover of *Hello!* magazine. Do you know that magazine? Very much the model of a modern major overhaul.'

'Huw? Come on! Huw?'

He smiled at her, blinking all the time.

Then he died.

His eyeballs went slack, and his head flopped back, and a puff of smoke trickled up out of his open mouth.

The smoke smelled of burned sugar, plastic and fæces.

Knifed by the same pain that had killed him, Toshiko fell to her knees, wincing.

'He lost the Amok,' a voice behind her said.

Toshiko looked around.

The tramp stood in the beating rain, watching her. He seemed huge, but that was because he was wearing too many old coats. His filthy beard was strung with rainwater droplets like a Christmas tree's decorations. He reeked of mud and factory waste. His arms were weighed down by two heavy carrier bags. Sainsbury's.

'He lost the what?' Toshiko asked, rising.

'The Amok,' the tramp replied. There was no way of telling how old he was. Thirty? Sixty? Life had run him down without stopping.

He set his bulging carrier bags down at his feet. 'Huw had the Amok, but he lost. Donny had it before him, and he lost too. Before Donny, Terry. Before Terry, Malcolm. Before Malcolm, Bob. Before Bob, Ash'ahvath.'

'Before Bob who?'

'Ash'ahvath,' the tramp said.

'As in the Middlesex Ash'ahvath's?'

The tramp sniggered and shook his head so hard raindrops flew out of his beard, like a dog shaking itself after bath-time. 'You're funny. I don't know no Ash'ahvath. It was just the last name on the list.'

'I see,' said Toshiko, slowly rising to her feet. 'Do you have the Amok now? What's your name?'

'John Norris,' replied the tramp, crouching down to sort through his carrier bags. 'John Norris. I was all right once, you know.'

'You're all right now, John,' she said.

'I'm not. I'm not. I had a good job. A company car. It was a Rover. GL. I had my own parking space. They called me Mr Norris.'

'What happened?'

'Workforce rationalisation. The wife moved to her sister's place. I haven't seen my boy in five years.'

The tramp began to weep.

'Mr Norris, we can sort this all out,' Toshiko said, stepping towards him. Her head was throbbing. 'Please, do you have the Amok?'

He nodded, sniffling, and rifled around in one of his carrier bags.

'It's in here somewhere.' He glanced up at her. 'Big big big,' he added. Emphasis on the middle 'big'.

'Just show it to me. The Amok.'

'Oh, right, here it is,' he said. He drew something out of the carrier bag. It was a ten-by-eight clip frame in which were pressed three photographs. A woman. A boy. A woman and a boy.

'Mr Norris, that's not the Amok, is it?' Toshiko said gently.

The tramp shuddered. He shook his head, shoulders hunched. 'No,' he whimpered. He struck the clip frame against the path and shattered it.

'Mr Norris?'

When he turned to face her, he was holding a sliver of the clip frame glass in his hand. The broken edges were so sharp, and his grip on it so tight, blood dribbled out between his dirty fingers.

'Oh shit,' said Toshiko, backing away abruptly.

The tramp lunged.

TWO

Fat radials hissed as the SUV came to a halt. Jack and Owen got out into the rain. Jack tried his mobile.

'No signal,' he said to Owen.

Jack looked around. 'Tosh? James?' he yelled. There was no answer.

'Let's try in there,' said Owen, making off towards the nearby pub. It looked bright and inviting, the frosted glass oblongs of its windows warmed from within by yellow light.

Jack followed him. Owen had gone a few steps when he paused and lowered his head.

'What?'

'Bastard of a headache I've got, all of a sudden,' Owen groaned, his hand raised to his temple.

'I thought you were going to have a quiet one last night,' Jack said sourly, pushing past Owen towards the door of the public bar.

'It's not that kind of headache,' Owen complained, his thin mouth more of a downward curve than usual. 'Buggering Christ, can't you feel that?'

'Your headache?' replied Jack. 'Funnily enough, no.' He hesitated. 'But I know what you mean. I can feel something.'

He opened the pub door and went inside. Owen followed. It was as cheerfully grotty as any of Cardiff's arse-end public houses, marinated in a smell of fags and malt. An aimless clatter-ping rang from the pinball machine and 'If You Don't Know Me By Now' issued from the jukebox.

'So where is everyone?' Owen asked.

The public bar was empty. So was the saloon. Empty chairs loitered around Formica-topped tables on which a few half-empty glasses and the occasional open packet of nuts waited. There was no sign of disarray, and no sign of any bar staff. The drawer of the public bar's cash register was open.

'Not a robbery,' said Jack, going behind the bar and lifting each of the drawer's spring clips in turn. 'There's a couple of hundred in here.'

'This is very wrong,' said Owen. He pointed. Two full pints of lager sat side by side on the counter's plastic drip tray. The glasses were sheened with condensation. 'These have just been pulled. No one walks away from a fresh pint in a pub like this.'

'Not in welsh Wales they don't,' Jack agreed.

They went back outside. The buildings beyond the pub and the little late shop formed an ominous silhouette against the lights of Cardiff Bay over the river.

They both heard the cry. Distant, robbed out by the heavy rain, but distinct. Not a scream, but a cry of alarm.

They both broke into a run.

Toshiko sprang back to avoid the slashing glass. The tramp was mumbling and blinking.

'Mr Norris,' she warned. 'Put that down. You're hurting yourself, and—'

The tramp stabbed at her again, and forced her to retreat further down the riverside path. Toshiko looked around for options. The overgrown embankment and the high chain-link fence against which Huw had died was on her right. To her left, a glistening black edge of curb-stones showed where the river wall dropped way. She could hear the river, and smell it, but it was invisible below her. It sounded a long way down.

'Mr Norris…'

'You can't have it!' he cried. 'It's not your go! It's my go!'

He came at her for the third time, moving with alarming speed for such a dishevelled, unhealthy soul. The makeshift blade glittered as he swung it, and the motion whipped out a fan of blood from his lacerated fingers.

This time, despite the pain in her head, Toshiko managed to do more than evade. She side-stepped, pirouetted on one foot, and planted a heavy side-kick into the tramp's sternum.

He *woofed* and jerked backwards, but the multiple layers of clothing he was wearing insulated against the bite of the kick. He surged back at her with a strangled cry, and drove the tip of the glass blade at her throat.

Toshiko ducked it, turned, and grabbed the extending forearm with both of her leather-gloved hands as it came over her. Hauling on his arm, she slammed her shoulder up into his armpit, and threw him right over her onto his back.

He landed with winding force, and lay twitching, face up in the rain, his mouth moving slackly behind his beard.

She kicked the shard of broken glass away.

'Right then,' she said.

Something that felt as big and heavy as a speeding bus slammed into her from behind without any warning at all.

'Down here!' James yelled. Gwen made a scrambling descent of the embankment after him towards the murky riverside. Wet cow-grass and rhododendrons slapped at her face. They came out on a cinder path along the dirty flood wall. A little way along, the body of a young man lay twisted against the fence.

'James!' she cried.

'Never mind him!' he shouted back, still running. 'Fighter Command!'

Fighter Command. Thank you so much, Captain bloody Analogy, she thought, struggling through the headache to form any kind of coherent thought at all. Fighter Command meant 'Scramble and drop everything'. Spitfire pilots sprinting in their flying jackets and Mae Wests the moment the field telephone started to jangle, cups of tea and faithful dogs and card schools left behind. The urgent call to action.

'Sodding well wait up!' Gwen yelled, and then shut up.

Twenty yards ahead of them, two figures were struggling violently on the path. One was Toshiko. The other was a big man in jeans and a lumberjack shirt. He had Toshiko by the throat, and was shaking her to and fro as if he wanted to work her head off. Toshiko was flailing helplessly. Nearby, an old, filthy tramp was crawling around on the ground, mewling to himself pitifully. Gwen could hear the horrible barks of pain being forced out of Toshiko.

James flew past the tramp and threw himself at the big man. Gwen was right behind him.

'Oi! Bloody leave her be!' she yelled.

The big man in the lumberjack shirt obliged, tossing Toshiko aside. But only, it turned out, so he could jerk around to get James off his broad back. The big man was six six, his neck as thick as his shaved head. He smelled of a beer-sweat that was showing no mercy to industrial-strength applications of Lynx. He roared something, and rotated so wildly that James's feet left the ground altogether. A beefy, jabbing elbow did the rest. James yelped and fell off him onto the path, clutching his face.

Grinning, the big man was about to place-kick James in the ribs when Gwen tackled him like a full-back.

He went down on his face, felled like a tree, and cracked his teeth on the ground, biting the tip off his tongue into the bargain. Gwen struggled onto his back, and bent one of his meaty arms up behind his shoulder-blades.

'That's enough!' she ordered. 'Stop fighting me, or I'll break your bloody arm off, so help me!'

The man beneath her hollered something through broken teeth.

'Yeah, yeah, I've heard it all before!' Gwen snapped. She cinched the twisted limb up beyond 'pinned' to 'painful' to make him shut up.

Running footsteps approached from the opposite direction. Jack and Owen appeared out of the rain, racing down the riverside path. Jack's greatcoat was flying out behind him like wings.

He skidded to a halt, looking at Toshiko and James writhing on the ground, and Gwen straddling a blood-spitting thug.

'Going well, I see,' he remarked.

'As bloody usual,' snapped Gwen. 'Give me a hand with this one, for Christ's sake!'

More than a hand was needed. The big man bucked and unseated Gwen. She flew off him and landed on her backside. The big man got up on his feet, blinking and looking around, spoiling for more. He found himself face to face with Jack Harkness's perfect white smile.

'Rough night?' Jack asked.

'Fwuk yoh!' the big man spat, his words mangled by his cracked front teeth and swollen tongue. 'Iss mihhn! Mhhy ttuhhn!'

'Your turn?' asked Jack. 'OK, fellah.'

Jack threw a perfect, Marquis of Queensbury right hook that slapped the big man's head to the right. Drops of blood sprayed out, like *Raging Bull*.

''ahstard!' the big man snorted, and swung a punch back that was so telegraphed, it might as well have been announced by a butler. 'Big big big!' he yelled, his slurred emphasis resting on the middle 'big'.

'Yes, you are,' Jack replied, 'but you know what they say…' A jab to the gut folded the big man over. An upper cut finished the job.

The big man curled up on his side on the ground, groaning and dazed. Jack stepped back, rubbing the knuckles of his right hand, and smiled again.

'And the winner is,' Owen remarked snidely, helping Toshiko up. She was bruised around the throat and having trouble breathing.

'All right?' James asked Gwen. She nodded and held out her hand to let him pull her to her feet.

'You're bleeding,' she said, pointing.

'Just a split lip,' he replied.

'Tea, cakes and Band-Aids later,' said Jack. 'Were we all just brawling for fun, or—?'

'Those bags,' coughed Toshiko, pointing down the path to the two, forlorn Sainsbury's carriers. 'It's called the Amok.'

'Is it, indeed?' asked Jack, cocking his head in curiosity and stepping forwards.

'It's mine!' the old tramp moaned. He was cowering by the fence. 'It's mine! It's my go!'

'Not any more, I'm afraid,' Jack told him. 'Stay there.'

Jack approached the bags. The rain pattered off the bulging plastic. He could smell the contents, and the experience wasn't pleasant. He crouched down. Gwen and James appeared on either side of him.

Jack glanced at them with a rueful grin. 'Lucky dip,' he said. He put his hand into one of the bags.

Behind them, the tramp wailed out a deep, anguished howl. It almost obscured Toshiko's call of 'Be careful!'

Jack pulled out a few objects that made him, Gwen and James grimace. 'Oh, joy,' Jack said. 'This is why I love the job so.'

'Just tip them out, I would,' suggested Gwen.

'And if it's something volatile?' asked James. 'Something delicate or sensitive or, you know, explosive?'

'Just tip them out anyway,' said Gwen. 'That's got to be better than having to stick your hand in shit.'

Jack turned both carrier bags out onto the path and began to sift. The rain rinsed the exposed contents: pieces of clothing, matted with black dirt; a crushed Marlboro packet filled with a collection of stubbed-out cigarette butts; part of a Rubik's cube; the fashion cover for a mobile phone; something furry and mauve that had once been a motorway services sandwich; the tail of a kite; a toothless comb; more bits of torn, stinking clothing; a single, scuffed Adidas trainer in a child's size; eight disposable plastic forks and spoons held together by a red Post Office elastic band; a Happy Meal toy; part of an electric toothbrush; another clip frame, smaller than the first, holding a photo of a mother and father proudly displaying a small baby on a windy beach somewhere; a safety pin; an out-of-date copy of *Exchange & Mart* with several pages torn out; a Bic pen with no innards...

'There!' James said, excitedly. 'What's that by the phone cover? Is that it?'

Jack held the object up. 'It's a Pikachu-head Pez dispenser,' he said solemnly. He checked. 'It's OK, though. It's not loaded.'

'Oh,' said James. 'It looked like—'

'Like what?' Jack inquired.

'A Pikachu-head Pez dispenser, now I see it, obviously,' scowled James.

'My head really hurts,' said Gwen, 'otherwise I'd be laughing and taking the piss right now.'

'All right!' James snapped. 'It looked like...'

'What?'

James muttered something.

'Say again?'

'A piece of exotic technology,' James said slightly louder and reluctantly.

Gwen pursed her lips. 'Even though my head does hurt, that's fantastically funny. Should I alert the rest of the team James just made a tit of himself?'

'No need,' said Owen. He and Toshiko had joined them. He looked at James. 'End of the World, huh?' he asked. 'If it hadn't been for us pesky kids?'

'Shut up!' Toshiko growled. She was still rubbing her throat and the colour had not yet returned to her rain-streaked face. 'This is still serious. Something's affecting these people. And us, or am I the only one whose head feels like it's about to pop?'

'What do you know, Tosh?' Jack asked.

Toshiko coughed, tryng to clear her voice. 'Whatever Torchwood has been tracking this last week is here, in this vicinity. It's aggressive and it's spiking. It's driving people in range out of their minds. Background cerebral flooding. We're all feeling it. It's killed one boy already. His name was Huw.'

She gestured back up the path at the pale, tangled heap of limbs.

'Huw,' said Gwen, with a glance at James. He was dabbing at his split lip.

'The victim was talking about abstract numbers before he died,' said Toshiko. She pulled a compact digital recorder from the pocket of her coat and sourced the right playback with expert flicks of her gloved thumb. 'Here...'

'There are… there are numbers, and there are two blue lights and they move, and they move about, like this,' a tinny voice said through a background rustling of rain and pocket lining. 'They move. They move. They move about. They're big lights. Big big big.'

'Lights? And numbers?' Toshiko's voice asked.

'Big big big. Flashing and moving. Blue. Oh, sometimes red. Red is dead. Blue is true. Big big big.'

'Big big big,' echoed Jack, mimicking the emphasis.

'That's what his girlfriend said too,' said Gwen.

'Along with a load of old bollocks,' James added.

'Then the tramp there arrived,' said Toshiko, 'and said—'

She thumbed the playback again. 'Huw had the Amok, but he lost,' the ragged voice recording declared. 'Donny had it before him, and he lost too. Before Donny, Terry. Before Terry, Malcolm. Before Malcolm, Bob. Before Bob, Ash'ahvath.'

'Before Bob who?' they heard Toshiko ask.

'Ash'ahvath.'

'As in the Middlesex Ash'ahvath's?'

There was a spluttery, sniggery sound on the playback 'You're funny. I don't know no Ash'ahvath. It was just the last name on the list.'

Toshiko clicked the device off.

'*Huw had the Amok, but he lost,*' repeated Jack, deep in thought. '*Donny had it before him, and he lost too. Strange.*'

'Yeah,' said Owen. He frowned. 'Uh, how?'

'He said "lost", not "lost it",' said Jack. 'If it was an object, they'd have lost "it". But they just "lost", as if—'

'As if it was a game,' said Gwen.

'Exactly as if it was a game,' Jack agreed.

Toshiko held the recorder out again and clicked it on. They all heard the tramp's voice crying 'You can't have it! It's not your go! It's my go!' She clicked it silent.

'The lumberjack told me it was his turn,' Jack said. 'I didn't really understand what he meant at the time.'

'So…?' asked Owen.

Toshiko turned away from them and stared at the tramp. He was still cowering in the overhang of the slack chain link.

'Where is the Amok, Mr Norris?' she asked.

'Shooo! Shoo!' he cackled back, spitting and warding them off.

'Well, he's no sodding use,' said Owen.

Toshiko aimed her index finger at the pile of garbage they were huddled around. 'Shoe,' she said.

Jack picked up the child's trainer, sensing at once the weight of it. He tipped it up, and something rolled out of it.

It was a geometric solid about five centimetres wide that looked as if it had been stamped or cast out of copper. It had the look, colour and patina of the twopence pieces that had been in circulation since Decimalisation. It clinked as it rolled across the path on its geometric corners. Staring at it, they all felt a sudden revulsion.

Though it was perfectly symmetrical in every aspect, none of them could sufficiently explain its geometry.

Or even bear to look at it.

'Is that a…' James began. 'What is that? A dodecahedron? No, a… a…'

'I can't describe it,' Toshiko began.

'I'm gonna be sick,' said Owen.

'Don't,' said Jack.

'I really can't describe it,' Toshiko repeated.

'I really am gonna be sick,' said Owen.

'I meant don't to either of you!' Jack demanded. He closed his hand around the object. 'You can't describe it because it's got more than four dimensions. You can't stand looking at it for the same reason.'

Owen nodded, wagging a finger in agreement, and turned aside to be sick anyway.

'Jack?' whispered Gwen.

'Oh,' said Jack, smiling broadly. 'Oh, I see what they meant about the two blue lights. Moving.'

His smile melted away. He sat back on the path, cupping the object in both hands. He was staring into the rain-swept distance.

'Moving,' he said. His voice had dropped to a dull sound they could barely hear. 'Moving about. Big, blue, flashing lights. Oh.'

Toshiko reached towards him. 'Jack? Let it go and let us—'

Still staring into the distance, Jack pulled away from Toshiko's touch. 'It's my turn,' he said.

'Jack?'

'Big,' said Jack Harkness. 'Big, big,' he added, stressing the middle 'big'.

Then he fell back and went into convulsions.

'Jack!' Gwen screamed.

'Bugger Jack!' cried James. Gwen turned. They all turned. They saw what James had noticed.

Dozens of people were shuffling and twitching down the overgrown bank towards them, coming up smack into the rattling chain link and still trying to plod forwards, dead-eyed and grasping. Others were hobbling along the path from both directions. The patrons of the empty pub, Owen was sure, staff from the late shop, families from the nearby row of houses. It was all far too George A. Romero to be remotely funny.

'Oh bollocks,' said Owen. The shambling figures were all muttering as they bore down, their voices overlapping in the rain. They were all saying the same thing.

'Big big big. Big big big.'

Emphasis on every middle 'big'.

THREE

Shiznay rather fancied Mr Dine. He'd been eating in the Mughal Dynasty for sixth months, every Monday and every Thursday, like his life was regimented. Always the same thing: shashlik, followed by a lamb pasanda, then a bowl of chocolate ice cream. He drank one bottle of lager with his meal. He paid with a card, signing *Dine*.

He was a lean, straight-backed man, with hard cheekbones and a head of white-blond hair cropped back like flock across his skull. He always wore a suit, sometimes grey, sometimes black and occasionally blue, and a tie with some club insignia repeat-embroidered on the jet-black field. A crisp white shirt. He was always respectful, though never talkative. Shiznay imagined an IT job, a nice car parked in the nearby Pay-and-Display, a regular run to Bristol and Bath and Swansea, whatever was in his area. She wondered who he visited. Big offices in the Bay most likely. New European businesses probably. Yeah.

Two weeks before, on a Thursday night like this one, although lacking the rain, Mr Dine had come in and sat down at his usual table. When she'd brought him the menu, he'd looked up at her, and smiled, and asked her, if she didn't mind, what her name was.

'I've been coming in here for such a long time, and I don't know what you're called,' he had said.

'Shiznay,' she replied, blushing.

'Shiznay,' he repeated, turning the word over and over.

This Thursday, she produced the bottle of lager he hadn't asked for yet, and set it down next to the upturned glass.

Mr Dine smiled. 'Thank you. You read my mind, Shiznay.'

'My pleasure. Have you decided yet, sir?'

'A moment.'

Shiznay retreated to the kitchen door and waited. As ever, the restaurant was nothing like busy.

'What are you doing?' her father asked, bustling out of the kitchen. 'Are you loitering?'

'I am waiting for Mr Dine, Father,' Shiznay replied.

Her father looked out across the empty restaurant and spotted Mr Dine at the distant table.

'You favour him,' he observed.

'He's a customer, Father, and a regular. What do you want me to do?'

'Not get any ideas,' her father said.

Shiznay had plenty of ideas. Mr Dine knew her name. Mr Dine had smiled at her. He had wanted to know what her name was. He liked her.

She caught sight of herself in the floor-length mirrors beside the restaurant door. Her father insisted they all wore authentic clothing at work – even though neither of her parents had ever been out of South Wales in their lives. Authentic clothing revealed her midriff, and also revealed what the local white boys called a 'muffin top'. But authentic clothing also accentuated her bosom.

Shiznay was proud of her bosom, but she was also fairly sure she had a pretty face.

'He's a breast man,' her mother had told her.

'Mother, what?'

'That Mr Dine. I've seen the way he looks at you. He's a breast man.'

'What is a "breast man"?' she had wondered.

'There are four kinds of men… the breast men, the backside men, the leg men, and the others.'

'The others?'

'The ones who'll go for anything. Mr Dine—'

'Mr Dine is a very nice man, and a regular customer.'

'Mr Dine is a breast man, Shiznay, you mark my words.'

Shiznay turned way from her reflection and looked across the Mughal Dynasty at Mr Dine. Are you a breast man? she wondered. What exactly does that entail, being a breast man?

Mr Dine had put his menu down.

25

She crossed the floor to him, breathing in to minimise her muffin top and push out her bosom. Maybe, maybe, he'd ask her out on a date. What would that be like? A walk down to the Pay-and-Display, him holding the door of his nice car open so she could get in. A trip to—

But, no. Revise that fantasy. He'd have eaten, of course, he'd already have eaten. No fancy restaurant on the Bay for the two of them. Unless, of course, he asked her out on an evening that wasn't a Monday or a Thursday…

She wondered what French food was like. What Welsh food was like. How would it taste if Mr Dine was sitting opposite her?

Shiznay didn't really care if he was a breast man. He was a nice man, and he'd smiled at her, and he knew her name, and—

'Are you ready to order?' she asked.

He looked up at her and smiled. 'Yes, I am, Shiznay. Shaslik, and a—'

'—lamb pasanda?' she finished.

He frowned. 'Am I so predictable?'

'You know what you like.'

'I study the menu,' he confessed, picking the tri-fold card up again, 'and I look, but always the same things seem agreeable. Meat, spiced, then meat and carbohydrates. The alcohol is a treat for me.'

She smiled, not quite knowing what to say. 'And chocolate ice cream?'

A broad smile etched itself across his lean face. 'There's nothing like it where I come from.'

'Well,' she said. 'Well, thank goodness we've got some.'

'Would you… can you… sit down?' he asked, indicating the chair opposite.

Shiznay sat down. This was it. The moment. Her breathing had become rather rapid, but she didn't mind. It did splendid things to her bosom.

'Shiznay, I've been coming here for a while now. I want to ask…'

'Yes?'

'What is chocolate ice cream?'

She paused. 'I… uh… that's not what I was expecting you to ask. Chocolate ice cream? Well, that's animal fats and flavouring, pretty much.'

'Oh,' he said. He sighed. 'No wonder I love it so.'

'Is that… will that be all?' she asked, rising.

'Yes. Thank you, Shiznay.'

She got up and hurried back to the kitchen.

* * *

'Jack!' Gwen yelled. 'Jack! Come on!'

She and Toshiko were trying to hold Jack's convulsing body still. The shambling, mumbling figures were closing in all around them.

'What do we do?' James asked Owen. 'Start throwing punches?'

Owen took a shiny, black, custom side-arm from his coat and racked the slide. 'We do whatever we have to do to get out of here alive,' he replied.

'You brought a gun?' James asked.

'You didn't?'

'No—'

'I thought this was the End of the World?'

'Look—'

'Shut it, the pair of you,' said Gwen. 'The SUV's got a weapons locker.'

'Well, that kind of requires us to be where the SUV is,' James told her, 'rather than being, you know, up a certain creek without a particular implement.'

'Just get behind me,' said Owen.

'They're coming from all sides!' James objected.

'Just get behind me *in spirit*,' said Owen.

They could all smell the ketosis on the breaths of the advancing figures. A girl of eleven in a *Powerpuff Girls* nightshirt was in the front rank, a middle-aged man with flecks of potato crisp around his mouth, a woman in a housecoat and fluffy slippers.

'You're cheerfully going to shoot them?' James asked.

'Not cheerfully, exactly,' Owen admitted.

Jack made a sudden, deep exhalation, as if surfacing from a deep dive. He sat up, panting.

'Not something I'd recommend,' he said, blinking. He looked up at Gwen and Toshiko, and then back down at the object clenched in his hand.

'Hard to fight it. Really hard. We have to get this contained. I don't know how much longer I can keep it busy.'

'There's a containment box,' Gwen began, 'but it's—'

'—in the SUV,' James and Owen chorused.

'Then let's move!' Jack ordered, clambering to his feet with Toshiko's help.

They started back along the riverside path in the direction Jack and Owen had come from. Almost at once, they were pushing their way through the muttering files of automaton people. Hands clawed at them, catching at their clothes.

'Just run!' Jack barked. 'Push through! Just shove them aside!'

They fought their way forwards. A couple of the moaning figures went sprawling. Gwen got clear enough to start running. Toshiko followed her.

There were hands all over Jack, grabbing at him, and dragging him down. Someone had hold of his left leg.

'Dammit!' he cried out. 'Gwen! Go long!'

Still running, Gwen glanced back. Jack freed his right arm and pitched the object like a Rawlings ball.

'Pass it on!' he yelled. 'Don't hold onto it!'

Running backwards under the object's arc, Gwen kept her eye on it, and caught it neatly. She started to run towards the embankment steps.

The mindless crowd forgot about Jack and started to spill after her.

She could feel the terrible warmth of the object in her hand. She blinked. On the back of her eyelids, two blue lights shone, moving.

'Gwen!'

Toshiko was near the top of the steps, looking back at her. She held her hands out, begging. 'Gwen!'

Gwen blinked again. She didn't want to let the thing go. It was her turn.

A young man in a collegiate rugby jersey ran into her from the side, and began to fight her for the thing in her hand.

'Big big big!' he explained. 'Tokyo drift. Wood. Trees. Leaves. Nothing behind.'

'Get off!' Gwen told him.

He punched her in the ribs. A small, weasel-faced woman joined him, and started to kick and scrabble at Gwen.

The three of them fell back against a secondary stretch of chain link that had been fixed along the edge of the river wall below the embankment steps. The iron poles juddered as the weight of them hit the mesh.

'Get off me!' Gwen cried. She got her arm free and hurled the object up towards Toshiko. It was a poor effort. The weasel-faced woman had been hanging on her elbow.

'You throw like a girl!' Owen declared as he raced past her, heading for the steps.

The object had sailed through the air and missed Toshiko by about six feet. It bounced into the long grass near the top of the embankment, somewhere to the left of the steps. Uttering a very clipped and precise piece of Anglo-Saxon invective, Toshiko floundered through the long, wet weeds to retrieve it.

The mindless crowd on the path turned towards the bank, tottering up the steps or scrambling up through the long grass after Toshiko.

Pressed against the chain link, Gwen tried to push the bodies off her. They'd already lost interest in her, and were trying to extricate themselves, but they'd all lost their balance into the belling net of the fence.

There was a sharp, metallic ping, then another, and another.

The section of chain-link fence was pulling away from its end pole under their combined weight. The rusting bolt-pegs sheared with a staccato squeal.

Gwen felt herself pitching back off the edge of the wall into open space. The invisible river rushed below. The young man in the rugby jersey managed to flail backwards onto the path. The weasel-faced woman was not so well braced. As the fencing tore away, she went off the wall face first, and dropped into the blackness.

Gwen was holding onto the fence, her fingers and thumbs threaded into the links. She was already too far off her centre of balance to pull back.

The fencing tore back and unspooled all the way to the second pole, where it held. Gwen yelped as she fell, and ended up hanging over the river wall, feet dangling, clinging to the swaying, straining section of torn-away fence.

The bolt-pegs on the second pole began to shear.

Toshiko rummaged in the undergrowth. A man thrashed into her, and she chopped the side of her left hand into his throat to keep him busy.

There it was. A dull glint in the rain-soaked grass. Toshiko snatched up the Amok, and started to run up the slope and back towards the steps. There were people milling around her. The moment she had it in her hand, they surged after her. Some fell over on the wet undergrowth. A woman squealed in disappointment as she slithered right back down the slope.

Toshiko kept running. Her throat ached, and she was aware of plenty of bruises elsewhere on her person, but all that seemed to matter any more was the thing in her hand. She could feel it, like a hot coal, through the leather of her stylish gloves.

Someone grabbed the tails of her long coat, and she kicked them away. Someone else seized her by the arm, and she gave them a blunt elbow smack in the philtrum as a present. She had reached flat ground, a puddled square of broken concrete between the derelict buildings and the late shop. She could see the SUV forty yards away outside the pub, sitting under the streetlights in a haze of rain.

A wrecking ball swung in and struck her in the small of the back, walloping her off her feet.

She fell on her front in the puddles. It wasn't a wrecking ball, she realised. It was the big man in the lumberjack shirt. Twice in one night he'd poleaxed her.

He was raving, speaking in tongues, his mouth a bloody ruin and his face purple-bruised from Jack's punches.

Toshiko rolled away as he clawed at her. Her body hurt. Her mind hurt more. Her hand was hot. It felt as if the leather of her glove was burning away. As she blinked, she saw blue lights. They were moving, moving in ways nothing could be expected to move, not even two blue lights. And they seemed very big. Big big—

A gun went off.

It was so loud and so close, and the acoustic echo of the narrow yard so hard, Toshiko jumped out of her skin.

Owen came running up to her, his smoking weapon raised, shouting her name.

The big man in the lumberjack shirt turned, unfazed by the sight or sound of a high-calibre handgun, and socked Owen in the face. Owen looked as if he'd run into a clothesline. His legs kept going as his head snapped backwards. He bounced on his back as he hit the ground.

The big man turned back to regard her, ropes of clotted blood swinging from his nose. She was already up.

'Big big big!' he explained to her.

'Piss off!' she explained back.

As he ploughed on, she kicked him in the balls. He went down, but not before he'd caught her across the side of the head with his fist.

Two blue lights, moving, this way and that, and then the numbers, scrolling up across the darkness like the end titles of a movie…

Toshiko opened her eyes. There was rain in her face. She'd blacked out for a moment. The big man had fallen across her legs. He was writhing. The thing in her hand was red hot.

She tried to pull her legs free. The big man reared up, and grabbed her throat. There was an ugly noise, like canvas tearing and raw liver being hit with a mallet, both at the same time.

The big man's face deformed as muscle control became extinct, and any character and expression fled from the sack of meat his mind had occupied.

Blood gurgled out of his mouth like an overflowing drain. His head folded over on one side and he pitched forward.

A blade of clip-frame glass two inches wide was buried in the nape of his neck.

The tramp stood over her, his hands bleeding. 'It's my go!' he protested. 'You can't have it!'

Toshiko scrambled away, kicking the big man's body off her legs, crawling furiously. *Dawn of the Dead* rejects moaned and staggered after her.

'Tosh!'

She saw James, at the mouth of the yard, nearly in the street.

Toshiko leapt up, ignoring the tramp's hands as they closed on her back, and yanked the glove off her left hand. She dropped the Amok into it – thankful at least that the retinal pattern of blue lights went away – and launched the wrapped object down the yard towards James.

He caught it as neatly as Shane Warne at the gas-holder end. Turning, he ran out into the street towards the SUV. The mob followed him. Some of them kicked or even stood on Toshiko in their urge to pursue him. She curled up in a ball to protect herself.

The South Wales Police Unit, a flash-marked Vauxhall Vectra, had been responding to a call concerning a disturbance in the West Moors area. It was doing just under thirty miles an hour as it pulled in along the terrace by the pub. It caught James on its front bumper, hoicked him up over the bonnet in a thumping tumble, and bounced him off the windscreen. The windscreen crazed. The police car squealed to a halt. James rolled off the other side of the bonnet and fell on the road.

'Jesus bugger it!' said one of the officers as he leapt out. 'Where'd he come from?'

The officer ran over to James and bent down. 'Call it in, for Christ's sake!' he yelled at his oppo. 'Get a bloody ambulance!'

He knelt beside James. 'S'all right, mister, it's all right,' he said. The man they'd run down was in his early thirties, blond, clean cut. He was wearing black jeans, a white shirt, and a black leather coat. Good quality, all of it. The officer, who was twenty-two years old and whose name was Peter Picknall, had a feeling it was a bit odd someone so well dressed should be running out of a derelict lot. Running out of a trendy club, maybe.

'Is it coming?' he yelled.

'It's coming!' his oppo, Timmy Beal, yelled back. Squawks on the radio. The rain hissing.

'What the hell is this?' Timmy Beal called.

Peter Picknall didn't look up. The man they'd run down had been holding a black leather glove. When Peter picked it up, he realised there was something heavy inside it. The something heavy fell out and bounced on the road surface in the back-splashing rain.

It was something metal. Something oddly shaped.

Peter picked it up. Immediately, he knew it was the best thing he'd ever done. He felt like he'd won the lottery. Twice. During sex.

There were people all around him. There were people milling around the unit, people knocking Timmy Beal down and kicking him out of the way.

Peter heard Timmy Beal cry out in pain. He hardly cared. He stood up. He looked at the people closing in around him.

'Big big big,' he agreed. 'Now piss off, it's my go.'

Shiznay brought Mr Dine his shashlik, along with a side of shredded iceberg lettuce and a wedge of lemon.

'Thank you,' he said.

She shrugged.

'Shiznay?'

'What?'

Mr Dine studied her face. 'I have a feeling I've upset you somehow. Or let you down. I'm not very good at reading facial expressions where your kind is concerned.'

'My kind?' she asked, astonished that he could be so openly racist.

He considered her response. 'I feel I may have put that badly. I meant—'

'What? What did you mean?'

'What did I do to upset you?' he asked.

'It doesn't matter,' she said.

'Whatever it was, I'm sorry,' he replied. 'I never intended any slight or prejudicial slur. Really not. The cultural briefing, it's so vague really, when you get down to it. So many useful things they don't tell you.'

'What are you talking about?'

'I like you, Shiznay. I really do. I like you, and I like the spiced meat and the animal fats. And the alcohol.'

She shook her head sadly. 'I don't get you.'

He shrugged. 'No, I suppose you don't. But I do like you. You are kind. You have a physical aspect that is—'

'Oh, so you are a breast man, are you?' Shiznay sneered, and turned away.

'I was intending a compliment! Did it not come out right either?'

'Not so much,' she said.

He shrugged. 'Shiznay, all I want to say is that I'd hate to do anything to upset you. That was never my intention. You've been kind to me. I…'

'You what?'

Mr Dine sat upright suddenly, his back straight. His bright, wide eyes switched back and forth in his head. With his flock hair, he reminded Shiznay of the Eagle-Eyed Action Man her brother had once played with.

He stood up, bumping the table.

'I have to go,' he said.

'What?'

'Something's happened. I have to go.'

'But,' Shiznay protested, 'you've ordered.'

'I have to go.'

'You have to pay first.'

'Next time.'

'You have to pay. You've ordered food.'

'Next time,' he insisted, striding towards the door.

'Mr Dine!'

'The Principal,' mumbled Dine. 'The Principal is under threat. I must go.'

Shiznay ran after him. 'Waitaminute!'

Her father was blocking the door of the Mughal Dynasty. 'You have to pay, sir. Do you hear me, sir? You have to pay before you leave.'

Mr Dine raised his right hand, as if he was brushing away a fly. There was nothing in it, no force. It was a gesture. Nevertheless, Shiznay's father was suddenly sitting on the carpet and Mr Dine was gone.

Shiznay ran out into the street.

The lights of passing cars were blurred by the heavy rain. There was no sign of Mr Dine.

She looked around, baffled at how he could have disappeared so rapidly. Out of the corner of her eye, Shiznay had a fleeting impression of something leaving the pavement in a fluid leap that took it up onto a two-storey roof fifty yards away.

But that could only have been her imagination.

FOUR

The chain link bit into her fingers. Gwen wailed in pain and fear as the drape of fencing she was swinging from began to tear out from its moorings.

'Got you,' said Jack, and he had. He held her by the wrists. With a grunt of effort, he pulled her up onto the path.

'Oh shit,' she murmured. She had to lay where she was for a moment, her heart pounding. She rubbed at her throbbing fingers.

'I thought I was gonna—'

'But you didn't,' said Jack.

'But I thought I was—'

'But you didn't,' said Jack.

Gwen took a deep breath. 'Thank you.'

Jack shrugged off her gratitude. He seemed scratchy and aggravated, and not quite himself.

The mob had disappeared up the bank. Jack was already heading for the embankment steps.

'Coming?' he asked.

She got to her feet and followed him.

'Are you all right?' she asked.

'If this turns out not to be the End of the World, I'm going to be reading everyone the riot act when we're done.'

'And if it is the End of the World?'

Jack was taking the steps two at a time. 'Then I'll stick to the main points in the time available.'

'Jack?'

'Amateur hour,' he said, more to himself than her. 'This is a mess, even by our own high standards.'

'Jack!'

He ignored her. He wasn't stopping. They could hear voices up ahead, and see flashing blue lights strobing and bouncing off the shadowy buildings before them.

'I'll take that,' Owen told the policeman.

To emphasise his instruction, he clouted the policeman around the back of the head with the grip of his side-arm. The policeman slumped forwards across the boot of his unit. Owen dug the object out of his clenched fist. The rest of the crowd closed in, clamouring for him, grabbing at his clothes and his hair.

Pain was helping him heaps. The pain of being smacked in the mouth had lent Owen a wonderful sense of clarity and prickly anger that buoyed him up. He kicked and punched back at the crowd, relishing each pay-back impact, and began fighting his way clear of the milling, uncoordinated pack.

Something began to cancel out the pain, something very welcome and also very inviting. It spread out from his hand, up his arm, into his head and into his loins. Such a rush. Such a big big rush.

'Owen!'

'What?'

'Owen, let it go! Don't hold on to it too long! You can't hold on to it for too long!'

Owen blinked. The world was full of blue lights. The police car lights. Other lights.

'Owen!'

Owen blinked again, refocused, and saw James. James was pushing people out of his way, reaching at Owen. 'Give it to me! We have to get it into the SUV! Into the box, remember?'

'Not really necessary,' Owen replied.

'Give it to me!'

Owen raised his side-arm and aimed it at James's face. James stared back at the gun with wide, astonished eyes.

'Owen? Mate?'

'It's my turn,' Owen said.

* * *

Both Jack and Gwen felt it, like a sudden change in air pressure, or like chronic tinnitus when it suddenly stops. The rain suddenly felt colder.

They stepped out onto the street.

It was like the aftermath of a bomb blast. A few people were still standing, swaying aimlessly. Most of the others had fallen down in the rain. Some were sobbing or moaning, others limp and still, others looking around them in complete bewilderment.

The muttering had stopped.

Jack and Gwen stepped down past the stationary police car. Its cycling light bar reflected off the puddles like an Eighties disco.

'What's going on?' a middle-aged man asked them, leaning against the police car's right wing as if he was ill. His voice was tremulous, outraged. 'What the bloody hell is going on?'

They heard someone calling out someone else's name. A young girl splashed past, crying for her mum.

James was sitting on the road with his back against one of the rear wheels of the SUV. The SUV's hatch was open. A brushed-steel casket stood on the ground between his legs. James's face was in his hands.

Five yards away from him, Owen lay flat on his back on the tarmac, blinking up at the rain as he came round. He sat up sharply. 'What,' he began. 'The hell?' he added.

Gwen and Jack walked over to James. Toshiko appeared and, limping slightly, fell in step with them. James looked up at them as they drew close.

He smiled feebly and patted the locked lid of the containment box in front of him.

'Got it,' he said. 'Chastity belt. One hundred per cent chastity belt.'

No one spoke much on the way back to the Hub. Jack drove, hard and mean, as if there was some urgency left.

Ianto was there waiting for them when the cog hatch rolled aside and they walked into the gloomy stone vault. He was about to speak, but then thought better of it. It wasn't the tired, strung-out looks on their faces, or the bruises, the cuts or the torn clothing. It wasn't that James was limping painfully, or that Owen was helping Tosh.

It was the stone-hard glint in Jack Harkness's eyes. Ianto had only seen that once or twice before, but he knew it was something you didn't speak in the presence of.

Jack went straight up to his office, carrying the containment box. Shortly afterwards, they heard the old, heavy safe door clang.

Owen sat down at his work station, popped two painkillers and knocked them back with a swig of flat coke from an open can on his desk. He winced as the cold metal touched his puffed, bruised mouth.

'Right,' he said, 'med checks. Let's get them done right now, before I stop giving a toss.'

'You first, Tosh,' said James, leaning back against the lip of his station to ease the weight on his leg. 'You nearly got your head pulled off.'

'You bar-dived a moving car,' Toshiko countered. 'You've probably broken something. And Gwen's hands—'

'Gwen's hands are fine,' said Gwen, rubbing at the raw places where the chain link had stripped the skin off her fingers and palms. 'Gwen just needs some antiseptic spray, a stiff drink and a, oh I don't know…'

She looked at the others.

'… long holiday in the Maldives?'

Owen snorted, and wished he hadn't, as snorting made his nose bleed again.

'Christ alive,' murmured James. 'We're a bit of a mess, aren't we?'

They eyed each other up: the bruises, the lacerations, the swelling lips, the skinned knuckles.

'Still,' said James. 'Look on the bright side. It's not the End of the World.'

The four of them began to laugh. 'Stop it,' protested Toshiko, 'it hurts my ribs.' For some reason, this made it even funnier. Their combined laughter echoed out across the Hub.

'I suppose it is real funny.'

Jack was standing in the doorway of his office. He wasn't laughing.

'I mean,' he said, taking a few steps towards them, 'given what we're supposed to be. Real funny.'

'Oh, come on, Jack,' said Owen, 'if you can't laugh, what can you do?'

'I dunno,' said Jack. 'Not perform like a bunch of clowns maybe? What happened tonight was just embarrassing.'

'What?' asked Toshiko, stunned. 'Jack?'

'You heard me, Tosh. Did you see the mess we left behind us tonight? Forty-plus civilians with their lives bent out of shape. At least three dead. Hardly a covert operation.'

'We had to react fast,' said Toshiko. 'It was right on us. We had to improvise.'

'And excuse me,' said Owen, 'but plus, we were getting our arses handed to us.'

Jack shook his head wearily. 'I expect more. A lot more. This is Torchwood, not amateur theatre.'

He turned away.

'Oi!' cried Gwen.

'Save your "oi" for sometime when I care,' Jack told her over his shoulder, walking back into his office.

Gwen glanced at the others and then sprang up to follow Jack. 'Oi!'

'I'm not kidding around, Gwen,' Jack said. 'Don't "oi" me just now.'

She marched into his office anyway. He was sitting down behind his glass-topped desk.

'Where do you get off?' she asked.

'Wanna close the door?' he asked.

'No.'

'Do you suppose I might want you to close the door?'

'I couldn't give a toss, frankly. Where do you get off?'

Jack looked up at her. 'You tell me.'

'We got beat to shit tonight. Beat to shit. I know Tosh is hurt worse than she's letting on, and James must be banged up a treat. Owen too, but he's playing it all macho.'

'Good old Owen.'

'What is your bloody problem?'

Jack sat back. 'We should have been on top of that. We should have closed it down quick and clean, before anyone knew. In and out. That mess is going to be in the *Western Mail* tomorrow, Gwen. Mystery riot. Deaths. We can't paper over it. Fast bug out. No time to wipe memories or fake deaths. Just a big old mess.'

'We did the best we could, and—'

'That's what I'm saying. It wasn't enough. Not nearly enough.'

'I had an "and" then, by the way,' she said.

'So "and" me.'

'And we won, I was going to say.' said Gwen. 'We stopped it. We got it contained, even though it nearly killed us.'

Jack shrugged and rose to his feet. He looked at her. 'You know what I think? I think you're pissed at me, Gwen Cooper, because I called you amateurs.'

'Actually, no I'm not,' Gwen replied. 'I'm perfectly well aware of my amateur status. So's Tosh and James and Owen. See, the thing is, as far as we're aware, there *are* only amateurs in this line of work. 'Cept you, maybe. The things we have to deal with, Jack. The bloody things we have to deal with. We're only ever going to be amateurs, Jack.'

'That's what I'm afraid of,' Jack said.

Gwen sighed and shook her head. 'Sometimes…' she said.

'Sometimes what?'

'Sometimes you can be the biggest arse imaginable.'

'That all you got?' Jack asked, sitting back down. 'You done?'

'I think I am.'

'I think you are too. Walk away and check on the others. Don't come back until my headache's gone.'

'How will I know when your headache's gone?'

'I won't be armed.'

'Funny. Ha ha.'

'Look at my face.'

'Rather not,' she said, and swept out.

Halfway up the stairs to the medical area, she stopped in her tracks. *Rather not?* What was she, six?

'Just bruising,' said Owen, swinging the med-light away.

'Just bruising?' Toshiko echoed.

'OK, nasty, nasty bruising, but just bruising all the same.' Owen took another look at her throat. The pale skin was discoloured with brown fingermarks. 'Big bastard did a number on you.'

'Yes,' she said. 'Can I put my top back on now?'

Owen glanced back at her with a grin. 'Unless there's anything else you want me to examine?'

Toshiko shook her head and reached for her sweater. 'Check James, please.'

'If you wouldn't mind,' said James. He had stripped down to his jeans and was lying back on the exam bed. Owen had covered the stainless-steel surface with clean paper roll, but still he felt vulnerable. 'I feel like I'm waiting for my Y-shaped incision,' James complained.

Owen adjusted the lights. He palpated the green-black bruises and contusions on James's white torso.

'You really took a knock, didn't you, mate?' Owen said.

'Ow! Will I – ow! – live?'

Owen didn't reply. He waved his Bekaran deep-tissue scanner over James's torso and stared at the graphic displays.

'You've cracked a rib on the left side. I'll bond it for now, but go easy. No heavy lifting. Oh, and your left elbow's knackered up. Nothing fractured, but you've got serious tissue swelling. Hang on.'

He played the device over James's arm. 'Get that packed in ice and don't tit around with it.'

'Yes, Doctor.' James sat up.

They heard the metal creak of a locker opening. Gwen was up by the sink, going through the drug store for something to put on her hands.

'Let me do that,' Owen said.

'I can do it,' Gwen replied. 'Check yourself over.'

'Me?' asked Owen. 'I'm fine. I've had worse on an average Friday night off duty.' He sat down on a swivel chair, rode its castors across the tiled floor to the lower lockers, and leaned over. He winced, paused to take the side-arm out of his waistband and set it on the cabinet top, and then leaned over again and opened a drawer under the instrument rack. He produced a bottle of Scotch, screwed off the top, and took a swig.

'Medication, that's what I need,' he said, enjoying the burn.

'You should put that back in the Armoury,' said Toshiko, nodding at the gun.

'I will,' said Owen, 'though it's scragged anyway. Broken.' He looked at James, who was buttoning up his shirt.

'Sorry about, you know, pointing it at you,' Owen said.

'No sweat. You weren't yourself.'

Owen frowned. 'Still, bugger only knows how you disarmed me. Very kung fu.'

'It must've felt like it to you,' said James, 'but I was just flailing around. I think the thrall of the Amok made us all a bit slow. I only realised I'd knocked it out of your hand when I saw it on the ground.'

Dressing her hands, Gwen leaned on the rail and looked down at them. 'My head still hurts like a bastard,' she said.

'Mine too,' said James. Toshiko nodded.

'All in all, that wasn't nice, was it?' Gwen asked.

'Scale of one to ten?' asked James.

'Twenty-seven,' they all answered.

'What's up with Jack?' asked Owen, taking another swig from his bottle.

'Who knows?' replied Gwen. 'And right now, who cares?'

'Coffee?' asked Ianto.

Jack had walked upstairs to the Boardroom, and was sitting in darkness, looking down into the Hub.

'That'd be good,' he replied quietly.

'Rough night?'

'End of the World.'

'Analogously?'

'No, just almost.'

Ianto set the coffee down on the table beside Jack.

'They've been through the wars,' said Ianto.

'I guess. They're gonna have to get used to it.'

'Why's that?'

'More wars coming,' said Jack.

Ianto left him alone. Jack Harkness took the small, black tile out of his lap and looked at it. It was a piece of exotic technology that had been in his possession since the day he'd joined Torchwood.

The display hadn't changed. It had been blinking the same read-out for six weeks.

Jack Harkness didn't know exactly what the read-out meant, but he didn't need a doctor to know it wasn't in any way good.

They made last orders in a bar on Mermaid Quay. James got them in, but Toshiko and Owen had to carry the drinks because James was busy with the rubberised ice-pack around his elbow.

'Here's to the End of the World,' said Owen.

'Let's hope tomorrow's quiet,' said James.

'Let's hope tomorrow's POETS,' said Gwen.

They all looked at her.

'Oh, come on,' she said. '"P. O. E. T. S."? "Piss Off Early Tomorrow's Saturday"? The weekend approaches, people.'

'Speaking of which…' said James significantly.

'It hasn't?' asked Owen.

'It most surely has,' said James.

'Arrived?' asked Owen.

'At long last, as promised,' said James.

'The whole deleted series?' asked Toshiko.

'Oh yes,' said James, wiping beer froth off his upper lip. 'Came in the post this morning from my pal Archie in Burma. Three DVDs. The whole thing, unavailable in the West.'

'Bloody hell,' said Owen.

'So, I'm thinking,' said James, 'Saturday afternoon, three o'clock-ish, my place. I'll supply the in-flight nibbles. Owen, booze?'

'My middle name.'

'Tosh, some proper food, maybe, for half-time? Those Dragon Rolls and the tempura you made last Christmas, pretty please?'

Toshiko smiled and nodded.

'I can bring some nuts,' Gwen volunteered.

'They'll already be there,' grinned James.

'Do we ask Jack?' Gwen asked.

Owen frowned. Tosh shrugged.

'He pretends he doesn't like Andy, but he really does,' said Gwen.

'Of course he does!' James exclaimed. 'Everyone likes Andy.'

'Let's see what he's like tomorrow,' said Toshiko. 'Then decide if he gets an invite.'

Owen and Gwen nodded.

'But if he comes around makin' trouble,' said James in a beaky voice, 'I ain't gonna get in no flap.'

'I ain't gonna get in no flap!' echoed Owen, laughing.

'No, it's more nasal,' said Toshiko. 'Up in the nose. Listen to how James does it.'

'Hello?' said Owen. 'Punched in the face?'

'Oh!' said Gwen suddenly

'Oh what?' asked James.

'I just remembered. I promised I'd go to the pictures with Rhys this Saturday. *Pirates of the Caribbean 3.*'

'Can't you get out of it?' asked Toshiko. 'I mean, we're talking unseen Andy.'

Gwen pulled a face. 'Christ knows, I've blown him out twice this last week. I think we'll have issues if I muck him around again.'

'But it's Andy,' Toshiko protested.

'I know, I know…'

'You should just chuck him and have done,' said Owen.

'What?'

'Rhys,' Owen said, sipping his drink. 'You should just chuck the bugger and have done. He cramps your style.'

'Owen!' Toshiko scolded.

'I can't just chuck him!' Gwen said, outraged. 'I—'

'You what?' asked James quietly.

Gwen looked at James, and made a small smile. 'I live with him,' she said.

'Well, just make it if you can,' James said. 'It's going to be a blast. Thirteen episodes. Thirteen whole episodes.'

'I know,' said Gwen. 'I know.'

***

43

She got back in just after one, creeping like a mouse into the flat in Riverside. The flat was dark, but she could hear the telly still playing from the lounge-diner.

Gwen realised she was very hungry. Her head was still throbbing. She went into the lounge-diner. The TV was playing News 24, but there was no sign of Rhys. Some magazines lay on the couch. A pizza box.

It was empty.

She scurried into the kitchen area, and opened the fridge. Cheese appealed, and grapes. She found some bread in the bread bin.

Her bandaged hands were making heavy weather of slicing the cheese when a voice said, 'You're home, then?'

Rhys stood in the landing doorway, his hair tousled, his eyes heavy with sleep.

'Yes,' she said, as brightly as she could muster.

'What are you doing?'

'Making a snack. I didn't get anything earlier. Want something?'

Rhys shook his head, but then helped himself to a slice of the cheese she'd cut. She sliced some more.

'How was your day?' she asked.

He shrugged. 'OK. I taped *How Clean Is Your House?* for you. Aggie finds a rat in the kitchen.'

'Oh, yeah?'

'You're late,' Rhys said.

'Work,' she replied. She took a bite of her sandwich. Cheese fell out. 'What are we doing then, on Saturday?'

'I thought it was the pictures,' Rhys said, scratching his head. 'You get a better offer?'

'No, no,' she said. 'There's a work thingy, but I can just not go.'

'Be nice to spend some time.'

'It would.'

'Important work thingy?'

'Oh, no. Just some… some stuff that's come in from Burma.'

'Top secret, eh?'

'Deleted.'

'Ah,' Rhys said. 'What's up with your hands, babe?'

'I hurt them. It's nothing.'

'How d'you hurt them?'

'Work.'

Rhys was silent for a moment. 'You know, there comes a point...' he began.

'What sort of point?' Gwen asked.

'The sort of point when "work" ceases to mean anything, or be an answer for anything. It's the ultimate excuse, the ultimate get-out-of-jail-free card. It's like faynights.'

'What?'

'Faynights. You never say that in the playground? You're it! Faynights. You're tagged! Faynights. To cover all excuse. Diplomatic immunity.'

'Have you had a drink, babe?' she asked him. She'd lost her appetite. The sandwich went down on the counter.

'You say "work" the same way. You do.'

'Rhys, I've had a bugger of a day and I don't fancy a row right now.'

'A row? How could we have a row? Everything I say, you'd just answer "work". Where have you been? "Work". Why haven't I seen you this week? "Work". Why are you out so late? "Work". Why haven't we had a shag in a month? "Work".'

'Oh, give over! It's not like that!'

'It bloody is! It bloody is, Gwen!'

Gwen's head was kicking off again. She threw the butter knife into the sink and pushed past Rhys.

'Gwen?'

'Shut up!'

'Where are you going?'

She looked back at him. 'You know, this evening, someone I have very little regard for suggested I should chuck you.'

'Why don't you then?' Rhys roared back.

She glared at him. 'I have no bloody idea,' she replied. She turned and headed for the front door.

'Where the hell are you going now?' he yelled after her.

'Work!' she replied, and slammed the front door after her.

It was only after fifteen minutes of wandering the streets looking for a taxi that Gwen began to cry.

High above the city of Cardiff, Jack Harkness stood in the cold breeze and looked out at the stars. Sirens whooped in the amber streets below him.

Up high, he had time to think. To clear his mind. Being up high always put him in an expansive mood. He looked down at the city, the lit thoroughfares like interlocking bars of light in the black continuum below. He heard the throb of the late traffic, the wail of emergency vehicles plying the streets, their chopping lights moving like cursors along the bars.

His mind was easing a little. Tough night. Rough night. One of the worst, and it still wasn't over. Today, or the next day, or the next, the night was going to last forever. Even so, he began to relax a little. He felt safe and powerful up there, confident that he was the only being in Cardiff who could ascend so high and regard so much without being seen.

In both particulars, Jack Harkness was entirely wrong.

Mr Dine waited, crouching down below a parapet. He could feel the pull. He resisted. He had to check first. Be sure. It might just have been a false alarm.

He stood up and stepped into space.

Twenty metres below, he landed effortlessly, and began to run across the slanted roofs.

Owen Harper poured himself another measure of Scotch, and toyed with the glass. By his own standards, he was falling down drunk. Luckily, he was in his own apartment overlooking the Bay.

He gazed out at the lights.

'I used your soap, is that all right?' the girl said, coming out of the en suite.

Owen looked around. 'Yeah, sure.'

What the hell was her name again? Lindy? Linda? The only thing he was sure of was that she had the most tremendous rack in the history of tremendous racks.

'What are you doing?' she asked.

He stared at her. She wasn't wearing anything, and that helped to remind him why he'd brought her home with him in the first place. He took a sip of Scotch.

'Looking at you,' he said.

The bath was neck-deep and warm, and suffused with fragrant oils. Toshiko Sato turned the lights down until only the candles made a glow, and slipped off her bath robe.

She sank into the bath. The warm water enveloped and embraced her, soothing her bruises and her tired, weary body.

She lay back, and reached for her glass of wine.

James Mayer paused the television remote and cocked his head. Someone was definitely tapping on his door.

He got up, gingerly, feeling the pain in his body, and padded barefoot to the door.

'Hello,' said Gwen.

'What are you doing here?' he asked.

'Is me being here a problem?' she asked him.

'Hell, no, I was just surprised. I didn't expect—' He looked at her. 'You know today is Friday, just, don't you?'

'Yeah.'

'And you know the Andy Pinkus Marathon doesn't start until Saturday?'

'Yeah.'

'Gwen?'

'Are you telling me I can't stay here until Saturday?' she asked.

'No,' James replied. 'Have I ever?'

Her mouth met his. He pulled her into the flat.

Later, during a brief intermission, she got up, naked, closed the door, and turned the deadbolts.

SIX

Monday morning, with a sky like a dirty fleece above Cardiff.

As the kettle boiled, Davey Morgan fed the cat, and then made up his flask.

'So, anyway, I left it in the shed,' he said, bringing his story up to date. 'It didn't seem to want to be disturbed, so I thought, it's doing no harm here, I thought, and left it there.'

He took his digging jacket down off the door-peg in the little back kitchen. It was the top half of an old suit. He reckoned he'd been married in it, in '48, but Glynis had always insisted he'd been wearing it when they'd first met, at the social in Porthcawl, which would have been '46. Glynis had always had a keen memory for such details, either that, or she had always been better at asserting her version of the truth. He missed her.

The jacket had been pretty done in by the mid 1950s, but she'd refused to let him throw it out, for 'sentimental reasons'. So it had become his digging jacket, her name for it, reserved for the allotment in cold weather. Pretty good run it had had since then, for a demob suit with feeble stitching.

'I suppose I'd better check on it,' he said. The cat was as indifferent to this remark as it had been to the rest of his story. Bowl cleared, it sat down like a Degas ballerina, toes en point, and began to lick its arse.

'You be all right here for an hour or two?' Davey asked. The cat looked up briefly, the tip of its tongue slightly protruding, then went back to its ablutions. He wasn't talking to the cat anyway. He was talking to the picture on the hall table. But he always pretended he was talking to the cat, because if you talked to pictures, you had to be bonkers, didn't you?

He put on his cap and patted the pockets of his digging jacket. Glynis had died in 1978. Complications, the doctor had said, which had seemed a reasonable diagnosis. As complications went, dying was a considerable one.

Every Friday night, she'd slipped a packet of mints into the pocket of the digging jacket for him to find every Saturday morning out on the allotment. He still checked, even though there hadn't been a packet of mints to discover in twenty-nine years. There was a wrapper, though. A twenty-nine-year-old scrap of foil and paper. He'd never had the heart to throw it away.

He went out into the yard, and locked his backdoor. Leaning against the wall, he put on his wellies, then walked off down the backyard to the lane behind the houses that joined with the allotment path.

A pneumatic drill stammered like a frantic blacksmith. They were building new homes on Connault Way. The land buy-out had included a large swathe of the allotment space that had once surrounded the streets of Cathays. Madness. Jim French, who grew winter veg on the plot three over from Davey's, had told him on the nod that the council were considering selling off their patches to the developers too. How could that be right, in any man's world? What would he do for lettuce and spuds and marrows then?

He could smell brick dust and rain on the air. The new houses looked like box skeletons over the hedge. Prefab rubbish, like Airfix kits, thrown up in a month, the speed of weeds. Not like the front-and-backs on his street. Decent brick, wooden doors. Course, his could use a lick of paint, but still.

There was no one on the allotments, not on a Monday morning. The iron gate squealed as he let himself through. More than half the plots had gone back to the wild. Nobody wanted the toil of an allotment any more, not when there were Kwik-Saves full of guavas and broccoli and pre-washed beans.

That was why he'd been digging in the plot next to his. He hadn't paid the annual fee for it, but it had been abandoned more than ten years ago, and he hadn't seen the harm of it. And that's when he'd found it. Just that last Saturday, forking the cleared earth while the stripped weeds crackled lazily in his brazier. He'd just had the clearest taste of a mint in his mouth, just for a second, the memory of a mint, when the tines of his fork struck it.

The boys had been there again, Sunday night. Empty beer cans on the path, a cloche kicked over. Davey still had the tub of black paint ready, in case they ever took it upon themselves to decorate his shed again, the way they had in the spring. Foulmouth buggers couldn't even spell. *Taff Morgan iz a old purv.*

Davey went up to the shed and undid the padlock. It was still there, where he had left it, propped up in his wheelbarrow, angled slightly as if it was looking out of the grimy window.

'All right, then?' he asked.

It made no more response than his cat had done.

'I was wondering if you had a name,' Davey said. 'Just to put us on civil terms. I'm Davey, but they all call me Taff. The wife even called me Taff.'

A little hum: no more response than that.

'Daft name, I agree. What do you call it now? A stereotype, is that it? Had it since '42. Royal Fusiliers, boys from all over, no older than me. Boys from Liverpool and Birmingham and Luton. Jock, see, he came from Aberdeen, so naturally, he was Jock. And I was Taff. Taff Morgan. The Welsh lad. Oh, it was a simple thing. You didn't argue. You were glad to be noticed.'

Another hum. A slight change in pitch.

Davey took out his flask. 'How about a cup of tea?' he asked.

Monday morning, rain-clouds like bruises over the Bay.

Gwen let herself into the Hub via the little information centre on the Quay. She could smell Ianto's coffee even before the cog-door rolled open.

'All right?' Owen asked her. His face had bruised up well since she'd last seen him on Saturday. He had even more of a pouty expression than usual.

'It looks like you've had collagen implants,' she observed.

'Thanks for that.' He paused. 'How's the head?'

Gwen shrugged. The weekend had been a serious unwind, though she knew there would be consequences. It was only come Sunday night, when she'd simply crashed, that she'd realised how deeply the effects of primary and secondary contact with the Amok had worked her over. They'd been so bothered at the time by their bruises and cuts and contusions, the physical cost of the operation.

Bruises would fade. Skinned fingers would heal. The mind was where the real harm had been done. It had eased, the tram-tracks of pain snowing over, but she still felt sick from time to time, and she kept getting a stabbing pain behind her left eye. She shuddered to think what they had all been exposed to, shuddered to imagine what it had all been about.

'My head's screwed,' she replied, 'to be perfectly frank. But it's getting better. Like an ache that's going away.'

'Like the day after the day after a bad hangover,' Owen agreed, nodding.

'Yes,' she said. 'Though in your case, it *was* a bad hangover. You were putting it away, Saturday.'

'It was a laugh, though,' said Owen.

She smiled and nodded. 'It was a laugh,' she agreed.

It had been a laugh, the four of them at James's place. A necessary venting, like safety measures at an overcooking reactor. Without downtime like that, the 'job' would do them in.

Gwen wondered how long she'd been putting inverted commas around the word job, and how much longer she'd keep doing it.

'Coffee?' asked Ianto, appearing like a genie from an expertly rubbed lamp.

'I love you,' said Gwen, taking hers.

'I love you more,' Owen told Ianto, 'and I'm prepared to have your babies.'

Ianto smiled patiently.

Owen went back to his work station and sat down. 'Hey, Ianto?'

Ianto came over.

Owen picked up the side-arm from the clutter on his station. 'This had better go back into the Armoury. Could you?'

'Of course.'

Ianto took the weapon and looked at it. 'It's mangled,' he said.

'I guess I dropped it,' Owen replied, punching up newsgroups on his screen.

'From what? Orbit?'

'No, I just dropped it. Why?'

Ianto shrugged and went off about his business.

'Jack in his office?' Gwen asked Toshiko as she came over to the lab space.

'I guess. I haven't seen him.'

'What are you doing?' Gwen asked. 'Isn't that…?'

Toshiko sat back, removed her eye-guards, and took a sip of her coffee.

'Yes, it is,' she said. 'Mmm, I love that man.'

'It's me he's marrying,' Gwen said. She peered at the pulsing suspension field the containment console was generating.

'The Amok.'

'Jack said I could run the numbers on it. Basic probes and diagnostic tests.'

'I thought you said you hadn't seen him?'

'He left me a Post-it. "Tosh – take the Amok and run the numbers on it, please, basic probes and diagnostic tests."' She showed Gwen the Post-it, the beautiful copperplate handwriting that nobody did any more.

'Can you tell what it is yet?' asked a bad Rolf Harris impression.

James was standing behind them. Gwen tried to act casual, but it was hard not to make the sort of eye contact that would set off sirens.

'No,' said Toshiko.

'OK. Is it safe?' James asked, peering at the thing suspended in the glowing field.

'Eight levels of safeguard insulation,' said Toshiko. 'Ward screens. Focus blockers. Chastity belt.'

'Good,' said James. 'I don't want another mind-screw like that.'

'Yeah, me neither,' said Toshiko. 'I'm still not thinking straight. I've got what my father used to call "hand-me-down head". Nasty. Befuddled. How are you?'

'Fine,' James said.

'How're the ribs?'

'Fine. No heavy lifting, Owen said.'

'What?' Toshiko asked, glancing at Gwen. Gwen had involuntarily sniggered.

'Nothing.'

'What?' Toshiko asked again, eyeing Gwen inquisitively.

Gwen shook her head. A memory, unbidden. James hoisting her up against his fridge-freezer in the small hours of Friday morning. Carrying her weight, lost in passion.

'Nothing. Well, that thing was a real twenty-seven, wasn't it?' Gwen said.

'Twenty-seven,' said James.

'Absolutely,' said Toshiko. She made to replace her eye-guards. 'Thanks for Saturday, by the way. I haven't laughed so much in ages. The Andy stuff was priceless.'

'My pleasure,' said James. He and Gwen walked away, leaving Toshiko to her work.

'You're never heavy lifting,' James whispered to her.

'Stop it!'

'You left this at my place,' he added, handing over her MP3 player.

'Oh, sorry. Thanks.'

'New listings,' he said as he walked away.

Gwen put her right earpiece in, and selected menu. Music began. He'd loaded 'Coming Up For Air' and eight other tracks by Torn Curtain, his favourite band. 'Coming Up For Air' had been playing during the fridge-freezer moment.

'Heads up.'

Jack appeared on the walkway above the work areas. 'Morning, all. I trust you've had your coffee. Busy week. James, can you get onto your source in the Land Registry and background check that commune in Rhondda? It could be nothing, but I've got an itch says it's a cult, and that web page you found doesn't fill me with confidence that it's entirely, you know, terrestrial?'

'On it,' James said.

'Good. Owen?'

Owen swung around on his chair. 'Still nothing on the missing pets in Cathays. I'm cross-referencing a police report of small bones found in a skip behind a youth club. Weevil-watch is clean for the last week. Oh, and the flying saucer seen over Barry turned out to be an escaped windsock. I'm also keeping tabs on that man in Fairwater who rang the Samaritans and told them a Baycar bus had eaten his wife. I think it's a Care in the Community issue, but you never know.'

'You never do,' Jack agreed. 'And the Mr and Mrs Peeters thing?'

'I'm still watching that one,' Owen said. 'You'll know as soon as I do.'

'If they start hatching, I'll want to know *before* you know,' Jack said. 'Tosh?'

'Still busy analysing the Amok,' Toshiko replied.

'Yeah, well, skip that for now. I've sent a file to your station. Check it out. Either I'm wrong – and please God, I am – or an auto mechanic in Grangetown is blogging on how to make a portable meson gun. In Sumarian.'

'I'll look into that.'

'Would you?' Jack looked around. 'Gwen?'

'Yeah?'

'Got a minute?'

Gwen walked into his office. Jack had newspapers spread out on his desk.

'Did we make the front page, then?' she asked.

Jack shook his head. 'Best we got was two inches on page eighteen.'

'So, that's good, isn't it?'

'Yeah. It's good. Everybody caught up in The Amok Incident was too damaged to remember anything coherent.'

'Well, that's kind of good.'

'Best we could hope for.'

Gwen waited. Then she said, 'I think I'd better apologise.'

'Really?'

'I was harsh, on Thursday. Really very harsh. I'm sorry.'

Jack sat back and sighed. 'No, you're all right. I should apologise. I was out of line. I didn't realise how ... how insidious the Amok was. I think it affected me more than I knew. Made me act—'

'It's OK.'

'It's not OK. It deserves an apology,' Jack said.

'Accepted.'

Jack nodded. 'We friends again, Gwen Cooper?'

'Always were.'

He nodded again. 'You have a good weekend?'

'Yeah.'

'Hang out with the others?'

'Yeah,' she said. There was no point lying.

Jack stood up. '*Andy Pinkus, Rhamphorhynchus*. The lost season. As good as James claimed?'

'Yeah, it was.' How did he know?

'I know everything, Gwen,' Jack said. 'Maybe I could borrow the disks sometime. I do like Andy. Smart-funny, like *Ren and Stimpy*, you know what I mean.'

'Yes, I do.'

'Well, let's get to work,' Jack said.

'The Amok,' Gwen said. 'Do you know what it was?'

'That? Oh, yeah,' Jack replied.

He flipped over one of the newspapers on his desk and tapped a finger on the back-page word search.

'A puzzle?' James said.

'Yeah.'

'We were nearly killed by a word search?'

Jack nodded. 'Kinda.'

'People died because of a word search?' Toshiko asked.

'OK,' Jack said, 'hurry up and get over that part. I was making an analogy. A Jamesian analogy. The Amok is a puzzle, a mental exercise. Like a crossword or – yes – a word search. Trouble is, it was built by and for a species who exist in more dimensions than we do. Their idea of a simple puzzle invaded our minds in ways we couldn't cope with. We weren't made for logic challenges on that scale. We are simple, sturdy, four-dimensional beings. An eleven-dimensional sudoku is going to be a bit of a head-melt to the likes of us. Addictive, inviting, perplexing, infuriating, involving... but beyond our feeble means to solve.'

'You're saying I was mullahed by a sudoku?' Owen asked, joining them.

'Yes,' said Jack. 'What news?'

'This just in. The Peeters are hatching,' Owen said.

'Damn! Fighter Command!' said James.

'Exactly. Let's roll,' said Jack.

SEVEN

The alley beside the Mughal Dynasty smelled of exhaust fumes and cooked garlic on a Monday morning. The sky was spitting gobs of rain and, from outside the restaurant, Shiznay could hear the shouts of the delivery driver from the meat packers.

She was wearing a jogging suit, her hair tied back, and was lugging four tied-up sacks full of kitchen waste from the Sunday buffet ('two for the price of one!').

Shiznay opened the lid of the galvanised dumpster. She heard a scurrying, a settling, and braced herself for the rats that often popped up out of the slurry. Kamil ought to have been doing this drudge work, but Kamil had been out with his mates the previous night, and had greeted their mother's calls with groans and rebukes. 'Shiz, Shizzy, be my good daughter and take out the rubbish.'

And she was, always, a good daughter.

She threw the bags of rubbish into the dumpster, swinging from the waist. She heard a stirring, and looked for something to flip the lid shut without having to get too close.

The noise wasn't a rat. It was coming from behind the dumpster.

Mr Dine unfolded himself and stood up in the light. He blinked at Shiznay.

She stared at him. 'You,' she said, 'should go away.'

'Shiznay,' he said, focusing on her. 'I… I'm sorry, I—'

'You should go away, right now! You're not welcome here!'

Mr Dine breathed in and exhaled slowly.

'Were you… sleeping behind there?' she asked. 'Did you sleep there last night?'

He shrugged. 'I crashed.'

She said nothing, just stared at him.

He looked back. 'I wanted to come back, Shiznay. To apologise. Is your father all right? I have a horrible feeling I might have hurt him the other day.'

'He's fine. But he doesn't want to see you around here any more.'

Dine nodded, understanding. 'Of course. I can appreciate why he feels that way.' He took something out of his jacket and held it out to her. 'I left without payment transaction. I wanted to repair that error. I trust this will be adequate.'

'I don't want any trouble. Just go. Go.'

'Please take this, Shiznay, and give it to your father, with my solemn apologies.'

He stank. He'd been sleeping in the dumpster, by the smell of it. Reluctantly, she put out her hands, expecting a few crumpled notes.

He put rocks in her hands instead. Grit, more like. She looked down. 'What is…?'

Diamonds. Eighteen rough-cut diamonds. Or specks of broken glass, but she was somehow sure they were actual diamonds.

'Who the hell are you?' she asked.

'A customer.'

'I can't take these.'

'Why not? Surely they sufficiently reimburse your restaurant for the meal I ran out on?'

'I don't know where you got them from. Are they dodgy?'

'Dodgy?'

'You know, shonky?'

'You have used two words I don't know.'

'Dodgy? Shonky? How the hell do you not know words like that?'

'I'm not from around here.'

'That much is certain. Where the hell did you get a handful of diamonds? You pick them up off the street, did you?'

He looked blank for a moment. 'I found them in the waste unit.'

'Right.'

'A pencil. A broken pencil. Just a stub. One of yours I think. The kind

57

you write down orders with, certainly. It was simply a matter of graphite compression.'

'What?'

'Nothing illegal was done. I performed the compression manually.'

'You what?'

'It was a simple action.'

Shiznay stared at him. 'Were you sleeping there all night?'

Mr Dine smiled. 'From time to time, I am suddenly alerted to action. I usually have little warning, and the priority takes over. I am invested. I can't argue with it. The calorific cost of alert is huge. I expend at a high level, and then crash rapidly. It usually turns out to be a false alarm.'

'I don't understand what you're saying.'

'I know. Please accept the payment. And please pass on my abject apologies to your father. My intention was not to hurt him. Alert protocols had taken over. The Principal appeared to be in danger. I have no choice but to act when that happens.'

'Mr Dine, I—'

'One last thing, Shiznay. Close your eyes.'

She closed her eyes, and heard a slight, whooshing sound. When she opened her eyes again, he had vanished. Which was, of course, impossible, given the geography of the alley.

Unless he had gone…

Shiznay Uhma looked up at the sky, into the sporadic rain.

'Come back when you want,' she said.

A fine Edwardian house on a quiet residential street in Pontcanna. A black SUV, the automotive equivalent of mirror shades, sitting outside under the council-tended elms.

This was not amateur. Gwen was quietly delighted at that part. Not so overjoyed about the mucus.

The Droon were migratory, and sometimes came to Cardiff the way that these things did. According to conversations, operational post-mortems, Torchwood had dealt with the Droon eleven times since Jack had taken charge. Three of those occasions had been since Gwen had joined the team. They'd had practice.

Mr and Mrs Peeters lived in that fine Edwardian house on that quiet residential road. They'd lived there for twenty-six years. Mr Peeters was a retired history teacher, and his wife still taught piano privately. The Droon lived inside Mr and Mrs Peeters. They'd lived there for eight months.

James and Toshiko had gone around the back of the house. Gwen and Jack had approached the front door. Owen watched the side gate by the neatly maintained garage. They had brought the essential kit: audio paddles, tongs, Loctite baggies, pac-a-macs, surgical gloves, wet-wipes, tight-res scanners and carpet cleaner.

The thing with the Droon was that they were generally harmless. On arrival, they took up residence somewhere warm and moist, like a sinus passage, and stayed there, in a kind of contented fugue state. The worst harm they ever did was to trigger mild, cold-like symptoms.

Unless they hatched.

Mostly, they went away again without hatching after a few months. Just went away, or simply died and were ejected, into a Kleenex or during a sneeze, without their place of residence ever knowing about it. It was unnecessarily difficult and risky to try to remove them in their fugue state: better by far, for the health of the host, to allow them go to away of their own accord.

But, one time in ten, they pupated and advanced to the next phase of their haphazard, incomprehensible life cycle. That one time in ten required swift reaction. Fighter Command.

Sudden elevations in alpha-wave patterns were a reliable overture to hatching. As soon as the Peeters had been identified as Droon carriers, Toshiko and Owen had snuck into their house one afternoon and wired it with pattern monitors.

'Spike's increasing,' Owen said, checking his compact scanner. His Bluetooth carried his words to the others.

Jack rang the bell.

Mrs Peeters was a nice, elderly lady with a terrible head-cold. She squinted at Jack and Gwen with swollen, half-shut eyes.

'We're from the Gas Board,' said Jack, igniting a toothy smile.

That didn't seem especially credible to Mrs Peeters. A pretty girl in a black bomber jacket and a matinee idol in a greatcoat, both of them wearing clear plastic pac-a-macs over the top of their outer clothes. Sniffing and rubbing her nose on a hankie, she asked to see some proper ID.

With a simple, deft gesture, Jack showed her an audio paddle instead. By the time Mrs Peeters had realised the thing in his hand wasn't a laminated ID, the paddle – a matt-black plastic instrument the size and shape of a flattened salad server – was pressed against her forehead and Jack had thumbed the small, red 'on' switch.

Mrs Peeters took it rather well, all things considered. She let out a sharp moan, staggered backwards with her fingers pressed to her temples, and pressurised slime cannoned out of her violated nostrils.

'Catch her,' Jack advised.

Gwen was already doing so. She secured Mrs Peeters' falling form around the shoulders, dragged her quickly and gently into the hall, and lowered her onto the hall runner. Jack stepped inside behind them, and closed the front door.

Mrs Peeters was effectively unconscious, but her body bucked and rocked with involuntary coughs and throaty choking noises. An impressively noxious quantity of viscous yellow mucus was flowing from her mouth and nose.

'Recovery position,' said Jack. 'Keep her airway clear.'

'Doing it,' Gwen replied. She had rolled Mrs Peeters onto her side, and reached her fingers into the lady's spluttering mouth, pulling out globules of mucal matter. Thank God for surgical gloves. And pac-a-macs. The blast pattern of Mrs Peeters' first sneeze covered the front of Jack's plastic slicker like glue.

'Give her another go,' Gwen said.

Jack bent down and administered the paddle to Mrs Peeters' head again. As they hatched, the Droon were especially vulnerable to infrasonic bursts.

Mrs Peeters began to rack and cough more violently. A much more considerable flood of mucus began to pour out of her head, thick and soft like sugar icing.

'Oh, that's nasty,' said Gwen, hard at work.

A voice called out from somewhere. A man's voice, calling his wife's name between phlegmy coughs.

'Tosh?' Jack advised over his headset.

At the back of the house, in a dew-damp garden of mature apple trees and hydrangeas, Toshiko and James started to move. James had already popped the catch on the French windows.

The back room was a sitting room, with a handsome baby grand and antimacassars over the chair backs. An aspidistra stood on a jardinière beside a rack of sheet music. A number of school photographs hung on the walls; tiers of uniformed kids staring at the camera in landscape format.

James and Toshiko went out into the hallway. The voice floated down from upstairs. 'Viv? Who is it? Who's that at the door?'

Back down the hall, by the front door, Jack and Gwen were dealing with Mrs Peeters. The poor woman was emitting wet, splattery sneezes and gurgles.

Without waiting for further instruction, James and Toshiko went up stairs.

'Whoo! Really spiking now!' Owen warned over the link.

'Understood,' replied James. An upper landing, with a blanket box and some framed watercolours and mezzotints of Snowdonia. A rattling, fluid cough coming from a nearby bedroom.

Mr Peeters had taken to his bed the day before. The room smelled of menthol and cough linctus. There were two boxes of tissues beside the rumpled bed. Mr Peeters had made it to the doorway, unsteady and flushed. He was wearing flannelette pyjamas and a worried expression.

'Who…?' he began to say.

'Health visitors,' said Toshiko smoothly. 'Your wife called us.'

'Just sit back down on the bed, Mr Peeters,' said James, 'you ought not to be walking around.'

Mr Peeters was too poorly to argue. He allowed himself to be manoeuvred back onto the bed. He was still confused, flu-stupid. He sneezed, and snot hung from his left nostril like an icicle.

Toshiko helped him wipe with a tissue.

'Why are you wearing plastic macs?' the elderly man asked.

'It's raining,' said Toshiko.

'Just going to take your temperature, Mr Peeters,' said James, producing an audio paddle.

'There we go,' said Jack. Gwen had already spotted it in the pooling mucus. A wriggling blob, pale blue and sickly, about the size of a cockroach. Jack fished in with the stainless steel tongs, grabbed the blob out of the jellied goo and bagged it.

'Watch closely,' said Jack, 'there may be more than one.'

'What's the maximum you've ever seen?' asked Gwen.

'Six,' said Jack.

'From one nose?'

'Unlikely as it seems.'

'There's another!' Gwen announced, with distaste.

This blob was more active, its blue casing slightly ruptured to reveal something sharper and blacker inside. It wriggled away across the parquet flooring.

There was no time for finesse with the tongs. Jack grabbed it with his gloved hands and shook it off his fingers into another baggie. He held the baggie up to the light and shook it, studying the tiny, grotesque thing wiggling inside.

'Just in time,' Jack said. 'That one had almost shed.'

Mrs Peeters had gone into a paroxysm of gagging coughs. The matter flowing out of her mouth and nose was thinner suddenly. Watery snot streaked with blood. The pool on the floor widened.

'Any more?' Gwen asked.

Jack scanned the woman. 'No,' he said, but he gave Mrs Peeters a third blast with the paddle to make sure. 'Her body is just voiding now,' Jack said. 'Cleaning out the nest. Go put the kettle on.'

Toshiko extracted the third organism from Mr Peeters' phlegm-stopped mouth and cleared his airway. She'd had to take the old man's false teeth out. The thing clamped in the jaws of her tongs was almost all the way out of its pale blue casing. It had begun to unfold. Black, barbed, needle limbs the length and thickness of pencils quivered as they filled with ichor and began to inflate.

'Yuck,' she said.

'Kill it,' said James. 'It's too well formed to just bag.'

With a grimace, Toshiko dropped the emerging thing into a bag, put the bag on the corner of the bedside cabinet and flattened it with a sharp blow from a hardback Wilbur Smith.

'I think he's clear,' said Jack. He had Mr Peeters' limp form rolled forward and well supported, so that the muck drooling out of him could pour onto the bedroom carpet. There was a lot of it, like wallpaper paste stained with brown sauce.

Toshiko scanned the unfortunate ex-history teacher.

'We're there. He's clean.'

Owen paced on the path beside the garage. Birds twittered obliviously in the wet trees above.

'Come on,' he called. 'Are we done yet?'

'Owen?' Jack replied, after a pause.

'Yeah.'

'Get the carpet cleaner and the scrub-packs from the SUV.'

'How does that end up being my job?' Owen complained.

They put the couple to bed, and wiped the place down. Owen grumbled as he went to work with the mop.

'This is disgusting,' he said.

'You should have been here earlier,' Gwen said. She'd made the rehydrating drinks as per Jack's recipe: salts, glucose, antibiotics, warm water, plus a subtle cocktail of drugs that wiped short-term memory. Gwen wasn't fond of using those.

'You want me to strip out the pattern monitors?' James asked.

'We'll come back in a week and do that,' said Jack. 'Better keep them under watch for a few days more.'

They bagged up the soiled macs and gloves and disposable towels in waste sacks, and locked up after them.

Later, when Mr and Mrs Peeters woke, tucked up in bed, they were both feeling very much better.

As the team got into the SUV, Gwen's cellphone rang. She checked the display. RHYS.

She pressed 'reject call'.

EIGHT

Sometime around four o'clock, after a bout of late rain, Davey Morgan heard voices outside the shed.

He'd spent the morning on the allotment, then gone in for his lunch. Some vague urge had brought him back out in the mid afternoon, some desire to potter around the shed, sorting through old seed packets and polystyrene bedding trays.

Davey had chattered away. The thing in the wheelbarrow had hummed once or twice. Davey wondered if the humming was actually his imagination. His hearing was not as good as it had once been.

He heard the voices well enough. He went outside and pretended to check on the brazier. It was just turning dark, the very edge of dusk. Three or four of the boys, the yobbos, were having a kick-about on a patch of waste ground in the corner of the allotment area. They were shouting, and calling each other all colour of filthy words. Davey prodded the brazier, trying to look as if he wasn't watching.

The yobbos ignored him, or didn't see him. There'd be a broken shed window or two, by the morning, in all probability. He worried about the thing in the shed. After a while, he went back into the shed, laid the thing down in the barrow, put a piece of potato sacking over it, and wheeled it out. He locked the shed, and carried on down the path towards the gate with the barrow. Its wheel squeaked annoyingly.

He heard the dense, pneumatic *thunt* of a ball being kicked, and flinched slightly as it soared past him and bounced across Mrs Pryce's plot, snapping fronds of kale, and throwing aslant a nice head of white celery.

Driven by jeers, one of the yobbos flashed past Davey, laughing, on his way to recover the ball. His trainers did more damage than the ball had managed.

Davey couldn't contain himself. 'Standing on the bloody veg!' he exclaimed.

Scooping up the ball, the youth glared at him with a mystified look. 'What?'

'You're trampling all over the bloody vegetables!' Davey cried.

The youth looked down. He was a thin, whippety man-boy, long of neck and ping-pong balled of Adam's apple. Eighteen or nineteen years old, stupid two-tone hair, and a narrow, pimpled face. Davey recognised him. He had a feeling his name was Ozzie. This Ozzie, looking down at his muddied feet, grinned, and hoofed another head of celery out of the black soil. Bits of it scattered on the path.

Davey looked on, expecting verbal abuse. He sometimes doubted they could do anything but swear.

The youth, Ozzie, stared at Davey and took a step or two forwards. He held the football against his chest, with a hand on either side of it.

A few feet from Davey, still staring at him, the boy suddenly fired the football at him, two-handed. Davey grunted in surprise, and jerked backwards.

It had been a feint. The boy hadn't actually thrown the ball, just pretended to. But it was enough to overbalance Davey. He teetered, and fell sideways into a patch of cow parsley. Going down, he banged his knee on the corner of a galvanised water tank.

Ozzie howled with laughter, and trotted off with his ball. His mates were laughing too, shouting and whooping.

They called Davey some choice names. He waited, prone, feeling the throb in his knee, divided by rage and fear. He waited until the voices fell away and his breathing steadied, then slowly heaved himself upright, using the edge of the tank for support. The boys were moving away along the south path, lobbing the ball to each other, their interest in him evaporated. He felt like shaking a fist and yelling, but knew that would only start the cycle again.

He didn't want that.

He waited a while longer, leaning on the butt and lifting his sore leg to rotate the foot gingerly. Bloody bastards. Bloody, bloody bastards.

The surface of the syrupy green water in the metal tank began to pucker and dimple. The rain picked up again. Davey buttoned up his digging jacket, raised the handles of the barrow, and started on his way again.

More slowly, this time, limping.

He unlocked his backdoor, and wheeled the barrow into the kitchen. It left muddy tracks that he'd have to mop over later, but there was only so far he could carry the thing. It was heavy.

He wondered where he should put it. Where would it be safe? Where would it be comfortable? Upstairs was out of the question, and the under-stair cupboard, where the Hoover and the gas meter lived, seemed inhospitable. He finally decided on the tub in the little downstairs bathroom. He moved the soap dish and an ancient spider plant that he'd somehow kept alive since Glynis's time, and laid the thing in the worn bath, propping it back against the calcified snouts of the taps. He adjusted it carefully, made sure it was steady.

Then he took the barrow back outside, set it handles up against the yard wall, and came back in. He put the kettle on.

'Cup of tea?' he called.

The cat appeared, and looked at him expectantly.

Davey took off his digging jacket and hung it on the peg.

'Well, I'm certainly never eating cheese fondue again,' said James.

'I didn't know you were fond of fondue,' said Gwen.

'I wouldn't say I'm unduly fond of fondue,' James replied, smiling.

'Give it a rest,' said Owen. His scowl was particularly pronounced, a weary look, though he half-smiled at the banter.

'Decent enough result, though,' said Toshiko. 'Mucus notwithstanding.' She looked tired too.

'Not exactly how I'd choose to spend a Monday,' said Gwen, 'but yeah. Decent enough. Least we didn't balls it up this time.'

'I'll drink to that,' said Owen. 'If I had a drink…' He looked up.

Half six. The small, cellar bar off the Quay was filling up. A herd of suits from investment firms, insurance brokers and the rest of Cardiff's big, anonymous plcs were flooding into the watering hole.

'I'll help Jack with the drinks,' Gwen said, getting up. James watched her disappear into the crowd.

He looked back at Toshiko and Owen. They were smiling at him.

'What?' he said. 'What?'

'Need a hand?' Gwen called over the chatter.

'Thanks,' said Jack, turning to hand back a couple of drinks from the bar. He waited for the barman to bring him his change.

'More to your liking?' Gwen asked.

'What?'

'Today. Performance more to sir's liking, was it, then?'

'Yeah.'

'I think we did all right.'

'What, are you writing your own pep talk now?'

'Ha ha,' she said. 'Look, there's something up, isn't there?'

'Come again?'

'There's something up. More than just this last weekend.'

'Why do you say that?'

'Oh, I dunno. My "tall, dark and brooding" detector's been going off more than usual.'

'Your what now?'

'You. You've been standing around looking a lot more enigmatic and windswept these last few days. A real look of destiny on your face.'

'What can I say? I'm working on the image. I hope to have the full-on Heathcliff by Christmas.'

'OK,' she chuckled. They edged their way back to the booth with the drinks. 'But you'd tell me if there was something, wouldn't you?' she asked.

'Do I usually keep you in the loop?' Jack asked.

'No. Usually, you keep tons of stuff from us.'

'Well, that's not likely to change then, is it?' Jack said with a toothpaste-ad grin. 'Gwen, I know stuff. I know all sorts of stuff. I know stuff none of you need to be bothered with. The moment you do need to be bothered with it, I'll tell you.'

'Blimey,' she said.

'What?'

'Did we just have an actual need-to-know conversation?'

'I think we did.'

'Christ, now I feel like a proper secret agent.'

'I'll see if I can find you one.'

They delivered the drinks. One of the city types had loaded the jukebox with coins, and 'Who Are You?' blared across the cellar.

'CSI,' said Owen. 'Can I get a transfer to them d'you think?'

Jack shook his head. 'Unfortunately, you have to be a doctor.'

James snorted his beer. Toshiko patted Owen a 'there, there' on the arm. Gwen's cell rang. She took it out, and switched it off.

'Shouldn't you answer that?' Jack asked.

'No,' said Gwen, raising her drink. James glanced at her.

Jack set his half-finished glass of water down on the table. 'Well, charming though this is, I have to be going.'

'Lightweight,' said Owen.

'I've got a few things to do in the Hub,' said Jack. 'Tosh, did you finish those costings?'

'Can I give them to you in the morning?' she asked. 'I still can't shake this headache.'

'Sure.'

'I'll walk you out,' said Toshiko.

Left on their own, the other three sat there for a minute or two without speaking. Owen looked at Gwen, then at James, and then back at Gwen.

He shook his head. 'I get it. See you tomorrow.' He got to his feet. 'Don't do anything I wouldn't do,' he said.

'That leaves us a lot of scope,' said Gwen.

James waited until Owen had vanished into the bustle of suits, and then said, 'Rhys has been calling you, hasn't he?'

'Yeah. It's all right though.'

'Are you going to talk to him?'

'At some point.'

'What will you say?'

She shrugged. 'That's why I said "at some point". I don't know yet.'

James nodded. 'If this is difficult for you—'

'Shush now.'

Over the din of voices, the jukebox flipped from 'Who Are You?' to 'Coming Up For Air'.

Gwen smiled. 'So, what shall we do?' she asked.

'Goodnight then,' said Toshiko.

'See you tomorrow,' Jack replied. Toshiko hurried away through the dinner rush on the Quay. There was rain in the air. The illuminated windows and signs of the restaurant-bars formed a loud band of light and colour under the low night sky.

Jack walked to a quiet part of the rail facing out towards the Barrage. He took the black tile out of his coat pocket and studied it. The display was the same. Ominous. Ticking.

'Need to know,' Gwen had joked. Jack needed to know, and there was no one to ask.

Owen walked around the Bay to his apartment, and let himself in, the bag of takeout banging against his raised arm.

He put his wet coat on the back of a chair, and went into the kitchen to find a plate and a fork, and a beer from the fridge.

He felt wired and restless. A headache nagged behind his eyes. His bruised mouth was sore. He dished out the food, carried it into the lounge, and set it down on the table, the beer beside it. Then he headed into the bathroom to study his lip in the mirror.

The girl – Miss Tremendous Rack UK – had left a lipstick by the sink. He picked it up and idly twisted it.

He decided he really needed an aspirin. Heavy rain began to sheet against the windows of the flat.

NINE

The bedside alarm display glowed 01:00 in bright red digits. James was asleep.

Gwen got out of bed in the dark and padded into the lounge. The uplighters were still on. A filthy night swirled outside. She wondered where James kept the painkillers. She had a rubbish head again.

A huddle of framed photos sat along the top of a shelf unit, surrounding a plush 'Andy' that Toshiko had bought for James. They were all represented there: Toshiko, Owen, Ianto and herself, along with James. Various combinations, laughing, joking. None of Jack, of course, but then Jack was notoriously camera-shy. There were a few other shots of people she didn't know. Parents, she supposed. Uncles. Siblings. James had a sister in Oxford, and a brother in London that he'd spoken of.

She picked up one picture of her, James and Toshiko. She couldn't recall the exact circumstances in which it had been taken, but the subtle differences in haircuts and clothes suggested it was going back a while.

It made her feel strangely deprived. The albums back at her flat, the photos on the fridge door and the pinboard, none of them showed James or Owen or Toshiko. Just her, Rhys and various friends. She didn't have the freedom to put up snaps of the team where Rhys could see them and ask who they were. Such was the divide between her domestic and work lives. The secret fold between two entirely different yet entirely real Gwen Coopers.

Except, she wondered, was that true any more? She'd lived a dual existence since joining Torchwood, but the older part of her was struggling to keep pace these days. It felt like the old Gwen, and the life-baggage she carried, was fading out, sloughing away like old skin. Her police career, her flat in Riverside, her relationship with Rhys; it was getting eclipsed. She'd always presumed – always been determined – to be both Gwens. She'd been happy with her lot, and had never intended to ditch it. But old stuff was slipping away and becoming irrelevant of its own accord.

That was a horrible word, she decided. *Irrelevant.* Cruel to think that. People moved on, that was organic, and you had to let things go sometimes. You had to let things go when you didn't need them any more.

God, it was going to be hard to do, but she owed it to Rhys to *let* it be hard to do. He deserved that much.

On the couch was a spill of CD cases. They'd been listening to music earlier. She'd picked through James's collection. For every cool band like Torn Curtain and The Buttons, there was a howler like Boulder and Foreign Hazard, which James put down to a misspent teenage with mates who were into metal and prog. She had a funny feeling Rhys still liked Boulder. She'd seen some in amongst the Genesis and the Rush and the Jerry Goldsmith soundtracks. How the hell had she spent so long with a man who had once suggested that 'Vader's Theme' might be an appropriate wedding march?

Poor soft, loveable, puppy-dog bastard. It was going to be so hard to do.

'Can't you sleep?'

She looked around. James smiled at her and stifled a yawn.

'No, sorry,' she said. She looked at him and raised her eyebrows.

'What?'

'You're what my mum would call very naked,' she said.

'So are you.'

Gwen felt self-conscious suddenly.

'It's all right,' James said.

'I know. I just can't remember the last time I paraded around naked at home.'

She noted that James let the 'at home' slide. 'Really?' he said.

'I just don't do it any more.'

'He'd get some funny ideas, would he?'

She shrugged. 'I think it was the worry that he *wouldn't* get any funny ideas.'

James nodded. 'Coming back to bed, then?'

They curled up together in the dark. Raindrops drummed against the window.

'It's all right me being here, isn't it?' she asked.

'What do you think?'

'I didn't mean like that. I'm imposing. Taking up residence.'

'It's fine. I like it.'

They were silent.

'It's only fair you speak to him,' James said. 'When you've got your head straight, I mean.'

'I know. I will. The next day or two. I hate lying. I hate the lies more than anything. I'll have to go back, face the music.'

She paused.

'And maybe pick up a few things.'

'Like what?'

'I dunno. All my stuff?'

He pulled her closer.

The artillery barrage was creeping closer, great white flower-blooms in the night, more pressure-slap than noise, the booming too loud to actually be heard. The world shook and rattled. Muddy vapour stung his nose, terror clawed like a cat in his chest, trying to get out.

Davey Morgan woke up. It was black, black like the Black Out. The luminous hands of his little wind-up alarm clock formed a tiny, green fuzz. He groped around and found his specs, put them on his face. Four o'clock gone.

The noise that had woken him, the noise that had penetrated his dream and whisked him back to '44, was just the storm. Pelting rain, and a juddering gale. Something was banging and knocking, persistently.

Cold to the bone, Davey swung slowly out from under the eiderdown and put his feet on the balding carpet. He found his slippers and his dressing gown. His knee hurt when he put his weight onto it.

The banging was close by. Like a door or a gate, tugged by the wind. Or maybe like some yobbo bastard thumping on his backdoor. Some yobbo bastard who'd been beering it up and fancied some fun and games at Taff Morgan's expense.

This late? In this weather? It seemed unlikely, but the trepidation wouldn't let go of him. Davey could still remember the dream, the terror of the dream. Fresh and real. Funny, it had been years and years since he'd dreamt about service life, years and years since he'd packed the raw memories of beachheads and the bocage up in some mental drawer and slid it tight shut.

What had opened that up again, after all this bloody time?

He followed the sound of the banging onto the landing. Shadows waved and jumped in the gloom: the wind waving tree branches in front of the street light outside.

He limped down the narrow stairs. More banging, sporadic.

'It's all right,' he reassured the picture on the hall table.

He entered the kitchen. So much rain streamed down the windows, the glass looked like it was melting. *Bang! Bang-bang!*

'Who is it?' he called. 'Who's there?'

Bang! Bang! Bang-bang!

Davey took a step towards the backdoor.

The door and windows blew in at him in a blizzard of glass and fire. Pots flew off the stove. Mugs jumped off their hooks and shattered.

Davey Morgan lay on his back, numb, ears ringing. His face was wet. Rain? Blood?

He could smell burned earth, heat, the fetid stink of deeply churned soil exposed to the surface for the first time in centuries. It was a smell he'd never forgotten, the smell of '44.

He could hear the crackle of flames, the tinkle of glass chips dropping out of broken window frames.

He got up somehow, hauling on the doorframe. There was a bright light outside, a leaping orange glare. Ribbons of smoke oozed in through the gap where the backdoor had been.

Davey Morgan reached the doorway. The yard had gone. The back path too, and the houses and allotments all the way over to Connault Way.

They had been replaced by hell.

The night was a black cave lit up by vast lakes of fire. The ground behind his house had been excavated and tilled by God's own wrath, torn up, heaped, broken, scattered with debris, splintered fenceposts, mangled chunks of metal and tile. Spools of wire coiled from the banked mud. Burning hanks of ash and soot fluttered down.

As Davey stood and gaped, volleys of mammoth explosions went off along the skyline, overlapping ripples of light-flash. Overpressure bent the air and fanned the flames. Carpet bombing, or heavy barrage, five miles out. He felt the delayed punch of it in his chest.

He thought about ringing the police, but that was just daft. Like they didn't know about this already. It would be on the news. He hadn't had the radio on all day. What story had passed him by, what international crisis that would have led to the systematic bombing of Cathays?

He saw a figure, fifty yards away, back-lit by the firestorms, striding slowly across the ruined ground towards him. A tall, thin silhouette, with sharp angles and slender limbs. Another, off to the left, slightly further away. Skinny, gangly, like some bloody teenage yobbo.

No, not even slightly. Too tall. Too thin. Eight, nine feet tall, arms like broom handles. Hands like bunches of bananas.

There were three of them now. Cartoon stick figures, with emaciated frames and giant hands. The firelight glinted off the nearest one. Flame-light off gunmetal, the wink of light catching brass or steel.

From somewhere off to his right, beyond the house, tracer fire started up, the coughing chatter of a heavy weapon. The luminous rounds raked the fire-broken earth and tried to get the range of the approaching figures. Davey ducked down, involuntarily. *Gunfire, find cover.*

The tracer rounds stitched explosive plumes of soil out of the ground around the nearest figure. It turned slightly, facing the origin of the gunfire, and something pulsed dull yellow on its head where its eyes should have been. Davey felt a scourging, invisible heat buckle the air. Off to the right, a crunching blast threw sparks up into the sky. The gunfire cut off abruptly.

Davey tried to edge his way back into the ruined kitchen. The nearest shape had resumed its slow plod towards him.

He saw it more clearly as it came closer, revealed by the light of the raging ground fires. Bone-thin legs, twice as long as a man's, took long, measured strides across the churned ground. The legs carried a tall, narrow torso of paint-chipped metal and a head – set on a long, thin piston of a neck – that was half-skull, half-sculpture. Burnished metal features, cadaver-thin cheeks.

'Go away!' Davey cried. 'Go away!'

The thing's gaze located him. A little hum, a slight change in pitch.

A pulse of dull yellow where the eyes should have been—

Davey Morgan woke up. It was pitch black. The luminous green hands of his alarm clock told him it was four o'clock gone.

He lay there, shivering in his own sweat, listening to the rainstorm throwing itself against the bedroom windows.

Just a dream. Just a bloody dream. Just a stupid—

The noise that had woken him came again. Something was banging and knocking, persistently.

Cold to the bone, Davey got up. His knee hurt when he put his weight onto it.

The banging was close by. Like a door or a gate, tugged by the wind. He'd had this already. He'd been around this dream once already, and he didn't want another bloody turn.

He limped down the narrow stairs. *Bang! Bang-bang! Bang!* He gently touched the picture on the hall table as he went by. He tasted mint.

He entered the kitchen. So much rain against the windows, the glass looked like it was melting. *Bang! Bang-bang!*

'Who is it?' he called. 'Who's there?'

Bang! Bang! Bang-bang!

Davey took a step towards the backdoor.

The fan light of the kitchen window was ajar. He must have left it open. The gale had pulled it off its brace, and now it was banging and jumping in its frame.

Bang! Bang-bang! Bang!

Davey fastened it. He checked the bolt on the backdoor.

He went into the bathroom and turned the light on, squinting in the hard electric glare. The thing lay in the tub where he had left it. A heavy, rounded tube of paint-chipped metal about three feet long, topped by a featureless ovoid the size of a rugby ball. Tube and ovoid were made of the same metal, and had been joined with such engineering skill, Davey could locate no seam or weld.

Davey lowered the toilet lid and made a chair out of it. He sat himself down carefully, holding onto the sink. The close air smelled of soap and mildewed bathmats.

He faced the thing in the tub.

'Right then,' he said.

A low hum.

A slight change in pitch.

TEN

Owen woke up with a murmur, rolled over, and fell off the armchair.

'Bollocks,' he groaned. He blinked. Some awfully cheerful pop music was blaring from the bedroom. He was in the lounge, on the floor. Things did not add up.

Nor could he make them add up for a moment. He had a vice squad raid of a headache kicking from room to room in his skull, and a mouth like the Lambies at low tide. His lip throbbed and every other ache and pain he'd taken the previous Thursday night seemed more acute than when they'd been inflicted.

'Bollocks,' he said again, and coughed. What day was it?

He took stock. The drapes were open, and pale daylight flooded in. He was still dressed. One shirt sleeve was torn, and there was mud on one leg of his trousers. He had no memory of a heavy night. In fact he had no memory at all.

He got up. That hurt. He swayed, dizzy. Swaying hurt too. He hobbled into the bedroom. Music was blaring from his clock radio. The clock radio on the bedside cabinet beside his unslept-in bed.

A nauseatingly upbeat DJ segued in. '… and that's the fabulous Four Play. Coming up on half nine now this Tuesday morning, and it's the news with Gayle…'

Tuesday. Right, Tuesday. That fits.

Half nine? His alarm had been playing for two hours without waking him. Even given that he was in the other room, that was good going.

'Christ,' he said. He started dragging off his clothes.

As he hopped through the lounge, unlacing one boot, he saw the plate on the table. The takeaway, untouched. A two-thirds-full bottle of beer beside it, standing in a small ring of water.

He stopped hopping, because that really hurt.

'What the bloody hell did you do last night, Harper?' he asked himself.

He went into the bathroom, turned on the shower, threw all his clothes and his boots into the laundry basket, cursed, fished his boots back out, and turned to look at himself in the mirror.

The hot rush of the shower was already beginning to steam the edges of the mirror over the sink. Owen saw his pale face looking back through large letters that had been scrawled, wildly, on the mirror in lipstick.

One word.

BIG.

'So where is everybody?' asked Jack.

'Well,' replied Ianto and made an open-handed shrug.

Jack looked around the Hub. 'And I thought I'd slept in,' he yawned.

'Coffee's on,' said Ianto.

Jack breathed in the aroma. 'I know. At least something's right with the world.'

'Other aspects are marginally more wonky,' said Ianto, handing Jack a piece of paper. 'This flagged up first thing this morning. I thought you'd want to see it as soon as.'

Jack read the page, nodding. 'You know what this is?'

'I seldom like to hazard a guess.'

Jack shook the piece of paper. 'This is a busy day ahead of us.'

'One other thing,' said Ianto.

'Shoot.'

The cog-door rolled open, and Toshiko hurried in, stifling a yawn. 'Sorry,' she called. 'Sorry, I slept right through the alarm.'

She started taking off her coat. Jack came over to her.

'You wanna talk about it?' Jack asked her quietly.

'About what?'

'Oversleeping?'

'Nothing to talk about, I'm just tired. Ever since last week. I can't shake it. Every morning I think I'm going to be back on form and—' Another yawn overtook her. 'Sorry. It seems to be getting worse. And the headache. I feel like I've been put through the pinger.'

'The what?'

'The ringer.'

'You said "pinger".'

'I didn't.'

'You did, actually,' Ianto called over.

'Well, that's how tired I am.'

Jack looked quizzically at Toshiko. 'That thing had real nasty after-effects, didn't it?'

'About that,' said Ianto, joining them. 'The thing I wanted to mention.'

'Oh, yeah. Go on.'

Ianto pointed over at Toshiko's work station. 'Should it be doing that?'

They crossed to the desk. The day before, Toshiko had locked the Amok away in its containment box. They could hear it. It was tapping against the metal insides of the container.

'Wow,' said Jack.

'I heard it when I came in. At first, I thought Owen had got himself locked in the cells again.'

Toshiko peered at the box. 'It was dormant when we first got it contained.'

'It's not dormant now,' returned Jack. 'It's sounding quite feisty.'

'We should check it,' Toshiko said, shooting a sidelong look at Jack. He nodded.

She popped on her eye-guards and slid the containment box back into the field zone of the containment console. Stainless-steel clamps automatically gripped the base of the box and rotated it into alignment with a whine. Toshiko closed the Lexan cover. The touch of a switch brought suspension fields up, bathing the box in a pulsing blue glow. Graphic analysis display projected across the dome of the Lexan hemisphere.

'I'm setting level ten safeguards. Maximum focus blockers, everything we have, and additional inhibitors. Grade K firewalls, Ianto. We know how aggressive this thing can be.'

Ianto nodded. At a neighbouring sub-console, he ran his fingers over the keyboard. Graphics scrolled on his relay screen.

'OK,' said Toshiko. She depressed a switch. The interlock collar of the containment box unbolted magnetically, and slid back. The suspension field flickered.

The Amok, manipulated by delicate hawsers of gravity, rose up out of the box and hung in the blue glow, revolving slowly. The graphics on the Lexan dome, and those on Toshiko and Ianto's screens, went into overdrive.

'The Killer Sudoku from the Planet Mind-Screw is not happy,' noted Toshiko.

'That much is obvious,' said Jack, staring.

'Firewalls?' Toshiko called out to Ianto.

'It's eaten through three, but we're holding it now.'

Toshiko pointed at the projection display. 'Elevated energetic behaviour. Some heat dissipation. There's some edge-spectrum stuff there I don't begin to understand. Nasty. Very agitated. Very angry.'

Jack nodded. 'I don't think it likes the fact we spoiled its games. I don't think it likes the fact we locked it up in a box that deprived it of all external sensory input.' He looked at Toshiko. 'I think it wants someone to play with it.'

Toshiko shuddered. 'I know we've got bleeding-edge inhibitors screening us from its effect, but I'm feeling ill just looking at it.'

Ianto raised a hand. 'Headache,' he reported.

'Psychosomatic,' said Jack. 'It's just freaking us out. It can't stand the fact it can't get to us.' He leaned closer and grinned at the rotating metal solid. 'Can you?'

He glanced back at Toshiko. 'Even so, box it up, lock it tight, and put it in an isoclave in the vault until we've got time to deactivate it or even disassemble it.'

'We don't have that time now?' asked Toshiko.

'No,' Jack replied. 'Pressing matters.' He handed her the sheet of paper Ianto had give him.

Toshiko read it. 'I don't understand this…'

'Seeing as no one else has turned up for work, looks like this one's down to you and me. Ianto, maybe you could give everyone a call and remind them they work for me?'

'On it,' said Ianto, reaching for his cell.

'I still don't get it.' said Toshiko. 'Where are we going?'

'We're going to the chapel, baby,' said Jack.

Despite careful oiling, the barrow's wheel still squeaked.

Davey trundled it up the path to the allotments. The sky was bare and white, like plain paper. A nothing day, caught in a trough between bits of weather. At least there was no rain yet.

The ground smelled strongly of the overnight downpour: rich earth smells and raw vegetation. Drains gurgled as they drank down the overspill. Birds sang in the hedges with sharp, whetted voices.

He'd intended to evict his guest in the small hours, after the dream. The storm had blown out around four thirty, and the sky had cleared so suddenly there had been stars. Davey, dressed in readiness by then, had put on his digging jacket and gone out into the wet blackness.

But it had been a cold, sinister hour. A dome of sky like polished jet, the prickle of stars, the amber glow of Cardiff. Roofs and chimneys were key-tooth silhouettes against the air. Somewhere, a dog-fox was barking her pitiful saw-edged yap. It was coming from streets away across the plots, the baleful cry of winter's onset.

It had made Davey feel solitary and vulnerable. He went back indoors and decided to wait for morning.

He flicked on the light in the bathroom and sat down again.

'I'm sorry,' he said, 'but I'll have to move you back tomorrow. I can't—'

He had paused. The hum intoned softly.

'I can't have you in the house, I don't think. Sorry. I need my sleep, and I can't be having dreams like that. Your dreams, weren't they?'

No answer.

'I think they were. I think I just brushed against them. Anyway, sorry.'

In the cold daylight, he wheeled the barrow up to the shed and unlocked the door. A few things had blown over in the night, but nothing had suffered human disturbance.

He took it inside, and propped it up carefully, the way it had been before.

'You'll be safe in here, I promise. You won't get disturbed. I'll be back to check on you.'

Davey turned to go. 'You can dream all you like in here,' he said.

Back in his kitchen, the kettle and the radio on, Davey rummaged around in a drawer for his bus pass. He had already decided on a trip to the lending library.

He put a bowl of food down, and banged the tin with a fork, but the cat did not appear.

* * *

The flat was a mess, frankly, and smelled a bit stale. Dirty dishes were lined up on the counter, as if Rhys was in training for some washing-up record attempt, and the bins needed emptying. A carrier bag full of overflow hung from a drawer handle.

Gwen started in the bedroom, and filled a hold-all with a few clothes, some clean undies, two pairs of shoes, and a few personal items from the dresser.

She'd decided not to take much, just a handful of essentials to begin with. Clearing her stuff out wholesale while his back was turned would have been plain nasty. Besides, she didn't have very long. She was late as it was. They'd overslept.

Some favourite earrings from her jewellery box, a necklace her mother had given her, a locket that had belong to her nan. From the bathroom, her favourite soap and shampoo, her expensive perfume. Not the one Rhys had bought her duty free that time, which she wore to please him. The other one, the one she treated herself to because she really loved the scent.

Gwen carried the hold-all back into the lounge. Books, DVDs, CDs... sorting through them seemed particularly petty. She knelt down and slid her trinket box off a lower shelf. Her box of lovelies.

It was an old shoebox, covered in pretty gift wrap, and adorned with coloured twine and faded petals glued on with Pritt Stick.

She took off the lid.

Birthday cards, Christmas cards, congratulations-on-your-new-job cards; a dried flower from a wedding they'd been to; some photos; a week-to-view diary from 1994 with a kitten on the cover; old invites, still in their envelopes, clamped in a bulldog clip; a champagne cork with a coin cut into it; postcards from here and there; an interlock puzzle out of a cracker; a dead watch she'd worn in her teens; a charm bracelet that she'd been given when she was eight; some foreign coins; three old letters from a boy she'd loved a long time before Rhys, tied up with now-colourless ribbon; glitter-edged gift tags, 'To Gwen, with love'; a shell she'd kept for reasons that now escaped her; a broken fountain pen; some keys that no longer fitted anything; a tacky little *ddraig goch* in a snow globe.

There was a black and white photo of her aged three, on a tricycle. One corner had a fold across it, crazing the emulsion. Gwen turned the photo over, expecting the explanatory caption 'The Heartless Bitch, at an early age'. There was nothing written on the back.

The front door lock jiggled open. Gwen stood up very quickly.

Rhys came in. He stopped dead and looked at her. His face looked puffy, as if he'd been sleeping too little or drinking too much.

'Gwen,' he said, genuinely surprised.

'Hello,' she managed.

'What are you doing here?'

'I needed some stuff,' she said. *Nice footwork, Gwen. Not at all pathetic.*

He looked at the hold-all beside her feet and sniffed. 'Moving out, are we?'

'No.'

'Coming back, then?'

'No,' she frowned. 'I don't know what's going on. I just—'

He waved his hand. 'Please, spare me the "I need some space" bit, all right? Would you, please? Otherwise it's all going to get a bit too bloody *EastEnders* for my taste.' He hesitated. 'You looking after yourself?'

'Yes.'

'Good. You got someplace to stay?'

'Yes.'

'With a friend?'

'With… yes.'

'Got a number? A forwarding address?' He slouched off his coat.

'It's not like that.'

'What is it like, then, Gwen?' he asked. He walked into the kitchen and filled the kettle.

'I didn't know you'd be here—'

'Morning off, me. Dentist. Sorry to bugger up your plan to sneak about behind my back.' He was losing his surprise and gathering a little confidence and momentum.

'It's not like that,' she said. 'I came round this morning because I needed some things. I came when you were out because I don't know what to say to you. Not yet. And really, that's all.'

'Sounds very much like sneaking about behind my back to me.'

'It isn't. Not the way you mean. I'm not ready for a confrontation or a—'

'A what?'

'A long, meaningful talk.'

Rhys nodded. 'When will that be, then? When will that be, you suppose? Next week? After Christmas? Can you pencil me in around work?'

'Rhys—'

He saw the trinket box on the floor. 'Your box of lovelies. And you tell me you're not moving out?'

'I was just looking at it.'

'Bloody hell,' he muttered, shaking his head. 'How cowardly... how bloody *spineless* can you be? Coming in here to pick the place clean while I'm at work. Very classy, that. I've known burglars show more—'

'I don't want this!' she protested. 'Not now. Can't you grasp that? This is exactly why I dropped in when I thought you'd be out. I don't *want* this.'

'OK. Just so long as you can sort out what you want, we'll be fine. Just so long as you get what you bloody want—'

'Rhys!'

He glowered at her.

'I'm not ready to do this,' she told him. 'I'm really sorry this happened today, but I'm not ready to do this yet.'

The kettle began to steam.

'I gotta go,' said Gwen.

'You got a number, then? Somewhere I can reach you if I need to?'

'You can call me on my mobile.'

'Apparently, I can't,' he said. 'God knows, I've tried.'

'I'll answer you, promise I will.'

'We'll see.'

She put on her coat and picked up her hold-all. She paused to slide the trinket box back onto its place on the shelf.

'I'm sorry,' she said. 'I'll call you.'

'Right,' he nodded. He was staring at the window, not looking at her. The muscles in his jaw were tense.

'I will. Soon. Soon as I can.'

'Right.'

'Take care of yourself, all right?'

'Yeah. No one else will.'

She walked out and pulled the front door closed behind her.

Rhys sighed, and bowed his head. He turned the kettle off and looked at the front door.

'Oh, also, I love you,' he whispered.

She'd parked her car around the corner. Morning traffic hissed by on the damp road: a turquoise Cardiff Bus, a minicab, an Alpha Course transit conveying chattering OAPs to a church lunch, a courier van, a big-boned Chelsea tractor with a tiny mum at the helm. Somewhere a car alarm was whooping, and a crossing signal was pinging. Engines idled. Tail pipes quivered, fuming.

Gwen felt sick and she felt bad and, most of all, she felt wrong.

She got into the black Saab. The windows had steamed up. James was dozing off in the passenger seat.

'All done?' he asked, opening his eyes as the door shut.

She pushed her hold-all back over onto the rear seats. It wedged against the head rest. She gave it an angry shove to send it on its way.

'Gwen? What is it?'

Gwen fumbled with the keys, then sat back. 'Rhys was there.'

'Shit. Did he give you a hard time?'

'No,' she said, sternly. 'He's not like that—'

'OK, OK. I was just—'

'Don't.'

'Sorry.'

She looked around at him. 'He was so sad. So messed up.'

'Gwen…'

'I did that to him. Me. My fault. I tried to explain why I was there, but it looked bad, you know?'

'Everything will sort itself out,' James said.

'Is that a promise?'

'Yes it is.'

'Wish I had your confidence. It's going to get ugly.'

'It'll be fine.'

'I hate the lying.'

'So you said.' James waited a moment. 'So, did you tell him anything?'

'Like what?'

James shrugged.

'No. Nothing about that. It's too soon.'

'OK. You're right. Too soon.' He looked a little downcast, but right then she didn't especially care.

He wiped the window with his cuff and looked out. 'Ianto called.'

'Did he?'

'Wondered where I was. Wondered if I knew where you were. Something's gone off.'

She started the engine. 'Hub?' she asked.

'No,' said James. 'I've got an address. He told us to meet Jack there.'

She pulled out into the traffic.

ELEVEN

Butetown, the old heart of industrial Cardiff, used to run right down to the Docks. It still did, in the opinion of dyed-in-the-wool locals.

But Cardiff was post-industrial now. Chimney soot and coal ash from the steel works no longer occluded the midday sun. Smutty trains no longer clanked in and out along the Taff Vale line. After three billion pounds-worth of facelift, the Docks were no longer called the Docks. They were the Bay, gleaming new and millennial, where suits lunched, and bistros thrived, and a few hundred thousand bought you a penthouse in the Quay developments with views of the Barrage. Those stalwart locals still called it Butetown, though, fighting the onset of a change already done and dusted.

All that remained of Butetown, all that actually perpetuated the name, had coiled up in the heart of the central area and laid down in surrender, a sprawl of brick link tenements and fatigued 1950s high-rises, criss-crossed by the ghost veins of railway embankments, rendered in decaying Victorian stonework.

Shiny black, brooking no objections, the SUV chased up Angelina Street like a slipped greyhound. Terraces swept by, a mosque. Traffic on the road, a street market, shop fronts with battered shutters still closed at mid morning on a Tuesday, like knights in the lists with their visors shut for the tilt.

'Chapel?' asked Toshiko for the seventh time.

'Patience. We're getting there,' said Jack.

He turned off into Skean Street, then braked as a refuse lorry blocked the way. He turned his head, resting his left arm across the seat backs, and reversed as far as Livermore, then switched left and then right again. Cobbles bumbled under their tyres.

He drove them down a narrow gulf between old machine shops, and swung out wide in the gravel bed of a dead lot. Fossil cars, up on bricks, gazed at them with rusted eyes.

'Here?' asked Toshiko.

Jack pulled the handbrake. 'Here. What have you got for me?'

She shrugged, and leaned forward, punching up the dashboard displays, working between one body of data and the next with the trackball set into the dash.

'Nothing?' she suggested.

'Go on.'

'An absence of fact. A lack of data. What do you want me to say?'

'Exactly that,' Jack said. 'There's nothing here.'

'So why…?'

'Nothing at *all*. You see?'

'Uh, no?'

'Not even bricks and ground,' Jack said softly.

'Ah,' said Toshiko. 'I see now. Hang on. No, I don't.'

'Let's take a walk,' said Jack.

He got out. She followed him. The slam of her door sent pigeons mobbing up into the rafters of a nearby ruin. The air was wet, suffused with a mineral scent. Bird lime spattered the ground. The overarching iron rafters were black against the plain white sky. They looked like the ribs of a leviathan fish.

Jack popped the SUV's back hatch. He took a compact scanner out of the equipment boxes and tossed it to her. Toshiko caught it neatly.

'And this is for?'

'Keeping tabs on the nothing that still isn't there.'

Toshiko switched the scanner on. No reading, no bounce, no tone lock.

'You know why I love working with you, Jack?' she asked.

'No?'

'Me neither. I was hoping you could help me out with that.'

'Come on,' he said.

They crossed the weed-infested gravel, and crunched onto a slurry of tiles that had cascaded down from the roof at some point. Cobwebs strung between bent girders encrusted with twinkling dew diamonds from the night's onslaught. They walked into shadow under what remained of a warehouse roof.

'What are we looking for?' Toshiko complained.

'All in good time. Try appreciating the vernacular architecture,' Jack said, his voice coming back hollow and echoing. 'This was the Millner and Peabody Number Three Coal Depot. In 1851 alone, this place factored and then sent out eighteen million tons of coke to fuel the engines of Empire. Doesn't that just make you crazy?'

'The quantity?'

'No, Tosh, coal. Like that was ever going to work in any lasting way.'

'Right. I'm still getting nothing,' Toshiko called, trying to reset her scanner.

'Nothing? That's good. That's what we want.'

She ran to catch up with him. Loose stones scattered under her boots.

'Through here,' he said, leading her out of a crumbling doorway into another bare tract.

A little church sat in front of them, derelict, windows and doors boarded up, graffiti wound around its flanks. It was sitting inside the plot of the warehouse.

'St Mary-in-the-Dust,' said Jack, pleased with himself.

'St Mary in the what?'

'It was built in 1803 and demolished in 1840 to make way for the depots.'

'But—'

'I hadn't finished—'

'I hadn't started. Demolished in 1840? But there it is.'

'Exactly. It keeps coming back, once every thirty-five or thirty-nine years.'

'It… what?'

'We can count ourselves lucky. It wasn't due back until 2011.'

'Again, what?'

'Come on,' Jack said. He drew his revolver out from under his coat.

'Oh, *now* I'm reassured,' said Toshiko.

Davey got off the bus as it came to a stop.

'Cheerio,' he said to the driver.

The driver ignored him.

Davey limped up the street, the three books he'd borrowed from the lending library swinging in a string bag. It was going to rain again. He could feel it in his water.

He wondered where the cat had got to.

He hobbled up to his front door and searched for his key.

'It's Taff! It's Taffy!' a voice cried.

Where was his key? Under his glasses case, deep in his pocket. He rummaged.

'Taff! Catch the ball, Taffy! Go on, catch it!'

'Go away!' he called, not looking around.

The boys were gathering. The yobbos. Ozzie and his mates. Bored and looking for a laugh. He could hear them. He could smell them: beer and weed. Yes, he bloody did know what weed was. He was old. He wasn't stupid.

'Taffy, Taffy, give us a song!' they chanted.

'Go away!'

Finally, finally, he got his key out and into the lock. He turned the key. The door stuck sometimes in wet weather. He had to push it.

Something hit him in the back of the head, hard. It hit him so hard, it slammed his face into the door.

Davey Morgan fell down. He flopped back against the door of his house, his own bloody house, and sagged, feeling the warm drip coming out of his nose.

'You bloody bastards,' he whispered.

On the path in front of him, a ball bounced to rest. *Thunt-thunt-thunt.*

They'd thrown it at him, thrown it at his head.

Bastards.

He looked up. The yobbos had gathered on the pavement, crowing and laughing, pointing and whooping. Ozzie and the other man-boys. Stupid haircuts, stupid skinny faces, stupid clothes, trousers that didn't pull up past their hips and left a waistband of underpants on show.

'You bloody bastards!' he spat.

'Oooh, Taffy! Such strong friggin' language!' Ozzie shouted.

'Mess him up! Mess him up!' the others sang. Scrawny boys. Scrawny bloody bastards.

Ozzie gathered up the ball in his hands and tossed it over and over. 'One on one, eh, Taffy? You and me? One on one?'

'Go to hell, boy,' Davey said, picking himself up.

The ball walloped him in the face. As he fell down again, his swollen knee shooting pain up his thigh, all he heard was wild, mocking laughter. They'd broken his nose. His cheek too, it felt like. Bloody, bloody bastards.

Davey blinked away tears. Ozzie was picking up the bouncing ball again.

'Want another go, you old git?' he asked.

Davey found an iota of strength from somewhere and hoisted himself up. He leant on the door and turned the key. As the door swung open and carried him in, he felt the ball ricochet of his back. More laughter.

The umbrella stand lived just inside the door, exactly where it had stood since Glynis had put it there in 1951. It held his old black brolly, her neat beige collapsible, a walking stick.

Davey Morgan reached for none of those. He took hold of the other object leaning innocuously in the stand.

Upright, he turned in the doorway.

'One on one, eh, Taffy?' Ozzie called, bouncing the ball. His chorus of bastards whinnied and shrieked.

'Go on, then, you bloody bastard,' Davey said.

Ozzie chucked the ball at him.

It struck Davey and somehow, miraculously, stayed put on his hand. The yobbos fell silent for a second, puzzled.

With a slow fart, the ball deflated. Davey Morgan slid it off the blade and let it *paff!* on the ground.

Army-issue Bayonet No. 1. A little dulled with age, like him, but still seventeen bloody inches long and sharp as a bugger. Like a bloody sword, it was, the size of it.

Davey raised it. The yobbos gawped.

'Bugger off, you tossers, or I'll do you up a treat!' he declared, brandishing the blade.

They looked on. They stared. They fled like a bunch of nancies down the street, scattering in all directions.

Davey picked up his string bag of books and went indoors. He put the bayonet back in the umbrella stand, and locked the door behind him.

He made himself a cup of tea. There was still no sign of the cat. The bowl of food had been left uneaten.

He sat down with the three books he'd borrowed. Each one was an illustrated volume on modern sculpture. He was sure he'd seen the thing in the shed, or something like it, before. Glynis had loved sculpture. They'd once gone all the way to Bath, to see a modern art show. 1969. He'd gone along with it because he had loved to see her happy.

It had meant nothing to him then. It meant something to him now. He flicked through the pages, stopping at various images: Brancuzzi, Epstein, Giacometti. That's what he had seen. Lean, attenuated bodies made of metal; cramped, pigeon-chested torsos; flaring slipstream limbs; burnished, angular heads.

But not still. Moving.

Humming.

Walking.

Gwen pulled the Saab into the dead lot. They could both see the SUV parked ahead of them.

They got out.

Gwen looked around. James fitted his Bluetooth.

'Jack? Tosh? Hello?'

He paused, listening. His expression had turned sour.

'What is it?' Gwen asked.

'Jack says boiled egg,' said James.

They started to run.

TWELVE

Old warehouses lacking roofs. The bones of the city's vanished industry. High-walled stone sheds with bare socket windows and roof-tile avalanches on the floors. Pigeons, weeds, puddles of rainwater.

No Jack. No Tosh.

'Spread out,' James said. They wandered around the derelict spaces, keeping each other in sight. There were scraps of metal tracks inlaid into parts of the concourse hardpan where freight trucks had once shunted. Broken lead raingoods spilt green stains down scabby brick work. In places, there were little caches of junk – wrappers and cartons, doorless fridges and defunct cookers. The residents of Butetown evidently used this place to dump their junk. Oddly, there was no evidence that the homeless lingered here, in what Gwen thought would be a typical location. What kept them out? Old attempts at fencing and boarding had long since perished and given up the ghost.

Ghost. An unfortunate word to bring to mind. It was broad daylight, closing on noon, but the place felt clammy and haunted.

Gwen paused below a massive brick archway that demarcated the plots between two warehouses. Part of a bas-relief inscription decorated the curve of the arch:

MILL ER & PEA ODY MBER FOUR POT 1 53

Lower down, newer signs had been fixed to the brickwork with wire and rivets. Red lettering on white fields:

KEEP OUT DANGEROUS STRUCTURE DANGER OF DEATH

She tried her phone again. She'd lost count of the number of attempts she'd made to reach Jack in the previous forty minutes. Since the 'boiled egg' message to James, nothing had been heard from their illustrious leader.

Dialling tone, connecting.

'Please wait,' said a voice. 'We are diverting you to the voice mail box.'

'James! I've got voice mail!' Gwen called, keeping the phone pressed to her ear. That was an improvement. Until then, they hadn't even got a connecting tone.

James hurried over to join her from the far side of the place.

'Hi,' said a recording of Jack's voice. 'This is Jack. Message me up good.'

'Jack, it's me. Where are you? We're here. Where are you, for God's sake? We're looking everywhere. Call me back. OK? It's Gwen. OK?'

She hung up.

She glanced at James.

'I left a message.

He nodded. 'If it's…'

'What?'

'I was just thinking. If it's boiled egg, well, it'll be *hard* boiled by now. We've been here half an hour.'

'Forty minutes, actually. This can't be the right place.'

'Ianto's directions were specific. Besides, the SUV is here. They're here too, somewhere.'

'Somewhere.'

'Maybe they went for a beer.'

She frowned. 'What?'

James pointed up at the arch inscription. 'Well, it's MILL ER time.'

Gwen glared.

'Not the moment for a bad joke? No?'

'No.'

'You'd think I would have sensed that.'

Gwen turned in a full circle on the spot, slowly scanning the abandoned site around them. 'Nobody's here. Nobody comes here. Nobody *would* come here.'

He nodded. 'Not unless they wanted to make an Ultravox video. And it was 1981.'

'Except for that, maybe. Let's go back to the SUV and sweep out from there again.'

They started walking. Gwen's phone started ringing.

She hoped it wasn't Rhys.

There was no caller ID on the screen.

'Hello?'

'Gwen?'

'It's Jack!' she hissed at James. 'Jack? Where are you?'

Something unintelligible gurgled back, something with the vague semblance of Jack's accent. It sounded as if he was on a train, in rush hour, and going through a tunnel.

'Jack? Jack? Say that again! Where are you? You sound like you're on a train!'

'Gwen we- did- can't really Mary- seriously…'

'Jack? Jack?'

The line went dead.

'Bugger!' Gwen cried. She tried redial.

'Bugger!' she cried again.

Her phone rang again immediately. It made her jump so much, she almost dropped it.

'Yes? Jack?'

'On a train?' his voice said, clear as a bell. 'On a train? People on mobiles always say that. "I'm on the train," they say, like that. It's a cliché. Was that humour, Gwen Cooper?'

'Shut it! Stop babbling! I said the train thing because you sounded like you were on one. Quickly, before the line goes dead again, where are you?'

'We're in the chapel.'

'The what?'

'St Mary's.'

'Where the bloody hell is that? We're in the… Where are we, James?'

'The derelict warehouses Ianto sent us to. Off Livermore.'

'You get that, Jack?'

A fuzz of static.

'Jack?'

'I said I heard,' Jack replied. 'You're in the right place. St Mary's is smack in the middle of it. Little old chapel, used to be sweet and quaint, boarded up now. Can't miss it.'

'We missed it.'

'It's right there.'

'We've been here three-quarters of an hour and we can't find you.'

Silence.

'Jack?'

More silence.

'Jack!'

'I was thinking,' Jack answered.

'We'll don't.'

'Pardon me. Look, you parked where we did, right?'

'Right next to the SUV.'

'You just walk from there, straight through the doorway dead ahead. You—'

White noise, like surf across shingle, washed his words away.

'Jack? I'm losing you.'

'Gwen? I lost you there for a sec. Did you hear what I said? Start at the SUV, in Number Three Coal Depot, and head through the north door. We're standing beside—'

Scrambled, alien voices, static, gone.

'Jack? Jack, you bugger?'

The message on her mobile's screen read 'CALL ENDED'.

Her phone rang again, two trills, then rang off. Another feeble trill, and dead again.

'What did he say?' James asked.

Gwen looked up at the arch.

MILL ER & PEA ODY MBER FOUR POT 1 53

'Number four depot,' she whispered. She looked at James. 'We're in the wrong place.'

'We are?'

'We've overshot,' Gwen said, and started to run back across the echoing space.

As she ran, her phone tried to ring again, and gave up mid trill.

James caught up with her. They crossed back through an empty, dank vault of loveless Victorian stone, until they could see the SUV and the Saab through a crumbling doorway.

'Here,' she said. 'Here is where he means…'

They wove around each other, staring out at the brick shell enclosing them.

Her phone rang, sharp and echoing in the cold space.

'Jack?'

'I keep losing you. The signal's bad.'

'Jack, we're right there. I can see the cars and the north door. Where are you?'

'Where are *you*? We're right here, outside the chapel.'

'What bloody chapel?'

'The funny little chapel with the graffiti and the boarded-up windows.'

'There is no bloody chapel, Jack.'

A pause. She thought she'd lost him again.

'Gwen?'

'Yeah?'

'How many windows in the west wall?'

She turned and counted. 'Thirty-six. Three rows of twelve.'

'Middle row, third window along from the right. Big chunk of masonry missing from the lower left-hand corner?'

'Yes.'

'There's a broken chest freezer halfway along the east wall, under the third window. Zanussi. There's nothing in it except for an empty bottle of Tango.'

'Hang on.' Gwen hurried over. Zanussi chest freezer. Bottle of Tango. 'Yes.'

'Second-storey window above you. Three pigeons. One's got a white mark on its head. Looks like a balaclava.'

'Yes.'

'Right in the middle of the floor. A rainwater puddle making a figure of eight. Beside it, a piece of curtain track with seven, no *eight* curtain rings still attached to it.'

Gwen stared down at the puddle and the broken curtain track at her feet.

'Jack, how can you be seeing these things?'

'Because I'm standing right there. Right beside the puddle.'

'Oh God,' she said. She felt the *Wooof*. Gwen didn't get the Wooof much, not any more. The things she'd seen as part of Torchwood, it took a lot to properly Wooof her out these days.

But this did it, with bells on. Her skin prickled and crawled. The hairs on her neck stood up.

'Jack?'

'Yeah?'

'I'm standing beside the puddle too, and I can't see you.'

'Ah. I was afraid of that.'

'Jack?'

James was right beside her. 'Gwen? You all right? You got the Wooof then, didn't you?'

She nodded. James knew about the Wooof. In his capacity as the team's Master of Analogy and Jargon, he'd coined the term.

'Should I be scared?' he asked.

Gwen nodded again.

'Where's Jack, Gwen?' James asked.

'Right here,' she replied.

'Wow,' he said. 'Big Wooof. I'm tingling. You sure?'

'Jack?' Gwen said.

'Yes, honey.'

'Are you still there? Here, I mean?'

'Yes, Gwen.'

'I really… I really can't see you. Or Tosh. Or this chapel place you're going on about. Can you see me?'

'No. No, I can't.'

Gwen swallowed hard. 'Jack, one thing.'

'Go ahead.'

'Is this a joke? Because if it is, I'll knee you in the nuts next time I see you.'

'Fair comment. No, it isn't a joke. Swear to God, my skits are never this elaborate.'

'OK, so where the bloody hell are you?'

Dead air for a few seconds, then Jack answered, 'I have a nasty feeling Tosh and I may – and I do stress "may" – be kind of… in 1840. Strange as that may seem.'

'1840?'

'Yup. Kind of.'

'1840?'

'While you linger on that, Gwen, may I ask you a question?'

'Yes, Jack.'

'Is it getting dark where you are?'

'No.'

'Ah, OK. Just here then. Not a good sign.'

'1840?'

'As I said, kind of. Still, you have to see the up side.'

'What up side?'

'These phones,' Jack's voice said. 'Great coverage.'

Owen walked into the Hub, feeling like shit. It was noon. He had his 'sorry I'm late' all ready, but there was no one in sight.

Water lapped down into the basin. The air was damp and fresh. Data scrolled across the flat screens on vacant desks.

'Hello?'

Something with leathery wings clacked and took off from a perch high in the vault above him. Owen sneered up. 'Not on my head, not today. I know what you're like.'

He went over to his work station and hit start-up. The screen blinked as it came on. He started running through his daily log, and launching some software. X-Tension 07, Eye-Spy v. 6.1, Normal Mailer. Maybe there'd even be a message telling him where everyone had gone to.

He had a headache. He was coming to the conclusion that it was going to be his lot in life to have a headache all of the time.

A suspension field ignited in front of him. Data streamed across a Lexan dome.

This wasn't his work station. This was Toshiko's. What the hell was he doing here?

How did he know her passwords?

There was something in the blue glow of the suspension field. A containment box, unlocking itself with a clack and a hiss. The magnetic collar ring turned. Had he done that?

'Owen?'

'Ianto? Hey, mate? Where were you?'

'Having a lie down in the Boardroom. I've got a murderous headache.'

'Me too. Where is everyone?'

'Didn't you get the call?'

'I overslept,' Owen said.

'In the last hour or so? Didn't you get my messages?'

'No.'

'Owen?' said Ianto after a pause. No response.

'Uh, Dr Harper?'

'Yeah. Mmmh. What?'

'What are you doing?'

'I'm just…'

'I don't think you should.'

Owen looked around at Ianto. His eyes were bloodshot. 'Is Jack here?'

'No.'

'Then I'm in charge. Me. I'll do what I want and you'll do as you're told.'

Ianto smiled. 'I don't think it quite works like that.'

'Does today!'

Ianto stepped closer. 'Owen. You're sitting at Tosh's station. You are systematically disabling the firewalls encasing the subject specimen. I can't allow you to do that.'

'Go and make me a nice cup of coffee, would you?' Owen replied.

'Don't make me hurt you.'

'You wish. Funny. I'm laughing, see? Aha ha ha.'

'Owen.'

'Get lost!'

Owen's fingers were racing across the keyboard. Inhibitor codes were flashing up, and were being cancelled, one by one.

'Listen,' Ianto said. 'Jack told me this thing had to be locked away. Vaulted. In an isoclave.'

Owen kept typing code. 'Jack doesn't know what he's talking about.'

'Owen—' Ianto warned. He looked at the screen beside him. He saw the firewalls closing down, one after another.

'Coffee please,' Owen said, working furiously. 'Coffee. Please. Now coffee. Make it a big one. Big big one.'

Owen reached over to press a key. His hand stopped dead. Ianto had grabbed it, holding it back.

'Coffee!' Owen cried, and slapped Ianto in the face with his other hand.

Ianto reeled, but recovered. He looked mortified. Without further words, he slugged Owen. Owen fell backwards off his seat onto the deck, dragging Ianto down with him.

Owen shook and went still. Ianto scrambled up. He saw the screens. He saw the last of the firewalls collapse.

Suspended in a cold blue glow, the Amok trembled and rotated.

Ianto punched blindly at various keys. It was too late.

He sank back, gazing at the wobbling light.
'You're big,' he said. 'Big *big* big.'

THIRTEEN

James had used his spare key to open the SUV. He lugged a portable scanner system and some other bits of kit into the empty warehouse space that was not as empty as it looked. He started to unpack the anonymous, brushed-steel flight cases.

Gwen completed a third circuit of the shed. She tried her phone again. Jack had been cut off mid conversation by a squall of interference, and there had been nothing from him since.

She dialled a different number instead. 'Ianto? It's Gwen. Why aren't you picking up? Ianto, it's urgent. Call me or James as soon as you get this.'

She walked back over to James.

'Something's wrong,' she said.

'I thought we'd pretty well established that.'

'No, more wrong than just this. Something's going on at the Hub.'

'Ianto still not answering?'

She shook her head.

'We're not having much in the way of telephonic success today, are we?' he observed.

She sighed, and pinched the bridge of her nose, her eyes closed. 'Can't believe I've got that headache again, on top of everything else.'

'You too?' James stood up. 'I've had a killer head for about the last five minutes. Came on like a switch.'

'Just like Thursday's?'

'Just like Thursday's. You don't suppose there's another one of those things around, do you?'

Gwen didn't answer. A breeze hustled litter across the ground. The muted sensation of haunting that had clung around the site earlier had been replaced by a palpable feeling of malice.

'Can you even begin to explain what's going on here?' she asked James.

He was still setting up the system, snap-extending the aluminium legs of the folding stands that the sensors clipped to. There were six altogether, and he was arranging them in a wide ring around the centre of the warehouse. 'Some kind of Rift phenomenon?' he suggested. 'A crack, a fold, an overlap? A spatio-temporal slip? A cleft? Dimensional transcendence? A chronal bifurcation with—'

'Whoa. You're just saying long words now, aren't you?'

'Yes I am. Actually, I'm trying to reassure you. I thought if one of us sounded like they were in charge…'

'Oh, I'm in charge,' said Gwen fiercely. 'I'm in charge, me, so very in-charge. Look at me, being in charge. Come on, boy! Get those scanners set up! Pronto!'

He grinned. 'Yes, boss. You could help.'

'I'm in charge,' she replied. She stared at their surroundings. The sky visible through the incomplete roof was an ugly shade of white, bruised with grey clouds. 'This place has got a really nasty feeling about it, hasn't it?'

'Yup. Getting nastier by the minute. Oppressive. Very much like my headache.'

'What do you really think is going on? And skip all that bifurcatory hooey this time.'

James fitted the last sensor in place on top of its tripod. 'Well,' he said, 'I have a hunch Jack and Tosh have stepped on an insanely malignant cold-spot and been drawn away from us against their will by the unliving appetite of some spectral entity.'

Gwen thought about that. 'Pooh,' she decided. 'That's cobblers.'

'Of course,' said James. 'Being positive didn't work, so I was shooting for negative reinforcement.'

'You're a nutjob, is what you are.'

James knelt down by the scanner system's master unit and pressed some switches. A vague filigree of green light spread out from the tripod-mounted sensors: thin rays they could barely see in the daylight criss-crossed and overlapped like a spirograph pattern.

'Actually,' James said, 'I was only half-kidding. I don't believe in ghosts.

"Ghost" is a word people use to explain things that Torchwood can provide much better, scientific explanations for. But in this instance…'

Gwen narrowed her eyes. 'Stop it.' She took a deep breath. 'Saw a ghost once…'

He shrugged. 'If you say so.'

Gwen got back to business. 'Getting anything?'

James fiddled with the master control, adjusting wavelengths. 'Umm… no.'

Gwen's phone rang. She snatched it out.

'Hello?'

She heard silence at the other end. Then, the very faintest murmur of something.

'Hello? Jack?'

The call ended. The phone immediately rang again.

'Hello?'

'Gwen?' It was Jack. His voice sounded thin and very, very far away. Thin, rushing sounds came and went, like gusts of wind. 'I've been trying to get through for ages. Gwen?'

'I'm here. Are you all right?'

'I can barely hear you, Gwen. My phone's on low battery. Can you hear me?'

'Just.'

'It's getting dark, Gwen. Really dark. Nightfall. We've gone inside the chapel. Tosh says she can hear noises outside, but I don't hear anything. She's telling me she can. Something walking around. Footsteps.'

Static.

'Jack?'

'Gwen? Gwen, how are things your end?'

'We're… we're trying to find you, Jack. Hold on.'

'Battery's low, Gwen. I—'

Dead.

Gwen looked anxiously at James. He returned her look with one of slight exasperation. 'I can't get the system to align properly,' he said, getting up and walking around the ring of tripods, adjusting each unit in turn. 'I'm just getting feedback. Interference patterns.'

'Listen,' he added, 'I'm sorry about the roast thing. I didn't mean to Wooof you out.'

TORCHWOOD

'What roast thing?'

'What?'

'You just said you were sorry about the roast thing,' Gwen said.

'I didn't. I said ghost.'

'You bloody didn't.'

James opened his mouth but didn't answer. He met Gwen's eyes. They each knew what the other was thinking. They'd been here before.

The pull came on him, without any warning, as it always did.

'Steady on, mate!' the traffic warden said. 'Are you all right?'

The lean man in the black suit had sprung up off the bus stop bench and barged into him.

'I said, are you all right?'

The man was swaying slightly, glancing around in some confusion. Drugs, thought the traffic warden. The man didn't look the type – too old, too well dressed – but nobody looked the type any more.

'Mate?'

The man took a step, halted, looked around again, and met the warden's eyes.

'What did you say?' the man asked.

'Are you all right? You look a bit spaced.'

'Alert protocol,' the man said, as if that explained everything. 'Threat to the Principal. Jeopardy. Investment is beginning, but the pull is wrong. The pull is wrong.'

'Ri-ight. Whatever you say, mate. Just mind how you go.'

The man ignored him and began to stride away down the pavement. He bumped into an old woman with a tartan shopping trolley, and then clipped a pushchair with his hip.

The mother gave him what for. The man ignored her too, and moved on, start-stop, a few quick steps, then another bewildered glance around. He changed direction several times.

Definitely drugs, thought the traffic warden, shaking his head. The man was scurrying backwards and forwards, like Jerry Lewis doing his 'confused' shtick, except there was a curiously fluid grace to his movements.

Designer drugs, the traffic warden decided. He'd read all about those.

City Road was bustling. Tuesday lunchtime. Bookmakers with coloured-bead door curtains; army surplus stores selling camo-pants and Air-soft guns; slot arcades with doormen; Dragon Burger bars ripe with grease; conga lines of carts outside the Happy Shopper; resigned queues outside the Post Office; bunting-trimmed forecourts of pre-owned cars with stickered windows; hot-dog stands sizzling with onion smoke; bhangra pumping from minicab sound systems; reversing hooters and car alarms; hand car wash and valeting, redolent with pine scent; a council worker in Day-Glo overalls, picking up litter with a squeezy claw and dropping it into his yellow cart; kids with sherbet fountains outside Poundland, laughing at the man by the crosswalk proclaiming Jesus' constant love to an uninterested crowd; men carrying cue-cases like shouldered arms as they wandered upstairs to the snooker club; double parking; hazard lights ticking; two Somali men arguing in a doorway; chuggers with clipboards asking for just a moment; the stable-smell of straw and pellet food exuding from the pet shop; two women in chadors; Telecom engineers erecting an orange hazard guard around the manhole they are about to lift; someone shouting to get Ronnie's attention; the pip-pip-pip of the crossing posts; the air-horn of a boy racer's GTi rendering 'La Cucaracha'; carentan melons like bald scalps in the fake grass trays of a fruit and veg; people, people, people.

Too many noises, too many smells, too much movement. Too much input. The pull was wrong. The pull was wrong. He couldn't get a clean fix on the alert. Location? What was the location? How could he respond if he didn't have a definitive location? The upload was pulsing into him, but it was patchy and contradictory. It pulled him one way, then another, as if it was uncertain, as if it couldn't make its mind up.

'Where? Where is it?' he demanded out loud. Faces in the crowd looked at him, confused, amused, alarmed, but they were just faces and he didn't care what they thought. Some of them spoke to him, but he didn't care what they said either.

Where was he needed? Where was the Principal? How could he have lost the fix on the Principal? Why couldn't he focus? Why was the upload so disjointed? Was it being jammed?

'Principal,' Mr Dine muttered. 'Majesty. Where are you?'

He felt his metabolism start to hike as the alert protocols took full control. His composition altered. He felt a surge as the investment began and power was relayed into him, unsleeving the deep-seated caches in his genes and bone marrow, and lighting up his higher senses. Still no fix. The pull was still wrong. Indecisive.

Turning wildly, he bumped against a news-stand, and a row of magazines slithered off onto the pavement. The vendor started to remonstrate with him.

'I'm talking to you, twat! Oi!'

No time for an altercation. Mr Dine raised his hand. The vendor jerked backwards into his stand and ended up sitting on a heap of scattered tabloids.

Some of the faces were shouting at him suddenly. What did he think he was doing? Who did he think he was? Jackie flaming Chan?

Mr Dine ignored them. He turned left, then checked himself and turned right instead, stepping off the kerb.

There was a squeal and a crunch. A woman screamed.

The Autospares van, an older, commercial-bodied Escort, had come to a stop so suddenly, its rear end had swung out. The driver's side door opened, and a chubby man with sweat patches on his beige, short-sleeved shirt got out and stared at Mr Dine, his mouth a goldfish 'O'.

'I didn't…' the driver began. 'I didn't see you. Are you…?'

People were gathering. Mr Dine was still on his feet, still glancing to and fro in a twitchy, panicky way. He realised he was the focus of particular attention suddenly. He looked down.

His legs had stopped the van dead. Ramming him had been like ramming a deep-seated bollard or a gate post. The bumper, number plate and grille had folded in around his thighs. The leading edge of the bonnet was crumpled like a bed-sheet. Dirty fluid gurgled out of the split radiator and pooled under the front wheels.

'Jesus flippin' Christ!' the driver stammered. 'How the—'

Mr Dine stepped away from the arrested vehicle. Bent bodywork groaned as his legs came out of the form-fitting impression. The bumper fell off.

No fix. Still no fix. The pull was wrong. Still no definitive focus from the upload, despite the fact that his body was now accelerating to full combat investment, hyping to maximum.

In another ten seconds it would automatically switch over to battledress. That was something that could not be allowed to happen in plain sight.

'Excuse me,' he said to the chubby driver.

'But you can't… you should go to hospital and—'

'I have no further time for this digression.'

Mr Dine started to move. By the time the gathered crowd had realised the man in the black suit was shoving his way through them, he had somehow

– inexplicably, in the opinion of many – already vanished.

The recorded voice said, 'The phone you are calling is out of range or has been switched off. Please try again later.'

Gwen cancelled the call. Her head was throbbing so much, she was having difficulty accomplishing even simple tasks. It felt like a six-inch nail had been driven in through the top of her skull. She wanted to cry. She wanted to lie down. She wanted to cry and lie down.

Fiddling with the master control box, James let out a dull moan. His hands were visibly shaking.

'Gwen, I can't do it. I can't work it. I can't think straight.'

'I know.'

'Gwen, can you see the blue lights?'

'No,' she lied. 'Try again.'

He looked up at her. His eyes were horribly bloodshot. Dots of sweat clung to his forehead and made his hair lank. 'I can't. I can't. I can't get the fœtus to align.'

'The fœtus?'

'The focus, focus.'

'It's OK. Just try one more time.'

'One more climb? Climb what?'

'I said time.'

'No, you said—'

'James! Please!'

He bent back over the control box.

Gwen held up her mobile, blinking away tears. She willed it to ring.

It rang. She answered. 'Tosh?'

'Gwen Cooper. Good to hear your voice.'

It was just a whisper, desperately far away, deep in a well.

'Jack!'

'My phone died. I'm using Tosh's, but her battery is fading fast too. Something here is sucking energy up. Something hungry.'

'Jack—'

'Listen to me, Gwen. I don't have long. It's gone dark here. Pitch black. Scary dark. We're both feeling pretty wretched, headache and nausea. I guess if this place leeches power out of cellphone batteries, it leaches power out of organics too. Anyway, we're not doing too good, all told. And there are footsteps out there. I can hear them too now. Circling the chapel in the dark. Creepy. This is not—'

'What? Jack?'

'This is not how I pictured my demise.'

'It's not going to *be* your demise, Harkness. We'll get you out of there! We'll—'

'Gwen. You're a good girl, but I know when I'm beat. I've flown from one side of this galaxy to the other, and seen a lot of strange stuff—'

'Don't you go all Han Solo on me now, you bugger! I get enough of that from Rhys! We're getting you out of there!'

'How?'

Gwen looked at James.

'How?' Jack repeated down the line. 'Gwen, you still there?'

'Yes.'

'How are you going to get us out of here? I don't even know where here is. All I know is there are footsteps coming closer and they ain't friendly.'

'We'll find a way.' She had a lump in her throat. 'We'll find something.'

A moment passed before he said anything. 'Gwen, I made a bad call today. Learn from that. I rushed in here with Tosh, and it was a bad call. Dumb. I don't know what I was thinking. Major error of judgement. Something was affecting me, something… putting me off my game. I don't mind paying for that, but I hate the fact that Tosh is paying for it too. Error of judgement. Not like me at all. Never rush into a situation unsecured. These are the things you have to remember. The things you have to learn.'

'Why?'

'When you take over. Recruit and rebuild. It'll be down to you. You'll need to learn from my mistakes.'

'Take over? Torchwood?'

'No, the Cyncoed Choral Society. Yes, Torchwood.'

'Jack, there won't be any Torchwood without you.'

'There damn well better be, girl. The Rift won't police itself. I'm counting on you—'

Static wilted his voice. A dry buzz. A flicker of rasping voices lacking any real words.

'Jack?'

Buzzing, buzzing.

'… come back and haunt you forever, you hear me?'

'Jack?'

'Did you lose me there?' Jack's tiny voice asked. 'I lost you. God, it's dark, Gwen. You wouldn't believe. Footsteps. I didn't think I could get scared like this any more. Battery's so low. I think it's about to fake out.'

'Say again? Did you say "fake"?'

'No, I said fade.'

'You said fake. I heard you. Jack, you said you had a headache. Headache and nausea. Is it like last Thursday at the riverside? Jack, is it like that?'

'I suppose, but—'

'Jack, listen to me. We're up to our necks here. Somehow, I don't know how, the Amok is affecting us again. Either that, or there's another one loose. Splitting headaches. We can barely thick.'

'By which, of course, you mean "think",' called James.

'Right. Think. If you weren't so deep in shit, we'd bail on you and head back to the Hub. Try and sort it out.'

'You should do that. Right now. Leave us and sort it. If the Amok – or an Amok – is operational, it's priority one. Not us. You hearing me, Gwen?'

'Oh, shut up and listen! I can barely cling two words together—'

'Uh, "string" maybe?' advised James.

Gwen put her hand over the mouthpiece. 'You're not helping, you know that? Work harder.'

James shook out his neck and turned back to the box.

'Jack?'

'Still here, caller.'

'Jack, I think you can feel the Amok's effects too. Your headache. Behind the eyes, is it?'

'In this life, ultimately *everything* is behind the eyes.'

'Spare me the cock philosophy.'

'You meant "cod" there, right?'

'I know what I meant! Jack, if you and Tosh can feel this like we're feeling this, how bloody far away can you be? You're not lost. You're… right there.'

'Faraway, so close, huh?'

'Does it make sense?'

'Kinda. You got a game plan?'

Gwen thought about that, which was especially hard. Crying and lying down still seemed like the best offer going. 'Yes,' she said. 'I've got a game plan.'

'So let's hear it before my battery expires.'

'The Amok… The Amok is calling us. It's hooked us and it's calling us. It wants us to obey it. It wants us to go and find it, wherever it is.'

'Fair point. I can feel it too.'

Gwen bunched her left hand into a tight fist. 'So… give in.'

'What?'

'Give in. Answer the call. Follow it.'

'Because?'

'Because it'll bring you here. Because here is where the Amok is.'

Silence.

'Jack, did you—'

'Hang tight, Gwen,' Jack said. Over the line, she heard movement, a bump or two. She heard Jack talking to Toshiko, urging her to get up. She heard Toshiko's frail complaints.

Jack began insisting. Gwen heard Toshiko call him a bad word. More bumps and scrapes, muffled.

'Gwen?'

'Yes, hello?'

'We're heading for the chapel door. Footsteps or no footsteps, we're going to do like you suggested. We're going to give in and—'

'And?'

'I dunno, hope for the best? Cross your fingers.'

Gwen wanted to, but in her befuddled state, she couldn't remember how.

Over the live link, she heard something heavy and wooden scrape back. She heard Jack mumbling to Toshiko. A fragile response.

'We're outside,' Jack said, though not to Gwen. 'Dang, it's dark.'

'Jack? Jack, just follow the call.'

'Christ almighty!' James said. 'Look at this!'

Gwen moved in behind him. She stared over James's shoulder at the monitor on the master control box, her phone still pressed to her ear.

Something had appeared on the dim screen, like a radar echo, a light-bouncing outline. It was a chapel, except it wasn't exactly. It was the ghost outline of a chapel, a luminous diagram. Struggling, the ring of scanners were painting something half-solid.

'Jack? Jack? We can see the shape of the chapel on our system! Jack?'

Jack Harkness said something in reply, but it was too distorted to make sense of. On the monitor, two phantom figures appeared, ephemeral and half-formed. They were stepping out of the outlined chapel's outlined doorway.

Gwen looked up. In the hard daylight, there was nothing to see inside the ring of mounted scanners.

'Jack?'

'They're coming out,' James said. 'I…'

He faltered. He looked up at her, pain lacing his features. 'Gwen, I feel really sick. I—'

James collapsed on the ground, quivering, his feet kicking.

'Oh God! Oh Christ! James!' Gwen exclaimed, bending over him. She tried to hold James's body steady and hold the phone to her ear at the same time.

James went still. Blood dripped out of his left nostril.

'Jack?' she whispered.

'Gwen? We're right outside. In the dark. It's really dark. Are you there?'

'Yes, Jack. Follow my voice. Scrub that, follow the Amok.'

'OK.' Jack sounded like a scared child. It was not a tone she associated with him, nor one she wanted to.

'Gwen? Gwen, I think it's here.'

At first, she thought he meant the Amok, but that wasn't it. Over the open line, she heard the footsteps. They were coming closer, hobnails on loose flags, *clack clack clack clack*.

Big *Wooof*. The sound of those footsteps was by far the scariest thing she would ever hear in her life.

FOURTEEN

Mr Dine vaulted off the burnished roof shell of the Millennium Centre and landed on the dry boards of the Quay below in a single bound.

He landed in a shock-absorbing crouch and slowly rose upright. Combat modulated, flicker-fast, skin-sheathed in battledress, he read the area. Environment appraisal, a super-vast sensory processing that took barely a nanosecond from initial data-capture to final tactical assessment. The gleaming finger of the water tower smelled especially hot to his elevated senses. He shot towards it.

Visitors and tourists milled around the area, all the way down Roald Dahl Plass, chattering in the colourless sunlight and taking pictures. None of them saw him, even though he passed amongst them. None of them recorded him in their pictures, even though he was right there in shot many times.

This was because he was simply moving too fast. Hyper-acceleration zigzagged him in and out of the bustling traffic as if he was occupying an entirely separate time scheme. The people were slo-mo to him, swaying, lumbering, cumbersome. It was also, partly, because he was invested for war, and the matt-grey sleeve of the battledress shrugged off light and colour like smoke.

In extremis, Mr Dine had switched to autonomous running. The upload was conspicuously unreliable, unacceptably compromised, and the fix undefined, so Mr Dine had muted the upload's data stream. He didn't need the confusion. For the sake of the Principal, he knew he had to act logically, and make the sort of executive anticipatory decisions all loyal bodyguards of the First Senior were expected to make when it came to the crunch.

This was the crunch. In selecting him, him out of all the exalted First Seniors, for this tour of duty, the Lord of the Border had placed enormous trust in Mr Dine, and Mr Dine wasn't about to betray that trust. Protect the Principal. Protect the Principal. All other issues were secondary. That was why he had been inserted onto the Earth.

He was buzzing, his body singing with the immense power the investment had bestowed upon him. This was his purpose, in its purest, most ineluctable form, these brief, shining moments of performance. This was the fleeting joy of being what he was, what he had volunteered to be. This was why he had been made the way he was.

A selfless, devoted soldier. An implacable force. An instrument of war. There was nothing on Earth in this time that could match him, like for like. Nothing *from* Earth, at least.

There were plenty of things from elsewhere that might give cause for concern.

A blink, he arrived beside the base of the water tower. Clear rivulets of water poured down the steel flanks of the naive human monument. Tourists laughed and backed off as the Bayside wind carried the spray out at them. None of them saw him.

None of them except a three-year-old boy, pulling on his mother's hand as the family posed for a father's Kodak digital. In Mr Dine's experience, very young human children sometimes possessed a knack of subtle intuition that adulthood stole away. The boy stared at him, goggle-eyed.

'Mummy, who is the grey man?'

'Look at Daddy, Kyle. Look at Daddy and say cheese.'

Mr Dine raised a grey-thorned finger to his lips and winked at the boy. The boy's eyes widened further and he grinned.

Mr Dine turned and took a deep breath. He could smell the technology buried under the flagstones. It reeked, hot and sharp, like cooking pheromones. Down below, deep under the Bay, exotic tech screamed to him like a newborn baby.

Autonomous running. Executive decision. Assess the options. Another nanosecond of deep reflection. He had no true fix on the Principal, so he had to work with the data available. If he couldn't find the Principal himself, he could locate and neutralise that which was threatening the Principal.

The water tower. His systems lit up, hungry.

Here. *Here.*

There was a lift mechanism under one of the paving stones, cloaked by a perception filter. Interesting. Unexpected. He nodded his head. A simple hindbrain connection with the lift's systems overwrote all the security measures.

Mr Dine began to descend as the lift kicked in.

He was lowered into a dank, twilight place, a lair of some sort. Gloom, concrete, old tiling, the background smell of the under-dock vault. The sleek flanks of the water tower extended down into the place, down through ground level into a recirculatory basin. Mr Dine tasted the heat of a network of high-level human computational systems and allied electronics: live work stations, woven sheaves of fibre-optic trunking. Very impressive, by local tech standards. Primitive to him.

He also read other things. Dead things, dormant things, slumbering things, dreaming things, things encased and secured and screened and boxed and locked away. A treasure trove of non-human artifice that had no business being either here or now. He approved of the way it had been so diligently sequestered.

But not all of it had been. Something was loose and live, aware and predatory. The lift had about five metres still to descend, but Mr Dine stepped off it. He landed on the grille decking with a quiet *clank*, and walked across the basin board-way towards the concrete platforms where the work stations flickered and hummed.

Two humans lay in a tangle of limbs on the floor, twitching, comatose. The loosed thing, the exotic tech, was a tiny object, revolving in a field of blue light. It felt him, read him and began to mew and wail in his mind.

Mr Dine's systems were robust enough to deny its initial advances. Shield buffers rose automatically to screen him. He assessed. No match. The technology was not known to the First Senior data-archive. He filed his findings for future reference. Product of an unknown species, origin/ manufacture unknown. Tech level sixty-plus. Powerful suggestion fields. Hazard (type 2) grade persuasion/manipulation protocols enabled by a quasi-sentience. Aggressive intercourse.

He took another few steps towards it. The tiny object began to spin more rapidly. To his surprise, his outer sets of shield buffers impacted suddenly and shattered. The inner sets held. Mr Dine accessed reserve investment and erected a custom barrier shield to bolster his defences.

'What are you?' he asked.

It answered in a rattling string of colours, lights and concept impressions. Abstract numbers. It was as swift and ferocious as a hail of gunfire. Abstract numbers. Two blue lights, moving.

Mr Dine winced. His inner shields exploded without warning. Instinctively, he set a second custom barrier behind the first.

'So, you want to play, do you?' he asked.

Gwen found herself sitting in her Saab, turning the engine over. The starter motor gagged and wheezed. She flooded it.

How long had she been sitting there? How long had she been trying to—

She got out of the car. She felt like a zombie that barely, just barely, realises it is a zombie. She tottered back into the adjacent warehouse.

James was sprawled on the ground. He looked distressingly dead. The ring of scanners was whirring. She remembered her intention. She'd been trying to drive back to the Hub. The Hub, from where the Amok was calling to her.

'Oh my God,' she mumbled. Her head hurt like it had been crushed between cymbals. She could barely walk straight. There was a ringing in her ears.

Her phone. Her bloody phone.

She took it out, opened it upside down, turned it over.

'Yeah?'

'Gwen? For God's sake, help us! We can't find—'

'Jack?'

She heard muffled voices, agitation, extraneous noises. Then, suddenly, clearly, she heard the footsteps again.

'Jack?'

A scream. Toshiko, screaming. Gwen went cold. The repeated booming of a revolver, straining the limits of her phone's speaker.

Laughter. Satanic, psychotic laughter.

Gwen squealed and hurled the phone away. It bounced across the ground, chipping and cracking.

'Gwen?'

She looked around.

Jack was standing in the middle of the ring of sensors. He was holding Toshiko to his side with one arm. She was clinging to him, weeping. Jack's face was drawn and haggard. He was shaking. His hair was lank with sweat.

In his right hand, his Webley wavered, uncertain, smoke coiling from the long barrel.

'Oh my God, Gwen,' Jack stammered. He sat down on the ground, and Toshiko folded up beside him.

One by one, in sequence, the six stand-mounted scanners exploded, their cases bursting open in clouds of sparks. Two of the tripods toppled. The master control box began to smoke and then caught fire.

Her own brain ablaze, Gwen tried to speak, but nothing came out.

The Amok spun around even more furiously, and then stopped.

'Yes,' said Mr Dine. 'Clever. But I believe I win.'

The Amok rotated left for two turns, then right for three.

'No, I do not want to play again,' said Mr Dine.

The Amok pulsed out a field of violet sulk.

Mr Dine reached forward and took hold of it. He grimaced as it burned his palm.

'Still fighting?' he asked.

It was. Mr Dine cried out as pain flared along his arm and into his head. The last of his custom barriers fell.

'You are tenacious, but I am of the First Senior. I am not impressed by your spite. I have given you fair warning. Accept the consequences.'

Mr Dine squeezed his hand. The Amok winced and shattered. Mr Dine toppled backwards and sat down hard. It had been tough. Astonishingly tough. Almost a match.

He let the powdered fragments of the Amok slide out of his hand and then began to try healing the grievous damage he had sustained.

Owen woke up. He looked around, aware that he was on the floor with Ianto crumpled on top of him.

'Hello?' he called. 'Hello?'

Something was sitting on the floor next to him. It was the size and shape of a man, but it was matt-grey, its bodywork comprising odd grey thorns and overlapping, segmented layers. A monster.

Owen had seen a fair few monsters in the course of his work. Weevils, for a start. This was altogether more nightmarish. So sleek, so machined, so artfully designed.

He felt funny. Muzzy. Sick. Maybe he was seeing things. Maybe there wasn't a monster there at all.

The monster turned its extended, streamlined, recurve head and noticed him.

There was an expression on its vaguely human face. An expression of pain and torment. It pointed a long, thorny finger at him.

'You will not remember me,' it said, its voice as level and heavy as the speaking clock.

'OK, fair enough,' said Owen, and allowed unconsciousness to carry him away again.

FIFTEEN

'Look, I'm all right. Really,' said James.

'No, you're not.'

'Owen, really, I—'

'Am I a doctor?' Owen asked. 'Am I?'

'You remind us often enough.'

'Then I ought to know, didn't I?' Owen replied smartly. 'And you know what's also true? You don't have to be a doctor – like me – to know that you're not at *all* all right. None of us are all right. We just took a damn serious seeing to. One of the worst I can remember since I started this bloody job. So sit still and shut up and let me do my thing.'

It was eight o'clock at night. Two hours earlier, a terrific storm, the second in two straight nights, had blown up out in the Bristol Channel and come swirling inland. High above their heads, Mermaid Quay was empty. Driving rain pummelled the dock walks and lamp-lit boards.

'How is everyone?' James asked, as Owen continued to examine him with the medical area's suite of instruments.

'Far as I can tell, sore, exhausted and traumatised,' said Owen, 'and we can be pretty damn thankful that's all we are. I haven't found anything more… serious. But I'm going to be checking everyone every day for as long as it takes to make sure there's no lasting damage.'

James nodded. He'd been told that he, Owen and Ianto had all fugued out, and that he had been unconscious the longest. Gwen had come close to joining them, but she'd kept it together, just about. Jack and Toshiko had said very little about what they'd experienced, and it seemed likely that they had suffered the effects of the Amok the least, insulated to some extent by... by wherever they had been.

Gwen walked into the medical area. Her face was drawn with fatigue, and there were dark shadows under her eyes. Unabashed, she went over to James and kissed him.

'I'm the doctor,' grumbled Owen. 'I'm the one who kisses things better.'

'Jack wants us in the Boardroom in ten,' said Gwen.

'OK,' said James.

'All of us,' said Gwen.

Owen nodded.

She climbed the stairs to Jack's office. He was at his desk, cleaning his revolver.

'Hi, come in,' he said.

She came in and sat facing him.

'Anything new?' he asked.

'Nope,' she said. 'Oh, one thing. Reports of civil disturbance down on the point this afternoon. Round about the same time we were up to our necks.'

'Where?'

'Exactly where we were last Thursday night. Where we recovered the bloody thing from in the first place. There was some fighting, a mini-riot. A couple of cars set on fire, windows smashed.'

'You're getting this from?'

'I checked the police system. The whole thing went away again as quickly as it started, with no one willing or able to explain what the hell had been going on.'

'It all went away again?'

'At about the same time our migraines eased and we started to remember how to spell our own names again.'

'And the police are saying?'

Gwen shrugged. 'Someone's suggesting it might be some kind of chemical poisoning event, a toxic spill at one of the Bay's industrial depots. Environmental teams are checking. It *has* happened twice in a week, after all.'

Jack smiled sadly. 'Well, they've written a cover story for us, at least.'

'We going to start this meeting, then?' she asked.

'Couple of things I want to say to you first,' Jack said, closing his old gun's frame and sliding it back into its leather holster. He screwed the lid back on the small bottle of gun oil, and put it away in the cleaning kit with the bristle push-brushes.

'Can they wait for the meeting?'

'No,' said Jack. He tossed two oil-smudged cotton wool pads into his waste bin and got up to put the cleaning kit away in a drawer. 'The first thing I want to say is thank you. You saved me today, Gwen.'

'Oh, no, I just—'

'You saved me,' Jack insisted, sitting back down. 'Me and Toshiko both. Despite everything, despite the… circumstances under which you were operating, you stuck to it. You stayed right there and, crazy though it was, you came up with a trick to get us out.'

He looked over at her. 'It was a damn crazy trick, Gwen. Damn crazy. Using one threat to combat another. How did you know it would work?'

'Honestly? I didn't. It seemed to have some resemblance to logic at the time. But – at the time – I was a girl with a jack-hammer going off in her head and serious big hand/little hand differentiation issues. So I think we were lucky, really.'

'I'll take luck, any time it's offered,' said Jack. 'Again, thank you.'

'Please,' she said, 'you're going to make me blush.'

'Yeah, well you'll hate the second thing, then. The second thing is sorry.'

'Oh, what for?'

Jack sighed. 'I know I've already apologised about tearing you all off a strip last week, but seriously, I need to do a lot more. I handled this whole thing really badly. Like—'

'An amateur?' she suggested.

'Oh yeah,' he grinned. 'I had no business calling you that.'

'I told you the other day,' said Gwen, 'the best we can ever hope to be at this is amateurs. You too. We should be proud of that. Anything that doesn't kill us makes us learn for next time. How can we expect to tackle the mysteries of the bloody Universe head-on and know everything about everything? A piece of alien technology put you right off your game today, Jack. But it's the end of the day, and we're all still alive, and Cardiff isn't a smoking hole in the ground populated by shuffling zombies, so, you know, yaaay us.'

Jack rose to his feet. 'Speaking of mysteries, there are some left, of course.'

* * *

The mood in the Boardroom was subdued. Everyone shuffled in like they were hung-over. Ianto brought in a tray of drinks.

'Decaff,' he said, handing them out. 'I thought that might be best.' He glanced at Jack. 'If that's all?'

'No, you sit too,' Jack said. 'You weren't a bystander today. I'd appreciate your input.'

Ianto hunched his shoulders and sat down.

Jack took a sip of his drink. 'Mmm. So, what are we calling that?'

'Twenty-seven?' said James. They all smiled, even Toshiko, who was huddled in a shawl and seemed to be shivering.

'Absolutely,' said Jack. 'I'm tempted to go even higher. This is the post-game analysis, so I want your comments. Speak freely. But first, hear mine. I was as much to blame as anyone for what went down today. More so, in many ways. So, sorry for that.'

No one spoke.

'OK,' said Jack. 'Moving on. It was a twenty-seven. Any other remarks?'

Owen half-raised his hand. 'I let it out. I acted like a prat. I think I smacked Ianto as well, so I suppose I'll be the one sitting on the naughty step.'

'You were under the influence,' said Jack.

'As usual,' Owen replied.

'You know what I mean,' Jack insisted. 'If it hadn't been you, it would have been someone else. Ianto tried to stop you because he was the only one of us who hadn't actually touched the darn thing. It's my belief that once someone touches it, it doesn't let them go, not even when it was dormant and contained. It was always going to get free again.'

'The riots this afternoon seem to support that idea,' said Gwen.

'It had a real range on it,' said James. 'It got to us over quite a distance.'

'There is a question none of us have asked,' said Toshiko. 'Where is it?'

'And why did it stop?' Jack added. 'I mean, it had us, and then—'

'I've had the Hub systems scanning for it,' Ianto said. 'Nothing, not a trace. It's gone. Maybe it went back where it came from?'

'Doesn't seem likely,' said James. 'Jack's right, it had us, it really did. It was winning.'

Jack looked at Owen and Ianto. 'You two were here. Either of you remember anything?'

They shook their heads.

'Hub monitors? Security?'

'I've been through the logs and the playback. There's nothing useful,' said Ianto. 'Though it's fair to say the records are incomplete. There's a whole chunk of the day's Hub-monitor log that's effectively blank, like it was jammed or erased.'

'Anything else?'

'There are signs that the Hub was violated,' said Ianto. 'Certain entry traces and system intrusions. But I don't think they're anything. I think they're all part of the damage the Amok caused. It got into everything.'

'Unless,' said Owen. 'Unless someone or something came in here and removed the Amok.'

'Like who?' asked James.

Owen shrugged. 'I dunno. Given our security, I guess that's too scary to contemplate.'

'I want us back to alpha scoping for the next week or so,' Jack announced. 'Extreme vigilance, twenty-four seven. If the Amok's still out there, I want to know about it. Any hint of it, *any* hint.'

Toshiko and Ianto nodded.

'So, are you going to tell us what happened to you?' Owen asked Jack.

'A little Rift-slip,' Jack replied. 'Something on the books I'd been looking out for. The Torchwood Archives have notes regarding St Mary-in-the-Dust. A phantom repeat-incursion. A temporal eddy trapping a little parcel of place and time like a fly in amber, and returning it to our reality on a fairly regular basis. I'd been keen to take a look around, next time it showed up.'

'What was it like?' asked Ianto.

'An old chapel,' said Jack. 'Thing is, there was a reason it kept coming back. There was something in there, probably the extra-dimensional presence that had edited the chapel out of our time in the first place. And it was hungry. Hungry for energy. It came back here to feed.'

'What…' Gwen began. 'What did you see?'

'I don't want to talk about it,' Toshiko said.

'Me neither. Ever,' said Jack. 'I'm with Tosh on that. We saw something, something I quite cheerfully shot at. Let's leave it at that. Gwen got us out before it fed on us. We're alive. That's all that matters.'

Silence.

'So, are we done?' asked Owen.

'There's one last thing,' said Jack. He took the small, black tile out of his pocket and put it down on the table-top where they could all see it.

'What's that?' asked Owen. 'Also, why's it flashing?'

'This,' said Jack, 'is one of my secrets. After what's happened today, I want to share that secret with you. I believe it's only fair.'

'Need to know?' Gwen asked.

Jack nodded. 'Exactly that. Today has shown me I'm not omniscient.'

'I could have told you that,' muttered Owen. 'And if I'd had to, that would have proved the point, kind of, wouldn't it?'

Jack refused to be baited. 'I know stuff, sometimes, and I keep it from you guys. It occurs to me I'd damn well better share, because there may come a time when one of you knows better than me. That time comes, like it nearly came today, you'd better be ready and know everything. Be ready to act, in case I can't.'

'So what is it?' asked James.

'Well,' said Jack. 'This is… frankly, I don't know what it is. I understand it to be an early warning, an alarm.'

'Where did it come from?' asked Toshiko, between shivers.

'No idea,' said Jack. 'It's been in the Institute's keeping since Victoria founded Torchwood. The notes say it pre-dates that foundation. This… thing has been handed down for eight or nine generations by families and antiquarians in the Cardiff area. It was entrusted to Torchwood for safekeeping in 1899 by a Colonel Cosley, a local landowner.'

'As in Cosley Hall?' asked James.

'Yeah, that's the one,' said Jack. 'Story goes it was given to mankind to bear warning of a terrible threat. A war, perhaps. It would sound the alarm if that threat ever came close.'

'Pardon me,' said James. '"Given to mankind"? Doesn't that rather suggest…?'

'Oh, yeah,' said Jack softly. 'It really does.'

'Why are you sharing this with us now?' asked Gwen.

'Because for the 108 years it's been in Torchwood's possession, and for all the time it's been in human hands prior to that, it's been inert. For the last six weeks, it's been flashing like that.'

'Meaning?' asked Owen.

Jack shrugged. 'Meaning something's coming. Or something's already here.'

SIXTEEN

Jack watched the sun rise from the roof of the St David's Hotel. Wednesday. Let it be a quiet day. A business-as-usual day, where everything turned out to be a false alarm. They deserved that.

The Cardiff skyline gleamed and shone in the first rake of daylight, like some heavenly city, like one of Blake's visions of Jerusalem. A beautiful city. A beautiful day. Let it be a beautiful day.

'This is nice.'

'I thought so,' said Jack.

'Very nice. A very nice start to the day.' Toshiko smiled at him. 'Can we do this every day?'

'Probably not. I thought I'd save it up for mornings where I had to check up on my friends.'

Sunlight streamed in through the café's wall of glass. Coffee and brioche had been delivered to their table.

'So, getting that part out of the way, are you OK?' asked Jack.

Toshiko nodded. 'Amazingly. I didn't think I would be. I was a wreck last night, exhausted and everything. I really didn't think I'd be right for days or weeks.'

'But you're OK?'

'Well, you being nice to me like this helps, but yes. Really. Clear-headed. Calm. I slept well. I don't think we realised how much that thing was in our heads until it went away.'

Jack asked a passing waitress for some water.

'How about you?' asked Toshiko.

'Famously robust,' Jack replied. 'Full of rude health.'

Toshiko buttered a slice of brioche. 'Do me a favour?'

'Absolutely.'

'Don't start apologising. It's not like you and it freaks me out. What happened yesterday happened. I'm fine. Just get to being flippant and cocksure and slightly devil-may-care. OK?'

'Sure. OK.'

'That's the Jack I know.'

'OK. This breakfast is on you, by the way.'

She grinned. 'Better. You're getting it.'

'There was this thing I was going to ask you, though,' said Jack. 'Just one thing and then I dump the sentiment completely, I promise.'

'Go on?'

'How long do you think I can keep people for?'

'Keep people?'

'In Torchwood. All sorts of things might whittle down the ranks, but I never considered attrition.'

'That you'd wear us out?'

Jack steepled his fingers in front of his face. 'That the work would wear us out. All of us, Tosh. Time was, not long ago, we'd handle a case every week, or every two, not counting false alarms. Then it was two or three a week. Now look at us. Look at this week alone. I'm trying to keep the team on track, and I'm thinking, "Wow, we're understaffed." I'm also thinking, "For God's sake, we're going to burn out." It's twenty-four seven, and it seems to be getting worse, not better.'

'We'll just have to take it as it comes,' Toshiko said.

'I never thought,' Jack said, waving a butter knife at her, 'that people would quit or, I don't know, *die* on me due to pressure. Nervous collapse. Mind-mulch.'

Toshiko sipped her coffee. 'If you'd asked me this yesterday, I'd have shared your worries, because yesterday was horrible. But today isn't, and it's not going to be.'

'You sure about that?'

'I'm a scientist. I have graphs, with arrows on them.'

'Uh-huh.'

'The law of averages owes us a quiet few days. A few Bartoks.'

125

Jack nodded. Then he half-frowned. 'Why *do* we call them that?' he asked.

He examined his bruised ribs in the bathroom mirror and flexed his arm. Not so bad.

Gwen called out something from the other room, but he couldn't hear her over Torn Curtain playing on the stereo.

'What?' he called back, rinsing his razor under the tap before rubbing shaving balm into his cheeks.

She wandered into the bathroom behind him, and dropped a bundle of clothes into the laundry basket. She was pretty much already dressed for work.

'I said, where did we put the sleeve of the Andy DVDs? And also, aren't you ready yet? We're going to be late.'

'I'm there,' he said.

'You all right?'

James smiled. 'Weird dreams last night.'

'About what?'

'Haven't a clue. I just remember them being weird.' He really couldn't remember them. They were a solid aftertaste in his mind, but try as he might, he couldn't actually bring back their content. 'You're very perky,' he remarked.

'I feel great.' She went out again. Then she called out from the other room.

'What? If you turn the music down, I can hear you.'

Torn Curtain dropped away a couple of dozen decibels.

'I said Andy. The box for the Andy disks.'

'It was there on Saturday.'

'I know. It's not here now.'

'What are you doing?'

'Nothing. Acting out of guilt.'

He was about to ask her what she meant by that when his nose tickled. He dabbed it. A tiny nosebleed, from the same nostril that had bled the previous day. James got some loo roll and blotted it. Just a tiny trickle. He peered at his face in the mirror, rotating his jaw and opening his eyes wide.

'Stop looking, I've found it,' she called.

James blinked, not hearing her. He continued to stare at his reflection. 'Gwen?'

'I said, I found it.'

'Gwen!'

She poked her head around the bathroom door. 'It was under the ficus.'

'Not that. Look at my eyes.'

'Your eyes?'

He turned from the mirror to face her. She came closer. 'Look at my eyes,' he repeated.

'Is this some kind of trick to get me in grabbing range, because we do not have time?'

'Gwen—'

She inspected his eyes. 'They're lovely. What do you want?'

'They're OK?'

'Yes. Why?'

'Just for a second there, they looked like they were—'

'What?'

'Different colours.'

'Your eyes?' she asked.

'Yes.'

'Let me look again.' She stared more carefully this time. 'Two lovely brown eyes, check.'

'The right one looked blue just then.'

'You imagined it. Now shake your tail-feather, we got to go.'

She walked back out of the bathroom. James took a final look at himself in the mirror. His eyes were brown.

'I just need to find a shirt,' he called.

'I ironed you one,' she called back.

'What?'

Gwen reappeared in the bathroom door and held out a clean, pressed white shirt for him.

'You didn't have to iron me a shirt,' he said, taking it.

Gwen thought about that for a second. 'Bloody hell, I didn't, did I?' she said, with genuine surprise. 'Sorry. Must be the guilt.'

'Yeah, what was that about guilt?' he asked, pulling on the shirt as he followed her into the lounge.

'I haven't even been here a week, and your flat was beginning to look like someone had conducted controlled explosions of your books, clothes and crockery.'

James buttoned his shirt and glanced around. 'Blimey,' he said. 'It looks like—'

'What?'

'It looks like... like the maid's been in.'

She grinned, cheeky. 'Like that, would we? Me in a little French maid's outfit and a feather duster?'

'You didn't have to tidy, or iron me a shirt.'

'I was feeling guilty,' she replied, picking up her phone and carkeys. 'Six days I've been staying here—'

'Living. I thought it was living?'

'Whatever it is I'm doing here, I've been doing it for six days, and it was starting to show. I never thought of myself as a slob, but your place was always so neat and tidy.'

'What are you saying? That I'm compulsive?'

'No. I'm saying I was a bit too free and easy with your home. I got up this morning and just noticed. Wine glasses on there. Plates stacked under there. Eighteen – *eighteen*! – mugs on that shelf. CDs everywhere. All the Andy disks out of the box, and it was Saturday we were watching those. And I won't tell you what I found behind the sofa.'

'Tell me what you found behind the sofa.'

'I won't.'

'Was it knickers?'

'Yes, it was knickers.'

'Gwen, you didn't have to straighten the place up.'

She looked at him. 'I didn't want you chucking me out because I was a messy bitch.'

'I'm not going to chuck you out,' he said.

'You promise?'

He kissed her instead.

They were on their way downstairs to the car when her phone rang.

'That'll be Ianto,' she said, taking her phone out. 'Hello? Oh, hello Rhys.'

Gwen looked at James and shrugged helplessly.

He shrugged back.

'No, I'm off to work right now. Fine, fine, you?'

James opened the front door as gently as he could and picked up some mail. She walked out past him onto the path, still talking. 'Yesterday? No, no, my phone was busy a lot yesterday. That's probably why. Sorry. Lot of important calls I had to take.'

James locked the front door and followed her down the tiled path into the street. It was a clean, fresh morning, with a golden tint to the sky.

'No, OK. Maybe at the end of the week. Or the start of next. See how things go. All right. All right, Rhys. Gotta go. All right. Yes. Bye. Bye now.'

She hung up.

'Everything all right?' he asked.

'Oh, he just wants to meet for a drink. Have a talk about stuff.'

'You ready for that?'

'Got to do it, haven't I?'

They got in the car. 'Do you think you and I should have a conversation before I have one with Rhys?' she asked.

'About what?' he asked. 'Why?'

'About… us.' Gwen looked at him. 'Splitting up with Rhys is a big decision to take. For me. For Rhys too. I'd hate to make a decision like that without consulting you.'

'OK,' he said.

'Moving on,' said Jack, sifting through the papers in front of him. 'The lights seen over Roath?'

'Bartok,' said Owen.

'Really?'

'Kids playing with a box of fireworks.'

'OK. The reports of vibrations and "odd, persistent humming noises" in St Fagans? I'm hoping that's not going to turn out to be another one of those harmonic tesseract thingies.'

'Nope,' smiled Owen. 'Bartok. It was traced to a gang of road-menders using a poorly positioned generator. Natural acoustics did the rest.'

Jack nodded. 'Great. OK, item six… "man-thing" reported on the commons by Sandhill Way?'

'Weevil,' said Owen. 'We got positive ID off the CCTV footage we borrowed from the police.'

'And when you say "borrowed"…?' said Gwen.

'All right, "stole",' replied Owen. 'It was a Weevil, anyway. Gone to ground now. We'll keep watching and move on it when it shows again.'

Jack turned another page. 'Missing pets in Cathays?'

'Gone quiet,' said James.

'Probably another Bartok,' said Owen.

'Let's keep an eye on that too, though,' said Jack. He flicked another page over. 'This one from yesterday. An adult male run down on City Road around lunchtime. It's flagged because, according to witnesses, the guy stopped the car that hit him dead and remained on his feet.'

'There's not much more available on that,' said James.

'The eye-witnesses also report the man as behaving oddly prior to the RTA,' said Gwen. 'General consensus is he was off his face on something Class A.'

'Probably wound up in A&E the moment he came down,' said Owen. 'I've seen that happen. People so high they wander around with a broken leg until the buzz wear's off and they notice.'

'OK,' said Jack. 'Put that one in pending. Right... the metallic object found on the construction site on Tweedsmuir Road?'

'Good thing we didn't move on that immediately,' said Toshiko.

'Yeah,' agreed Owen. 'We'd have looked pretty stupid storming in there mob-handed.'

'Why?' asked Jack.

'Because it's a Bartok,' said Owen.

'Why?' asked Jack.

'Because... that's what we call false alarms, isn't it?' Owen replied, glancing at the others for corroboration.

'No,' said Jack, 'I meant why is it a Bartok?'

'Because... uhm...' Owen answered, pausing again, as if it was a trick question, 'James's third-favourite TV show is *Eternity Base* and, between Seasons Three and Four, they changed the actress playing feisty head pilot Lauren Bartok, and the replacement actress was such a disappointment, there was a huge fan outcry, and the producers got the original actress back in for Season Five—'

'Owen,' said Jack.

'... hence "Bartok" meaning a disappointment and, by extension and usage, "false alarm"—'

'Owen,' Jack repeated.

'... What?'

'I know *why* we call it a "Bartok",' said Jack calmly, 'I meant why is *this* a Bartok?'

'Ooooh,' said Owen. 'Sorry. Well, because it turned out to be the cylinder block from a Hyundai.'

'A Hyundai?'

'Or a Subaru. Definitely a cylinder block, though.'

'You're remarkably happy today,' Jack said to Owen.

'I am. I really am,' Owen grinned. 'I feel great.'

Jack looked at the others. 'Good. So, summing up, everyone feels great, the sun's out, the day has nothing for us but false alarms, it's a wonderful time to be alive, and Owen's gone all geek on us. Anything else?'

'Costings,' said Gwen half an hour later, dumping a stack of files on Jack's desk. 'As requested.'

He looked up. 'Thanks. And the viability reports and evaluations?'

'Just getting to those.' She hovered, dawdling.

'Anything else?'

'No.'

Jack looked up at her again. 'You look bored.'

'That's very perceptive.'

'You might as well have been wearing a *Chairman of the Bored* T-shirt,' said Jack. 'Come on, the week we've had and you're complaining about a slow day?'

'No, just the bloody paperwork. I was thinking…'

Jack pulled an overly dramatic face and gripped the sides of his desk with both hands. 'OK,' he said, 'I'm braced. Go on.'

'You're so droll. I was thinking about that thing you showed us.'

'The trick with the paper clips?'

'No, that thing… the thing in your pocket.'

'I'm just as God made me, Gwen.'

'Oh, stop playing! The tile thing. The flashing thing. The secret you decided to share with us.'

'What about it?' Jack asked.

'Well, it's obviously bugging you that we don't know anything about it, not properly. I was wondering if I should go up to that Cosley Hall place and see if I could find anything out.'

'This wouldn't have anything to do with paperwork, would it?' Jack asked.

'No. Yes. But it's a cause for concern, isn't it? You're worried about it and you want to know what it is.'

'I do,' said Jack. He got up and removed the flashing black tile from his coat. 'But I've been up to the Hall on dozens of occasions. Been over the whole place with a fine-tooth comb. I don't know what you'd find that I didn't.'

She shrugged. 'Neither do I unless I look. Fresh pair of eyes and all that?'

'Torchwood's been studying this ever since it got hold of it,' Jack said, staring at the small black tile. 'Thanks for the offer, but I think there are more useful things you could do today.'

Gwen sighed.

'Hey!' Toshiko called from her work station below. 'This is potentially a live one.'

They quickly gathered around her station.

'I've been noting this for a fortnight now,' she said, tapping on her keyboard and calling up a spreadsheet. 'Llandaff/Pontcanna area. Complaints to the police and to the Chamber of Commerce about a bloke going door-to-door selling double glazing and loft insulation.'

'Oh my God, that's inhuman!' said Owen.

'Listen,' Toshiko said, ignoring him. 'Eighteen complaints, and six more came through today. The man is very nice, very polite, very credible. Comes cold calling, lovely chat, cup of tea. Then the homeowner signs up on the spot and forks out money. Cash.'

'How much cash?' asked James.

'As much as he can get. Sometimes he drives the homeowner to a nearby bank or cashpoint to get his payout. No cheques. He's making a killing.'

Jack shook his head. 'Look, I know everyone is anxious to find something to do, anything to get them out of here on a sunny day, but that's just fraud. A consumer protection issue. Goes on all the time.'

'Except,' said Toshiko.

'Except?'

'The police are unwilling to take action because they can't even get a partial description of the man. He spends hours at a time in the company of his victims, and afterwards they're at a loss to say what his hair colour is. Total blank. And he's not just praying on vulnerable people, pensioners or whatever, but affluent homes, people who should know better than fork over cash without a cooling-off period. People who already *have* double glazing and loft insulation.'

'Really?' said Jack.

'Really. This guy's getting money out of people who don't even want what

132

he's selling. People who tell the police afterwards they have no idea why they did what they did. No idea at all.'

'Maybe that is a live one,' said Jack admitted. 'Print me out what you've got.'

'I'll go have a nose around,' offered Gwen. 'I've only got paperwork.'

'No, thanks,' said Jack.

'Why?'

'Because you've got paperwork. I'll go check it.'

'Why?' asked Gwen.

'Because I haven't got paperwork.'

The SUV whispered up Cathedral Road into Pontcanna. The day was crisp and autumnal. Street cleaners were scooping up the carpet of fallen leaves into barrows. They drove past an ice-cream van tinkling along.

'So, what do you think? Hypnotic suggestion?' asked James.

'Got to be something of that order,' said Jack, at the wheel. 'A suggestion or perception technique. Maybe a piece of found tech.'

'Someone using something they shouldn't, you mean?' asked James.

'Usually the way in this town,' said Jack.

James peered out at the residential streets flickering by. 'Any suggestions how we look for a man without a description to go on?'

'Well,' Jack replied, 'I'm thinking he's going to look like exactly what he pretends to be. A salesman. Smart, suit, well-groomed, going door-to-door.'

'Because?'

'Because he's got to look the part to get inside in the first place, to walk down the street even. Whatever he pulls, he pulls it once he's in. Like close magic. If what he's using had a more powerful scope or range, there's a good chance we'd have picked it up already. No, I'm betting he looks exactly like a salesman.'

James nodded. 'And if anyone, like the police, did stop him in the street, he'd pull his trick on them too, and walk away?'

'Right. You'll notice from Tosh's printout that he's confident. He's not afraid of hitting the same street several times, on the same day if he feels like it. He's not afraid of being approached.'

'What's going to prevent him doing that to us?' asked James.

'We're Torchwood,' said Jack.

'Right.'

They drove on.

'Any particular reason you asked me to ride along with you?' asked James. 'Gwen was busting for an excuse to get outside.'

'No reason,' said Jack. 'Except... there was something I wanted to ask you.'

'What?'

'Everyone seems full of beans today. After yesterday, I was worried, but everyone has bounced back. Except you.'

'Me?' James asked. 'I'm fine.'

'You don't seem as fine as everybody else. Any headache? After-effects?'

'God, no,' said James. 'I'm bright as a button. Like Tosh and Owen both said, once the Amok stopped playing with us, everything felt so much better. We hadn't realised how it had been crippling us. You too, right?'

'Sure.'

'My ribs ache a little,' said James. 'And I had some weird old dreams last night. But that's all it is, I think.'

'Weird dreams? What about?'

'No idea. Can't bring them back to mind. But they were just weird dreams, that's all. Not alien mind-twisting crap.'

'All right, if that's all it is.'

'Yeah. I was telling Gwen about it when we—'

James paused.

'What?'

'I was telling Gwen about it, earlier.'

Jack smiled. He pulled the SUV over to the kerbside. 'You know I know, right?'

'Oh. Right.'

'It's cool,' said Jack.

'Why have we stopped?' asked James. 'We're not going to have some kind of formal talk are we?'

'Get over yourself,' said Jack. He pointed down the street. 'Look what I see.'

SEVENTEEN

Dean Simms was nineteen years old, but reckoned he passed for early twenties in his Top Man suit. He was always particular about his presentation: mouthwash, a haircut once a week, always cleanly shaven, and a nice splash of smelly, though nothing too strong.

His old man had once told him that the real secret to selling was clean fingernails. 'They always look at your hands, son,' he'd said, 'always at the hands. What you're pointing to, your gestures. And nothing kills a deal quicker than closing with grubby hands. If you get the papers out to run through them, and you've got dirt under your nails, forget it. Client's looking right at your hands at that stage, looking at the dotted line you're pointing to. Oh, yeah, and have a nice pen. Not a biro.'

Dean's old man had spent twenty-three years on the road in Monmouthshire and Herefordshire, flogging steam-cleaning systems door-to-door, so he knew the up and down of selling. Or 'non-desk-based retail' as he had preferred to call it. Dean had grown up paying close attention to his dad's pearls of wisdom. His old man had always brought in decent money.

When Dean left school, his old man had tried to get him a job with the steam-cleaner company, but the Internet had been murdering face-sales by then, and there had been no openings, not even for 'a lad with good selling potential'. A year later, his old man had been given his cards. That had killed him. Without a job at fifty-eight, he'd just withered away and died.

Determined to prove something, Dean had got himself a commission-only job with LuxGlaze Windows, but it had been a slog, and the product hadn't been all that, and LuxGlaze always sent him to areas where the homeowners had been pre-pissed off by LuxGlaze's carpet-bomb approach to telephone pitching. Twice, Dean had been chased off a plot by dogs, once by a man with a rake.

He'd switched to VariBlinds, then to Welshview EcoGlass, then back to LuxGlaze again for one awful, thankless, six-week effort to get himself a proper patch and actual customers.

There had come a time when Dean had started to think that maybe he wasn't 'a lad with good selling potential' after all.

Then he'd got his break, and found his feet, and these days he was in business for himself. He stuck to his old man's basic rules of salesmanship: presentation, clean nails and a nice pen. He'd always had the patter too, the charm factor that his dad had set plenty of store by. But Dean had something else, something his dad had never had. Dean knew the real secret of selling, and it turned out it wasn't clean fingernails.

Dean Simms had the real secret of selling in his briefcase.

He checked himself in his rear-view mirror, checked his teeth for specks of food, checked his nails, checked his tie and got out of his vehicle. Game on.

The street was quiet. His vehicle would be all right where it was for an hour or so. He crossed the road.

His old man had always talked about 'his patch' with a genuine measure of proprietorial pride. Dean knew what his dad had meant. These streets were Dean's patch, and he worked them hard. In return, they paid him well. Another few months, he reckoned, and he'd have to move area. Just to freshen things. You could go back to the well once too often, as his old man used to say.

He walked down the path, opening his zip-seamed briefcase, and looked at his list. It was easy to forget faces from one visit to the next. Early on, he'd hit the same house twice in a fortnight. Of course, the woman hadn't recognised him, but he had no wish to repeat the mistake. He had a list of addresses printed off the electoral roll, and he ticked them off.

Number eight. Mr and Mrs Menzies. He consulted his watch. Two oh five. Just after lunch. Perfect.

He walked up the pathway of number eight and pressed the bell, hearing it ring deep inside the house. He waited, whistling softly.

The door opened. Ignite smile.

'Good afternoon, Mrs Menzies?'

'Yes?'

'Good afternoon, sorry to bother you. My name is Dean Simms of Glazed Over, and I'm in your area this afternoon to introduce a remarkable domestic opportunity. Now, it's available for a limited period only, and exclusively, to a few, specially selected households.'

'Are you selling?' the woman asked. 'Are you windows?'

'I'm just here to talk about a remarkable domestic opportunity.'

'I don't want sodding windows,' scowled the woman, and started to shut the door again. 'Are you blind? We've got replacement windows back and front.'

'Let me just leave you with a leaflet,' Dean said, smiling. He reached into his unzipped case and squeezed the soft lump inside. 'Just a leaflet, Mrs Menzies?' He loved this bit.

'A leaflet?' she asked, slightly blank.

Dean's grin broadened. He made a gentle sweep with his hand. 'These aren't the droids you're looking for,' he said.

'Come in,' she replied.

'Oh, that's so got to be our man,' said Jack. He and James were walking briskly, side by side, along the pavement from the space where they'd left the SUV. Over a box hedge, they could see a young, suited man chatting to a homeowner in a front doorway.

'What do we do?' asked James.

'Ruin his day and queer his pitch,' replied Jack. They arrived at the gate. 'Excuse me,' Jack called pleasantly.

The woman in the doorway squinted at them from her doorway. The young man in the suit who had been talking to her turned slowly. He eyed Jack and James warily.

'I don't want to cause a scene,' said Jack, 'but could we have a quiet word?'

'A quiet word?' asked the woman.

'With your friend here?' Jack indicated.

The young man looked from James to Jack quickly, weighed his options, and then bolted. He vaulted the front garden wall and began to run away down the street.

'Oi!' cried the woman.

'Sorry to trouble you!' Jack called back to her as he and James gave chase. The young man in the suit was really moving. Head back, arms pumping, sprinting like a maniac.

James was leading Jack by three or four yards. 'Go left!' he yelled as they passed the turning to some backyard garages.

Coat flying, Jack broke left up the unmade track. James kept on, flying after their quarry. *Left at the next corner*, James willed, *just turn left and you'll run smack into Jack.*

The young man in the suit turned right and took off across the road.

'Damn!' James barked, and continued to pound after him, crossing the street diagonally behind a slow-moving car. He was force to halt sharply in the middle of the road to let another car go by the other way. By the time James had reached the far side and begun to pick up speed again, the young man in the suit was leaving him behind. James tried to up his pace, but the young man was putting increasing distance between them.

Jack ran out of the garage standing and back onto the street at the top. No sign of their quarry. Still running, he turned right and, in a moment or two, caught sight of James up head of him, running flat out away from him down the tree-lined avenue.

'James!'

James didn't appear to hear him. Much further away, with a good thirty-yard lead on James already, Jack could see the young man in the suit, leaning as he turned left again.

Jack crossed the road, edging between the cars parked under the trees, his feet slipping on wet leaves, and set off down a left-hand street running parallel to their target's flight path. If the young man in the suit doubled back, Jack would nab him around the next corner.

A man walking a dog frowned at Jack as Jack bombed past.

'Afternoon!' Jack called. Twenty yards to the corner, then right. He jinked around two men carrying an old bath out to a skip. He reached the corner, and skidded around it.

Jack's intercept prediction had almost been bang on. Left to his own devices, the young man in the suit would have doubled back again, and run headlong into Jack coming the other way.

But the young man in the suit hadn't made it that far. A few yards in from the opposite street corner, James had him pressed against the wall in an arm-lock.

Jack trotted up, breathing hard. The young man was struggling and mouthing off.

'Be still!' James told him. He looked around at Jack. 'Got him,' he said.

'How?' asked Jack

'I ran like a bastard and caught up with him,' said James. 'How do you think? Be still, I said!'

'Last time I saw you pair, he had thirty yards on you,' said Jack, panting.

'All in the finish,' James replied. 'He went off too early. Soon as he began to flag, I had him. It's pacing, Jack, pacing.'

'My ass it is. He was flying.'

'Are you going to help?' James asked. The young man in the suit was struggling harder.

'Get your hands off me! Get your filthy hands off me! I know my rights! Police brutality!'

'Turn him round,' Jack instructed. James manhandled the wriggling young man around to face him. The young man was sweaty and flushed, sucking painful breaths in after his exertions.

'You think we're police?' Jack asked him.

'Get your hands off me!' the young man replied.

'Do you think we're the police?' Jack asked him again, more slowly and deliberately this time.

'Y-yes?'

'Boy,' smiled Jack. 'This is going to be fun.'

They walked back to the SUV.

'OK,' Jack admitted. 'Not so much fun as I'd hoped. Or success.'

'You sure we should have let him go?' asked James.

'I'm telling you, that wasn't our guy.'

James pursed his lips. 'Unless, of course, he was, and he just hypnotised us the way he hypnotises his other victims, and we fell for it. Did you consider that?'

'Come on, that moron couldn't have hypnotised a… a…'

'A what?'

'Something that gets hypnotised very easily,' Jack replied, fishing the carkeys out of his coat.

'So you're certain it wasn't the man we're looking for?'

'You saw him as well as I did,' said Jack, slightly plaintively, 'You heard him. He was just a chancer, trying to case likely-looking homes by pretending to be doing a consumer survey. No cover story is that believably lame.'

'I suppose. He did seem scared.'

'Too right he was scared. Petty housebreaker, messing with me. Shame though, I thought he was the one.' Jack *blip-blipped* the key fob to unlock the SUV and they got in.

'Did he hit you?' Jack asked.

'What?'

'While he was struggling? Did he catch you?'

'What? Why?' James replied.

'Your nose is bleeding a little there.'

'Huh? Oh, yeah, I think he did.'

It wasn't yet three o'clock. Even with the secret, that was good going. Once you had them, you had to ease them in the direction you wanted them to go in, very gently. Some visits, that was slow going. Dean imagined it was a bit like steering a punt, although he'd never actually done that. He'd seen it on telly, however. Some fly-on-the-wall about arsehole toffs, punting.

Sometimes, during a visit, they resisted, due to inhibitions he didn't yet understand. Sometimes, he had to apply quite a lot of effort to get them moving the way he wanted them to go. Occasionally, there was nothing to get a purchase on, nothing but soft mud when he sank his punting pole in, so to speak.

Dean thought he ought to write a seminar. He could train people to use the secret, and he'd heard there was really big money in sales training. Not that he was about to give the secret away to anyone, of course. It was his.

Dean came out of number eight, and said goodbye to Mrs Menzies. She seemed very pleased with her imaginary loft insulation and replacement windows. Dean was certainly very pleased with the eight hundred and sixty-six not-imaginary-at-all pounds he'd been given by Mrs Menzies. He'd made sure to collect up all his bits of paper, all the forms he'd had her sign, here and here and here. They were only mail-away coupons and inserts from magazines, but the client always saw pukka, press-hard-you're-making-four-copies contract blanks. He tried not to ever leave any behind, but if he did, no one would give them a second look.

He walked down the street, whistling. He waited to cross back to his vehicle, and allowed some traffic to go by. A couple of saloon cars, a hatchback, then a monster black 4x4, a Porsche Cayenne or a Range Rover. It had gone past before he'd got a proper eyeful. Tasty. That's what he wanted next. A really nice ride like that. Yes sir.

He unlocked his own vehicle. It'd do the trick for the time being. No one ever looked at it.

Dean sat down, and flipped through his sheaf of electoral roll printout. Time for one more, then he'd call it a day.

The park would be closing soon. The sign at the wrought-iron gates advertised that they would be locked at nightfall in winter. Another half an hour. The white-gold sun was slipping behind the empty trees, and long dark shadows were running out across the grass like ploughed furrows. There was a slight autumnal haze, a softness in the light, and a smell of leaves decaying.

People were walking dogs. A few kids were playing, most of them on their way home from school, laden with knapsacks. A golden retriever chased energetically across the grass, hunting down a frisbee. Its owner shouted the dog's name. Leaves fluttered as it snatched up the red plastic disk and turned with it in its mouth.

Mr Dine sat on the top of the War Memorial, basking in the last of the sun. He was secure. No one could see him up there. He was out of sight to anyone passing by on the ground, and to anyone looking on from a distance. Besides, no one would expect a person to be up there. The Council had never bothered fencing the War Memorial with railings, because it was patently unclimbable.

He'd crashed, predictably, then switched to recovery mode. A warm glow that wasn't the sunlight suffused him. He could hear the distant, constant hum of traffic.

The upload had restarted about an hour earlier. Not an alert, just a routine data review. He sat listening to its melodious chunter. Key link-strands had not yet been clarified and restored to satisfaction. There was still some concern, expressed via the upload, that the Principal's status might yet be compromised and unsafe. A possibility of damage. Mr Dine was to monitor this carefully in the coming hours.

Mr Dine opened his hand and looked at the livid burn the adversarial object had left on the flesh of his palm. The wound was repairing, but it had gone through to the bone in places.

'You're joking! And?' asked Gwen.

'Well,' said James, 'he went off down Brunswick Way like he had an Exocet up his jacksie, and Jack and I went after him. This is the third time in one afternoon, bear in mind. I was not in the mood for another sprint. Anyway, he gets past me and Jack rugby tackles him on a traffic island.'

'Go on.'

'He's only a Jehovah's Witness, isn't he?'

'No!' Gwen exclaimed with a snort. 'Not really?'

'I swear. He starts trying to club Jack off him with a rolled up copy of *The Watchtower*.'

'What did you do?' Gwen asked, raising her wine glass.

'We apologised,' James grinned.

'But he'd run. Why had he run?'

'Apparently, two of his colleagues had been duffed up by youths in that area recently, and he thought we were out to get him.'

'Poor bugger.'

'Yeah. To make things worse, Jack sends him on his way with a cheery "Next time I see Jehovah, I'll put in a good word for you".'

The waiter brought the bill over. Gwen waved it to her.

'I'll do that,' said James.

'I invited you out, remember. My treat.'

She gave the waiter her card. 'Did Jack really say that?'

James nodded. He sipped the last of his wine and laughed to himself. 'He's a menace.'

'So, you never got him, then?'

'No, we didn't,' James said, sitting forward again and shaking his head. 'We're back on it tomorrow. Jack's quite fired up now, a matter of principle, I think.'

'Captain Jack always gets his man,' said Gwen.

'Well, Captain Jack was off his stroke this afternoon. Zero for three. First the oik casing houses, then the window cleaner who thought we were wanting words about a pliant hausfrau he'd dallied with. Then, the Jehovah's Witness.' James counted them out on his fingers. 'We were up and down Pontcanna all afternoon like a fiddler's elbow.'

'I thought that was in and out?'

'You're right. What's up and down?'

'A whore's drawers?'

'Thank you. I haven't run so far in years. My calves are like toffee apples.'

'What, crispy and sweet?' Gwen asked, smiling to the waiter as she punched her PIN into the reader he offered her.

'No, baked hard and round and… OK, not toffee apples. Either way, I'm totally exhausted.'

'Not totally, I hope,' she winked. She took her card and the tear-off strip from the waiter. 'Thanks.'

'Not totally, I suppose,' James said. 'Well, you paid for all this, and very nice it was too, but weren't we supposed to be talking?'

'We were talking.'

'I told you all about running around Pontcanna like a nong. We didn't talk about… talky stuff.'

'The night's still young,' she said.

James helped her on with her coat. They thanked the girl working the restaurant's front of house, and went out into the clear, chilly night. Fairy-light stars and an elegantly simple waxing moon stood out in the glassy blackness over the Bay.

'I paid extra for that,' Gwen said.

They walked along the Quay, hand in hand. The restaurants and bars were throbbing with music and bodies.

'You wanted to consult me, I believe,' James said.

'Yes, I did.'

'Consult away.'

Gwen leant on the railing. The oxide tang of the water was sharp.

'Rhys and I have been together for a long time. We're like socks that get rolled up together and dumped in the wash, week in, week out, just because we match. Never mind the holes that need darning.'

'But you match?'

She nodded. 'Always have. Never mind the holes. You can live with holes. That's why God made shoes. To hide the holes in your socks.'

'Can I ask, at this point, what shoes are representing in this elaborate analogy?'

Gwen chuckled. 'Bugger only knows. Daily life? I didn't really think that one through.'

James looked pensive. 'And – just so I'm clear, you understand – are you saying you only wash your socks once a week?'

She cuffed him on the sleeve. 'I'm being serious.'

'So am I,' James replied earnestly. 'Living with a woman who only washes her socks once a week, that could have long-term consequences.'

She looked up at him. 'Long-term? This is my point, you see? There's only one reason I'm even considering breaking Rhys's heart, and that's us. You and me. It's not a road I'm even going to think of going down unless there's you and me at the end of it.'

'I see. I thought you were tired of him?'

'I don't know what I am, as far as Rhys goes. Settled. Inert. Static. I'm being selfish, I know. I bloody know that, but I also know I want more. However, I don't want to hurt him over nothing. I'd only do it if it was truly important.'

'Right.'

'And for all I know, this may just be a bit of fun to you. A laugh. A fling. That's fine. I'd understand. But that's why I have to consult you. I'd like to know where you stand.'

'OK,' James said. There was a pause.

'No rush, no pressure.'

'OK.'

'In your own time,' she added.

'Right.'

'Bearing in mind I paid for dinner and this whole romantic seaview.'

He looked very solemn. 'So… whether you dump Rhys or not depends on whether I see a future for us? Or not?'

'In a nutshell,' she said.

'You like to put people on the spot?'

'It's in my nature as a policewoman.'

'Gwen,' he said softly. 'We've had a great time, this week. Despite everything.'

'We have.'

'I don't know how to say this,' he began.

Her face fell. 'It's OK. Just say it. Just say it, James, so I can hear it.'

'I'm really sorry,' he whispered.

'Right. That's all right, that's—'

He hushed her with a finger on her lips.

'I'm really, truly sorry, but you're going to have to break Rhys's heart.'

They caught a cab from the rank on the Quay. They sat as far away from one other as they possibly could on the back seat. Too close, they'd become volatile elements, intermix and explode. They didn't even look at each other as the street-lamps strobed by overhead.

'Keep the change,' James told the driver, the cab's engine purring hot gas into the night cool.

'Really, mister?'

'Oh yeah, really.'

'Have a nice night,' the cabbie called as he pulled away.

Gwen laughed as James failed to get his key in the lock at the fourth attempt.

'Not a good omen,' she giggled.

'Shush, my hands are shaking.'

'Nervous?'

'Yeah.'

The door opened and they blundered inside, wrapped around one another. The deep kisses felt like the first they'd ever shared. It was weird, charged, startling.

'Hang on,' he said, 'hang on a sec.' Pulling open the last few buttons of his shirt and ditching it, he headed into the kitchen. She heard the fridge door thump open, followed by a clink of glasses.

James reappeared with a bottle of Moët and two crystal flutes.

'I came by earlier, and put this in the fridge,' he said. 'In case… just in case we had something to celebrate tonight.'

'Oh God, that's so sweet,' she whispered.

Two hours later, they remembered the champagne and opened it. It was warm by then, but they didn't care.

EIGHTEEN

Flicker. Fast-cut: a bridge, a river, a palace. Shades on the high walls.

Too fast to follow, too jerky and chop-cut. Flicker. Edit. Edit. Smash-cut: the bridge, very old, very worn. Smash-cut: the thundering torrent of a river boiling along a deep, stone-cut channel under the bridge. The river is a mile wide. The bridge, therefore, worn and crumbling though it seems, is a mile wide too.

Smash-cut: the palace, made of silver-green bricks, towers reaching up into the clouds. The palace shimmers. Its high, silver-green walls are like the lustrous scales of a sleeping reptile. The sky is a silent bowl of black, marked by pinpricks of fire.

Smash-cut: the lurching segue of dream logic. Someone is running across the ancient bridge. Running fast. Fast footsteps on stone. Someone is running away from the palace across the ancient bridge. It's him. He's running away across the ancient bridge. Why is he running?

The shades on the high walls stir. Alerted by distant sirens, they begin to move, leaping and scurrying, like shadows, like whispers, like wraiths. They are barbed, and armed for killing.

They run faster than he does. Of course they do. They were made that way. They run faster, faster… faster than he could ever run. Leaping, bounding, they close the distance. They are catching up with him.

They are silent. They make no sound. Not even footsteps.

Still running, he looks over his shoulder. The shades are there.

One leaps—

***

He wakes. Bolt upright, wet with sweat.

'Babe, what is it?' she asks, head buried in the pillows beside him.

'Nothing,' he says. 'Weird dreams. Go back to sleep.'

Thursday morning, six o'clock. Still dark. Dean Simms gets up, and makes tea by the light of his single bulb. The B&B is quiet. He sneaks along to the bathroom and takes a quick shower.

Back in his room, he suits and boots as he sips his tea and checks over the electoral roll. Tovey Street. As good as any. He does his nails, digging the quick with the nib of a fresh orange stick. A splash of smelly. He pulls on his jacket and flicks his tea bag into the bin. Got everything? Keys? Briefcase? Secret?

He strokes the soft lump for a moment before zipping his briefcase closed. All set.

He goes out, locking the door behind him.

Outside, it's sharp and clear. Frost on the pavements. Glitter in the bushes. He hears a milkman clinking on his rounds down the street, the rising then falling hum of the milk float coasting point to point.

Dean crosses the street. The milkman nods good morning as he whirs past on his chinking float. A good day, a clear day. Dean takes a deep breath. Cold air.

A tabby cat slinks by along a wall, tail down. Dean reaches his vehicle and unlocks it.

He gets in. The vinyl seat is cold. The hard plastic wheel is cold. When he starts the engine, cold air breathes through the vents. There's frost on the screen, but nothing the wipers can't handle.

Mirror, signal. He pulls out of his parking slot into the street.

Gonna be a good day, he promises himself. Game on.

As the kettle boiled, Davey Morgan spooned out cat food into a bowl. He set the bowl down on the kitchen floor. There were two other bowls there already, untouched. He picked them up, banged their contents out into the bin and washed them up.

He hadn't seen the cat since Tuesday. Some one else was feeding him, Davey decided. The cat had got a better offer somewhere. Cats were like that. Fickle things.

Davey went into the bathroom and studied his face in the mirror. There was a scab of blood under his nose and his left eye had blackened. Bloody bastards. He'd come home from Normandy looking healthier. Still, his skin hadn't been translucent then.

'I've got old,' he told the picture on the hall table. 'I don't care what you say. Old.'

He wondered if the cat was all right. He put on his digging jacket.

Out in the yard it was brisk. His breath steamed. He rubbed his hands and pulled on his mittens. There was a proper mist that morning, swaddled all over the backyards and beyond. The sun was climbing reluctantly above Seraph Street, a thin, molten slice of light.

He limped up the path to the allotment gate. There was a funny smell in the air, like compost.

The grass was wet. As soon as he passed through the gate, he knew that something was up. Broken flowerpots, upturned planters, uprooted veg. The yobbos had been in overnight, ransacking. To get back at him, no doubt.

He reached his own plot and came up short. He blinked. He started breathing hard, breathing in short, sharp gulps. *Oh no, no, no…*

The windows of Davey's shed had been smashed in. Those responsible – Ozzie and perhaps four or five of his fellow yobs – were still outside.

What was left of them.

Taff Morgan had seen death, first-hand. The bloody debris left in the aftermath of a well-ranged mortar bomb. An entire advancing section atomised by a shell from a Nazi 88, nothing left behind except charred scraps of kit and pink mush. Friends he'd known cut up by heavy Spandau fire that sectioned them like hot wire.

He thought he'd been forced to see his share.

The bodies – there were no whole bodies, just pieces – had been scattered in front of his shed. It looked like a direct hit by an 88 round, except there was no crater, no litter of cordite ash. The poor bloody bastards looked like they had been pushed through a wood chipper. Bits of bone and half-limbs, some still partly clothed in meat, protruded from the soil as though they were heads of celery, carefully planted. Davey saw blood-black ribs, wet lumps of marrow, yellow, intestinal ropes glistening in the daylight.

Worst of all, whatever had killed them had preserved their faces. A row of Davy's gardening implements had been staked out in front of the shed door: spade, fork, hoe, shovel, rake. From the top of each handle swung a limp, meat flag; the flesh of a skinned human face, scalped off, lank and heavy in the dawn breeze.

Davey gagged. The stench of blood and ordure took him back to '44, and he had no bloody wish to do that. Hadn't he seen his share? Why was he being forced to confront this again?

Why?

Ozzie's boneless face stirred in the wind.

Davey threw up. Hot, acid tea spattered across the cold frame.

He staggered over to the shed door and pushed it open.

'What did you do?' he demanded, his throat hoarse. 'What the bloody hell did you do?'

The thing in the barrow wasn't in the barrow any more. It was standing by the broken window on slim, metal, legs it hadn't previously possessed. It turned its ovoid head to regard him.

It let out a low hum.

The hum changed pitch, then changed pitch again.

'Don't you give me that,' Davey Morgan snapped.

'Here you go,' said James, handing the serviette-wrapped object to Gwen. It steamed in the dank morning air.

'Ta,' she said. 'Oh, it's chilly.'

Leaning against the SUV, arms folded, Jack looked over. 'That's chilli? For breakfast?'

'No, I was saying today is chilly.'

'Oh. OK.'

He looked back at them a moment later. 'So what is that?'

'It's bloody delicious is what it is,' said Gwen, taking another bite.

'Did it once have a name?' asked Jack.

Munching, James turned his own order over and read off the printed serviette. 'It's a… "Croiss-ham-wich®".'

'Uh-huh. Like a croissant? With ham? Sandwiched in?'

'You're grasping the basic concept, I believe,' said James.

Jack shook his head.

'You could have had one,' said James. 'The place is just around the corner. Breakfast served until ten. I did ask you if you wanted one.'

'No, thank you,' Jack said firmly.

They ate on.

'You know what that stuff is doing to your arteries, I suppose?' Jack asked.

Gwen nodded.

'Croissant. That's like… butter in shrapnel form. Not to mention the processed flour. That's going to make you sluggish later.'

'At least,' replied Gwen through a mouthful, 'I'm not hypoglycaemic and tetchy.'

'I'm fine,' said Jack archly. 'My body is a temple.'

'Of course,' said Gwen.

James sniggered. He balled up his empty serviette and, with no bin in sight, put it in his pocket.

'Crumb,' said Gwen, and brushed his lip. She finished her own Croiss-ham-wich®, screwed up her napkin, and looked around for somewhere to throw it. James took it out of her hand and put it in his pocket with his own.

'You two are so sweet,' said Jack. 'Makes me want to barf.'

'So, are we going to do anything?' Gwen asked.

'I'm sorry,' said Jack, 'shouldn't that be: "Thank you, Jack, for letting me come out with you today"?'

'Hypoglycaemic and tetchy,' Gwen murmured sidelong to James.

'I heard that,' said Jack. 'What did she say, James?'

'I was saying,' said Gwen, 'my paperwork's all done, so I'm a free woman. Besides, I'm here as a foil.'

'A foil?' asked Jack.

'James reckoned you were so wound up about catching this bloke, you'd be a pain in the arse to be around all day.'

'He said that?'

James raised his hands. 'Don't bring me into this.'

'I'm here to make it more fun,' said Gwen.

'Kudos on that, so far,' replied Jack. He walked up and down, looking around. Traffic droned past. Somewhere, an ice-cream van tinkled its tune.

'OK, we've been here long enough,' Jack decided. 'Nothing going on. Let's ride around a little more.'

'What about him?' asked Gwen, pointing down the street.

Jack looked where she was pointing. 'He's from the cable company.'

'But *is* he?' she asked.

'He's got a cable company van, Gwen.'

'But *has* he?'

'He's not the guy, dammit,' said Jack.

'It could be an elaborate hypnotic cover,' said Gwen. 'James was telling me this bloke has the power to make anything look like anything he bloody wants. Jehovah's Witnesses, for example.'

Jack glowered. 'All right. All right. Just hold on.'

He set off down the street. They watched him have a conversation with the cable man. The cable man looked at Jack oddly. He said something to Jack. Jack walked back to join them.

'Don't make me do that again,' said Jack. 'Ever.'

'Was it not the guy?' asked Gwen innocently.

'It was not the guy.'

'Just as you thought?'

'Just as I thought.'

'Did he tell you to piss off?'

'He told me to piss off.'

'From which remark you deduced…?'

'That it wasn't the guy we are looking for, a fact I was pretty sure of before I went over.' Jack walked around to the driver's side door of the SUV. 'Come on.'

Gwen and James followed him to the car. 'How good at lip-reading am I, then?' she said. '"Piss off" from a whole twenty yards?'

James shrugged. 'I thought the hand gesture pretty much gave it away.'

On Tovey Street, Dean Simms said goodbye to Mr Robbins, and Mr Robbins said goodbye to six hundred pounds of the Darts Club raffle money. Mr Robbins was Darts Club treasurer, though Dean was fairly confident Mr Robbins wouldn't remain in that post for very much longer.

Thirty-eight minutes. Excellent result to start the day. In and out, no messing around, clean close. No heavy punting required.

He walked back to his vehicle. Dean had been intending to do another two visits on Tovey Street but on the way over he'd spotted a couple of choice-looking places. Double garages, bay windows, Dunroamin'-esque house names on cedar plaques. To Dean, that said money. That said bored wives of a certain age taking the odd nip of sherry while they Mr Sheened the giant plasma TV for the umpteenth time. Game on.

He patted his briefcase and turned the key in the ignition.

'This is dull,' said Gwen. 'This is… starting to make paperwork seem attractive. Are we going to do any running about at all?'

James yawned and leaned back in the SUV's passenger seat. 'With any luck, no.'

Gwen fidgeted in the back seat. She glanced out of the tinted windows to see what was keeping Jack.

James yawned again.

'You tired?'

He nodded.

'You had weird dreams again, didn't you? I remember you waking up.'

'Yeah. Very strange stuff.'

'About what?'

James shook his head. 'Still can't actually recall anything.' He stifled another yawn.

'But they're bothering you? These dreams?'

'Doing my nana.'

Gwen eyes widened. 'You were doing what? Oooh, I don't wanna know!'

He looked around at her. 'No, "banana". Like doing my head in. It's an expression.'

'Sounds more like a radical lifestyle choice to me.'

'I was not dreaming about my grandmother, Gwen.'

James seemed particularly sharp. She leant forwards.

'OK, keep your lovely hair on. I was only playing. God, it's really got to you, hasn't it?'

He hesitated. 'The thing is…'

'What?'

'Usually, I don't dream.'

Gwen frowned. 'That's silly. Of course you do.'

'I don't. I never have. Don't dream. Ever.'

'You're having me on, Mayer.'

He looked around at her again. 'Honestly. I don't. Maybe I'm not having weird dreams at all. Maybe I'm having normal dreams and they seem weird because I haven't had them before.'

She thought for a moment. 'I tell you what is weird.'

'What?'

'You.'

The driver's door opened and Jack climbed in.

'So?' asked James.

'His name was Colin,' said Jack. 'He was very polite, a bit of a floating voter

152

sexually, as far as I could tell. He was collecting for Age Concern.'

'Not our guy then?'

Jack sighed. He pulled out his phone and dialled. 'Tosh? This is becoming tedious. Got anything interesting?'

At her work station in the Hub, Toshiko sat with her chin on her hand, idly clicking her mouse to play Solitaire on screen. 'Nope,' she replied.

Jack hung up. He wound down his window and let in the outdoor smell of wet road and cold exhaust. 'Shall we just leave this?' he asked.

In the distance, an ice-cream van played its plinky-plonky tune.

Gwen looked up. 'Oooh, I could just go a choc ice now.'

Jack stared at her. 'On top of the fats you guzzled for breakfast?'

Gwen pouted. 'Just saying.'

Jack sat for a moment. His brow furrowed slightly. He looked back at her. 'Gwen… would you consider your appetite choices to be in any way freakish?'

'Freakish?' she asked.

'Unusual, then.'

'Generally, or by Welsh standards?'

Jack stared at them both and jerked his thumb in the direction of the open window. He had a certain look in his eyes. 'It's October,' he said. 'It's cold. School's in. And we can hear an ice-cream van at ten thirty in the morning?'

Toshiko's screen suddenly blipped. Solitaire folded up into the drag bar. A new window opened.

She sat up. 'He-llo,' she said.

She began to type.

'Owen!'

He was shooting hoops with Ianto down by the cog-door.

'Owen!'

'What?' he yelled back. 'I said you could play the winner.'

'Get here.'

He jogged up to join her at her station.

'What?'

She pointed at her screen. 'Say hello to my little friend.'

He squinted. 'Blimey,' he said. 'That's different.'

NINETEEN

They slammed the doors of the SUV. Jack led them across the street, his hands in his coat pockets.

The van had been parked on a meter between a Volvo and a Mondeo. Trees overhung from behind garden walls, and the broad pavement was slick with dead leaves.

'Mr Swirly,' Gwen read. The van was old, an old Commer, its paint job fading and peeling in places: decals of ice-cream cones and space-rocket ice lollies pasted over a pink and cream background. James pressed his hand against the back panel grille.

'Still warm.'

Cupping his hands around his eyes, Jack peered in through the hatch window. The interior was gloomy, but it was reasonable to conclude that Mr Swirly hadn't dispensed ice-cream products for a fair number of years.

'Look around,' Jack instructed, rotating his hand. 'He's got to be close.'

Jack went one way, Gwen and James the other. They walked along the damp pathway, past the raw smells of cyanothus and creosote-drenched fencing.

'Posh houses,' said Gwen. 'I hate posh bloody houses with names. Look. *Bindreamin*'. What the bloody hell is that about?'

James shrugged.

'*Bindreamin*'. I ask you. Do you think it's the home of a retired garbage collector?'

'That would be *Binladen*, surely?'

'Oh, *you're* going to hell then,' she said.

'You know what Julius Caesar called his house?' James asked.

She looked at him. 'This is a joke, isn't it? Hang on. *The Laurels*? No, no, wait… *Caesar's Palace*?'

'*Dunroman*,' he said.

She winced. 'I do not believe you actually had the nerve to crack that one,' she said. Her phone rang.

'Yeah, hello?'

'Concentrate. *Please*,' said Jack's voice.

They looked back down the street at Jack, and Gwen gave him a cheery wave.

'Will do,' she said into her phone and hung up.

They went past two more driveways.

'And as for friggin' gnomes,' she began.

James touched her arm. She followed his line of sight. Across the street, down a gravel driveway, a young, good-looking man in a suit was standing at a front door with his back to them. He had a briefcase under his arm. He was talking to a middle-aged woman in a housecoat. The house was called *Idlewhile*.

Gwen pressed a fastkey on her phone. She let it ring once then hung up. Far away, down the street, Jack turned and immediately began making his way back towards them.

James and Gwen started across the road. They approached the gate.

'Hang back,' Gwen said quietly. 'It'll spook him right off if he sees two of us.' James obediently stepped back behind a dwarf conifer at the gate post.

Gwen stopped in the open gateway.

'Excuse me!' she called.

The man turned and looked at her with a slightly baffled, slightly annoyed expression. The middle-aged woman didn't react at all.

'Excuse me,' Gwen repeated. 'Is that your van parked back there?'

'What?'

'Your van? The ice-cream van?'

'Who are you?' the man asked. He was stiff, wary. His briefcase lay in the crook of his arm, like a clipboard. It was unzipped.

'I'm only asking because I could fancy a Ninety-Nine just now. Any chance?'

The man took a few steps back up the driveway towards her. He stared at her. The woman remained in the doorway of *Idlewhile*, gazing into space.

'Are you joking?' he asked.

'No. I love Ninety-Nines, me.'

He took another step closer.

'Are you police?' he asked.

'Maybe I am. Maybe I'm here to check your ice-cream permit. Maybe I'm from the cones hotline. Maybe I've come to examine your wafer waiver. Geddit?'

'What?'

'Now I'm joking. Keep up.' She fixed him with a bright grin. 'How d'you do it, then?'

'How do I do what?'

'What've got in the briefcase? What's your secret?'

Dean Simms swallowed. He squeezed the soft lump in his briefcase.

Gwen took a step back. She got a sudden, strong smell of cut-grass and vanilla.

She turned and walked away. James stared at her as she went past him.

'What are you doing?' he hissed.

'Oh, there you are,' she smiled.

'What are you doing?'

She shrugged. 'I… I dunno…'

'Gwen?'

The man with the briefcase came out of the driveway behind her and saw James. His face darkened.

James moved towards him.

'These aren't the droids you're looking for,' the man said.

'What?' asked James. 'You what?'

Dean Simms gazed at James. 'These aren't the… you… you're supposed to…' He squeezed the soft lump again.

'Give me the briefcase,' said James.

Dean hesitated, then turned and ran off down the street. A second later, Jack pounded by in pursuit.

'Come on!' Jack yelled as he went past.

'Again with the running?' James wailed, and set off after them.

Gwen, wrinkling her nose, stood there for a moment. She watched the three running figures recede down the street.

'Y-? What- w-?' she said. She turned around, then looked back at them. 'Where are you going?' she shouted. She paused. 'Why am I standing here?'

she asked herself.

'Why am I talking to myself?' she added.

She started off after them. They'd all but disappeared, and she was only jogging half-heartedly. She took out her phone and dialled. It answered after three rings.

'James?'

The line was distorted and choppy with breathing noises. 'Running,' he replied, with effort.

'About that. Why are you and Jack running away from me?'

'We're not. We're. Running after. The Guy.'

'OK. What guy?'

'The guy. We're looking. For. He hyp. Notised you.'

'No, honestly? I don't remember that.'

'Well. You would. N't. Can't talk. Gotta puke.'

He hung up.

'Hypnotised?' Gwen said to herself, jogging to a halt. She brushed hair out of her eyes and frowned with the effort of thinking.

Her eyes widened. 'Ooooooooh,' she said, nodding.

She started to run.

'Is it my imagination, or is that getting worse?' Owen asked.

Toshiko's hands ran across her keyboard. 'It's not your imagination. That's really getting hot. How could it just pop out of nowhere?'

'Same way everything else does,' said Owen. 'Got a fix yet?'

'Area only. Cathays, I think. I'm narrowing the search focus. Should have a street name or a GPS fix in about three minutes. Less, if it keeps getting hotter.'

'Jack needs to know about this,' Owen said.

'Oh, absolutely,' she agreed.

'Ianto!' Owen yelled. 'Get Jack on the blower!'

Ianto picked up a cordless and pressed auto-dial.

'It's ringing,' he said.

Jack and James came around the street corner almost neck and neck. They had to break formation to go either side of a pillar box.

'There!' James yelled, pointing.

This street was busier than the residential roads they had come out of.

Some shops, some traffic, a muddle of people. Ahead of them, they could see the fugitive.

Dean had been forced to slow down, simply in order to duck and weave around the pedestrians in his path. He'd already bumped into one old lady. He risked a glance backwards.

The two men were still on his tail: the big, dark-haired guy in the long coat, and the leaner blond who'd challenged him. What were they? CID? He'd juiced the girl well enough, even though it had been off the cuff and desperate, but the blond guy hadn't even flinched.

How the bloody hell had he resisted?

'He got to Gwen,' James yelled, leaping a toddler on reins.

'That much was obvious,' replied Jack, turning his body sidelong to fit between two bewildered Bengali women.

Jack's phone started to ring. Still running, he hooked on his Bluetooth.

'This is Jack.'

'Owen for you,' said Ianto's voice.

'Jack—' Owen began.

'Kinda busy, Owen!' Jack replied, grunting as he barely avoided colliding with an opening car door.

'That's great. We've got a situation.'

'Gee, so have we. Call me back.'

In the Hub, Owen lowered the phone from his ear and made 'can you believe that?' eyes at Ianto.

'I swear, he never takes me seriously,' he said.

'Getting hotter!' Toshiko sang out from her station.

Owen stabbed redial.

Jack heard a crash and some squawking. He glanced over his shoulder. James had piled into an ageing hippy on a skateboard and they'd both gone over. Tin cans and potatoes clattered and rolled out of the hippy's split shopping bags. The skateboard shot out into the road.

'Sorry! Sorry!' said James, picking himself up.

'You're a bloody menace, mister!' the hippy yelled. James was running again. He'd lost ground. Jack had the lead, but the crowd was getting thicker. For a split second, the devil in him considered drawing his Webley and waving it around.

'Coming through! One side!' Jack roared, hoping his accent and gleaming grin would do instead.

His phone rang again.

'Seriously, Owen, it'll have to wait.'

'Don't hang up! Don't hang up!' Owen gabbled.

'Owen—'

'We've got a thing. A big thing.'

'Scale of one to ten?'

'Er…'

Jack hung up. He shoved through a crowd of teenagers outside a video shop. He saw the guy, ten yards away, stumbling over a dog lead. The guy looked back, saw Jack, and hurled himself in through the automatic doors of a mini-mart, banging against them when they opened too slowly.

Jack ran up to the doors, allowed them to reopen, and walked inside. His phone rang. He ignored it.

Bright strip lights. Soulless magnolia lino with trolley scuffs. Aisles of produce shelves and humming freezers. The smell of plastic, soap powder and vegetables. There were a few dozen people inside, most queuing at the tills, some pushing trolleys around the aisles. Everyone had come to a halt and was looking around, even the checkout girls. Muzak played.

Everybody stared at Jack. He walked past the stack of empty wire baskets to the chrome turnstile. It was still spinning.

He slid through it. 'Looking for a guy,' Jack called out. 'He came in here a second ago. I know you all saw him.'

The shoppers and the checkout girls gazed at Jack uncomfortably. They were thinking cops and robbers, they were thinking some dangerous nut with a weapon.

'Everything's OK,' Jack smiled, holding up his hands. 'There's no danger. I just need to know where he went.'

He looked at a football mum, who averted her eyes, then at an OAP, who shook her head in a *choose someone else* disavowal.

'Come on, help a guy out,' said Jack. 'Somebody knows where he is. Anybody?'

He caught the eye of the floor manager, a small, slope-shouldered, scrawny man in late middle age. The floor manager's supermarket uniform was ill-fitting. He was standing at the price-check post behind the checkouts. He said something inaudible.

'I'm sorry?' said Jack, cupping a hand to his ear.

The manager coughed, and slowly picked up the stand mic on the price-check post. He thumbed the 'on' button and cleared his throat, which caused a brief burp of amplified feedback.

'Uh,' the floor manager's voice came over the speakers, interrupting the Muzak. 'Aisle five. Frozen goods.'

'Thank you,' said Jack, with an honest nod.

'Uh, happy to be of service,' the floor manager replied over the speakers. He took his thumb off the button and the Muzak resumed.

Jack hurried along the aisle-ends, and then darted up aisle four, watching everywhere for movement. The few shoppers he passed cowered back behind their trolleys or simply stared at him in fascination.

'Hi,' he whispered to several of them.

The aisles had mid-length breaks. Jack sidled up to the aisle four break, his back against the shelves (cleaning fluids, bleach, disinfectant), and peered around the corner at the aisle five displays.

No one in sight.

He stepped around into aisle five, feeling the cold aura of the chest freezers. There was no one in the aisle except a huge black woman standing beside her trolley as if she'd been told to make like a statue. Her eyes were wide.

No sign of the guy. Jack hadn't expected to see him. Everyone in the shop had heard the floor manager rat out his position over the Tannoy.

Jack took a step forwards and leant on the nearest freezer compartment (pizzas, stone-ground, deep pan and thin-n-crispy, budget, double-topping) and bent down to peer under the eye-level ice-boxes at the bank of freezers that backed on to the aisle five units to form aisle six. Nothing.

He stood up again. He looked at the big black woman, and raised his eyebrows quizzically.

Remaining otherwise immobile, her eyes still wide, the big black woman extended her index finger and jabbed it repeatedly in the direction of aisle six.

She winked.

Jack beamed and mouthed a 'thank you'.

As quietly as he could, Jack climbed into the freezer full of pizzas. He gently rolled himself under the eye-level display and over into the adjacent aisle six freezer (chill-fresh prawns, seafood medley, haddock portions, individual boil-in-the-bag cod in parsley sauce, fish fingers). Frosty packaging crackled softly under his weight. The big black woman's eyes grew even wider.

Flat on his back in the freezer compartment, Jack braced, counted silently to three, and lurched upright.

The man in the suit was crouching down below the freezer's fascia. He started up at Jack's surprise appearance.

'Hi there,' said Jack.

Dean Simms reached into his briefcase.

Jack pounced on him.

They went down together in a bundle of limbs. Dean's briefcase fell out of his grasp and slapped onto the lino. Magazine inserts and a rather nice pen spilled out of it, along with a small, greasy beige lump that looked like a not-so-vital internal organ, the sort of thing that was hard to recognise in a quiz once you'd discounted liver, kidneys and spleen.

It flopped onto the hard floor and pulsed gently.

Struggling under Jack's weight, Dean yelled something. Securing Dean's arms, Jack gave him a slap that cowed him. Jack hoisted him up by the tie and leant him against the nearest freezer (summer puddings, freezer-to-oven apple pies, sorbets).

'OK, you're done,' Jack told him. 'Behave yourself.' He glanced down at the pulsing lump.

'Eeuww,' he said. 'You cough that up?'

Dean said nothing. His eyes blazed.

'Listen to me,' Jack began, 'here's what's going to happen. We—'

His phone began to ring.

Jack looked away for a second. All his life, Dean had listened to his old man's advice, keen to learn from him. Retail wasn't the only thing his dad had known about. Dean's old man had been an amateur welter-weight. Tough old bird, his dad.

Dean threw the jab, just the way his old man had taught him.

Distracted by his phone, Jack caught the fist square on the jaw. He reeled away, flailing, and hit the wall-freezers opposite (Ben and Jerry's, soft scoop vanilla, Cornish dairy cream, triple fudge sundaes). The glass door cracked with his impact.

Jack tried to right himself, his hand to his mouth. 'Jesus!' he exclaimed.

Dean had picked up the beige lump. He aimed it at Jack and squeezed it.

Jack blinked. He took a step back. He got a sudden, strong smell of bourbon and willow.

'I…' he said. He glanced around. He leant back against the cracked glass door and shook his head.

Dean started running, the lump in his hands. He headed for the checkout. Shoppers screamed as they saw him coming. Dean pushed through them, trying to work his way out via one of the narrow checkout lanes. A pot-bellied man was blocking his exit with a trolley heavy with crates of beer. A bulk purchase.

'Out of my way!' Dean yelled. He halted.

James was standing on the far side of the checkout, facing him. James said nothing. He stared at Dean, right in the eyes. The meaning was clear.

Dean roared and drove the crate-laden trolley at James. With the bulk purchases on board, the thing weighed fifty kilos.

Dean rammed it into James's legs.

'Bastard!' James yelped. He grabbed the wire cage of the ramming trolley, and threw it sideways. It flew the entire length of the shop front and crashed down on its side near the exit, castors spinning.

James turned, deftly ducking the punch Dean threw at him, and landed a punch of his own.

Dean hurtled backwards onto the checkout, breaking the code reader. He flopped unconscious. The checkout display flashed 'UNKNOWN BAR CODE'.

The shoppers and the checkout girls gave James a spontaneous round of applause. James stepped forward, and looked at the beige lump sliding towards him on the packing conveyer.

He pulled one of the crumpled serviettes out of his pocket and gathered the thing up. It was unpleasantly warm.

Gwen appeared behind him. 'Hello,' she said. 'Having fun?'

'Loads,' James replied.

'How did that happen?' she asked, pointing.

At the far end of the shop front, a broken trolley full of slumping beer crates was making the automatic exit open and close and open and close.

'No idea,' said James.

Jack's phone rang again. He straightened himself up on the edge of the nearest chest freezer.

'You all right, honey?' the big black woman cooed at him, peering under the eye-levels.

'Yeah, I'm fine. Thanks,' Jack replied. Who the hell was she?

He opened his phone.

'This is Jack.'

'Jack, for God's sake!' said Owen's voice. 'In answer to your question, twenty-bloody-seven!'

'On a scale of one to ten?'

'Yes!'

'Owen, why the hell didn't you call me earlier?'

TWENTY

'We'll meet you there,' said Owen.

Jack hung up. 'Owen says they'll meet us there.'

'Uh-huh,' said James. He was driving. 'Lunchtime rush. Cathays is going to be fifteen minutes minimum from here.'

'Punch it,' said Jack.

'You two OK?' James called back.

'We're fine,' said Jack.

'He got you both. Both of you,' James said.

'So you say. I don't remember,' said Jack.

'Oh, come on!'

'OK, OK, I'll take your word for it,' Jack looked at James in the driving mirror. 'How come he didn't get you?'

'I didn't give him the chance. You've got it bagged?'

'Bagged and stowed in a box,' said Gwen. 'Horrible thing, it was. Like an organ. Like a swollen appendix.'

'Looked like a sentient gland to me,' said Jack.

'And you'd have seen plenty of those,' said Gwen.

'One or two. Owen can give us a full slice and dice later.'

'If there is a later,' said James. He braked hard. 'Where are you going? Where are you going?' he yelled impatiently at a drifting taxi.

'Calm down,' said Gwen.

'I hate that we had to leave him there,' James complained, hauling on the wheel as they went over a roundabout.

'He's nothing without his mojo,' said Jack. 'We shut him down. Who's he gonna complain to? Who'd believe him?'

'I suppose,' said James.

'Besides, this is more important,' said Jack.

Gwen nudged Jack. 'James?' said Jack.

'Yeah?'

'Back there, did you throw a shopping cart full of crated beer the length of the store?'

'Yes, I did.'

'OK.'

'Because I have superpowers, obviously. What the hell are you asking me?'

'You didn't then?' asked Jack.

'Of course I didn't. I couldn't.'

'OK, then.'

'Why are you asking me?'

'Well, a cart got tossed—'

'Arsehole!' James shouted, and leant on the horn.

'Excuse me,' said Jack.

'Not you, that van. Look, the cart rolled and fell over. That's all it was.'

'The cart rolled and fell over,' Jack said to Gwen. 'So, you see, that's what it was.'

James glanced up and looked at himself in the mirror. He was sweating. It wasn't just the stress of hard-nosed driving.

He was a little bit scared.

And he couldn't tell anyone why.

'Where are we going again?' he asked.

Jack consulted the GPS. 'Wrigley Street. The open ground behind it.'

'Guess we're going to find out what happened to all those missing pets,' said James. He parped the horn. 'Get in lane! Get in lane, you idiot!'

Wrigley Street, Cathays. Noon. Grey clouds shooting spots of rain. Back-to-back tenements, front-and-backs, a relic of labourer's housing.

A blue Honda sports drew up with an ostentatious squeal of disc brakes.

Owen and Toshiko got out. She flipped out her phone and called Ianto.

'We're on the plot. Do you have a house number?'

'Number sixteen.'

'Ident?'

'David Gryffud Morgan. Lives alone. Pensioner.'

'Thanks, Ianto. Where are the others?'

'Eight minutes away, by GPS.'

'Thanks. I'm going to mute you but keep you live in my pocket, OK?'

'Yes, Tosh. I'm monitoring and recording.'

Toshiko and Owen walked up to the peeling door.

Owen rang the bell.

'David Gryffud, right?' he asked.

'David Morgan. Gryffud is the middle name.'

'Oh, OK.'

The door began to open. It rattled as someone inside shook it. It was sticking.

It opened. A tiny old man in a suit peered out at them. He had a black eye. He was one of the oldest people Owen had ever seen.

'Hello, yes?'

'Mr Morgan?' Toshiko asked.

'Yes?'

'Mr David Morgan?'

'Davey. Or Taff. They always used to call me Taff, even the wife.'

'Excellent,' said Owen, rubbing his hands together. 'Can we come in?'

'Are you from the MOD?' Davey asked cautiously.

Owen glanced at Toshiko.

'Were you expecting the MOD, Davey?' she asked.

'Of course. I rung them up.'

'All right then,' smiled Owen. 'We're from the MOD. Can we come in?'

Davey opened the door and limped around to let them through into the hall. They saw he was slightly scoliotic, and his frame so shrunken. So thin, like a bird. Owen thought if he stood in front of a light, they'd see his skeleton like an X-ray.

'About time,' Davey Morgan said. 'I was at a loss. He's very volatile, obviously. Very, very volatile. I was afraid to provoke him.'

'Uh, who?' asked Owen.

'Go through, the sitting room to your right.'

Toshiko and Owen went into the tiny sitting room. Two armchairs and a sofa. A wood-effect radiogram cabinet. An upright piano. A framed picture of the Scottish Highlands on the chimney breast. A stale aroma.

'Nice,' said Owen, looking around.

'It's all right. They're from the MOD,' they heard the old man say in the hall.

'Who are you talking to, sir?' Toshiko asked.

Davey followed them into the sitting room. 'Davey, just Davey, please.'

'Who were you talking to?'

'No one,' Davey said. 'Please sit.' He hobbled into one of the worn armchairs.

'So… *Davey*…' said Toshiko, 'how can the Ministry of Defence help you today?'

'Well,' he said, leaning forwards, 'I suppose you've come to bring it in. On the nod. I understand. A thing like that has to be on the secret list.'

'A thing like what, Davey?' asked Toshiko.

'Smart weapons. That's what they're called, aren't they? Smart weapons? I read about them in the papers. Not the kind of war I knew, of course.'

'What war did you know, Davey?'

Davey Morgan smiled. 'The last one. I went into Normandy with the landings. 1944. Royal Fusiliers.'

'Well, that must have been quite a thing, Davey.'

'Davey,' said Owen, cutting in quickly. 'Davey, old mate… what did you find? You said a smart weapon?'

Davey nodded. 'I would have thought you'd have known you'd lost it. Clever bit of kit, I'll grant you. Talking to me. I suppose that's computers and the Interweb and all that. I've been told about the Interweb.'

'It talks to you?'

'Of course. We've bonded, the two of us. Two old soldiers together. It sees my past in me, and respects it, which is nice. I have to say it's very clever, the way you built it to do that.'

'We are very clever, Davey,' said Toshiko.

'It knows me and I know it. We're mates. I fancy I'll miss it when you take it away.'

'Of course you will.'

'Thing is,' said Davey, scratching his head, 'as I said on the phone, it did a bad thing. Very bad. Oh, no one round here will miss *them*, but even so, it wasn't right.'

'Miss who?' asked Toshiko.

'The yobbos. The bloody bastards. They killed my cat, I'm bloody sure. And they gave me this eye.'

'Davey,' asked Toshiko. 'What did this thing do to these… yobbos?' She nodded to Owen, who got up and moved quietly towards the sitting-room door.

'Stitched them up, of couse,' said Davey. 'Stitched them up a treat.'

'Right. And where is it now?' asked Toshiko.

'In my bathroom. Would you like a cup of tea?'

Owen had slipped outside, into the cold, narrow space of the hall. The bathroom door was ajar, letting out a bar of light.

He pushed the door open.

'Oh bloody hell,' he started to say.

Mr Dine felt the pull. No prior warning. Alert protocols lit up his nerves in a warm surge.

He'd been enjoying the paintings. The gallery was pleasant and quiet, and no one bothered him. He rose from the settee in front of the Expressionists and walked towards the exit, his pace swiftly increasing.

Investment was beginning. The upload had connected by the time he reached the street outside. Significant threat to the Principal. Jeopardy.

But the pull was good, this time. A clean, steady fix. Definitive location.

He began to run. As he ran, he began to invest, to recompose and to vanish from human sight.

'Wrigley Street,' said Jack. James slewed them around the junction.

Gwen was listening to her headset.

'Ianto says he's had Tosh on the line, but he just lost her. He says the transmission's being jammed.'

'Still hot?' asked Jack.

'Smoking,' Gwen replied.

'No, no, no, no!' cried Davey, raising a warning hand. He pushed Owen behind him. 'It's all right, it's all right! He's a friend. Don't look at him like that.'

A low hum. A slight change of pitch.

'I think you spooked it,' Davey whispered to Owen.

'I spooked *it*?' Owen replied.

They were in the hall, with the front door behind them. At the other end of the narrow corridor ahead of them, the thing stood there, framed in the kitchen doorway. Toshiko was out of its line of sight, just inside the door of the sitting room. She caught Owen's eye, and made a pantomime shrug. He shook his head quickly. She couldn't see what he could see.

It was a human figure made of metal, thin and sharp. Its limbs were long and slender, like piston rods. Its hands were huge clusters of oily, steel hooks. Its torso, neck and head were narrow and sculptural, sleek like a missile, paint-chipped like a forgotten, unexploded bomb. The top of its ovoid head brushed the ceiling. It had no real features, just a burnished relief of lines and crests that vaguely suggested a human skull. There was a cold, tarry smell. The thing hummed.

'So that's… that's it, then?' Owen whispered.

'Of course,' said Davey.

The thing stirred slightly at the sound of their voices. Electric light from the bathroom slanted across it. It took a step. The hum changed pitch.

'All right, all right!' Davey called, soothingly. 'There's nothing to worry about! Don't be getting any ideas, now.'

The hum changed pitched again.

'Well, I realise that obviously,' said Davey, 'but you have to trust me.'

Another pitch change.

'That's what I said. You can trust me. We're going to sort it all out. That's why I called this bloke round. So we can sort things out. You do trust me, don't you?'

The hum warbled.

'That's right. That's right. You know me.'

Hum.

'Taff the soldier, that's it. Now let's be nice and calm. Nice and calm, now. Let's sit down and have a cup of tea, maybe.'

The thing stood still for a moment, then cocked its head slightly. Another hum.

'Davey,' Owen whispered. 'I need you to step into the sitting room with my colleague now.'

'Oh, no,' said Davey. 'That's not a good idea. I'd best stay in sight. It'll be reassured if it can see me.'

'Davey, you've done a great job sorting this out,' said Owen very softly, 'but this is our responsibility now. We'll take it from here.'

'You sure?'

'MOD work, Davey. Trust me.'

In the sitting room doorway, Toshiko quietly beckoned to the old man. Reluctantly, he limped into the sitting room with her.

Owen faced the thing.

'Wotcha,' he said.

It straightened slightly.

'Let's not do anything rash,' said Owen. 'We've got to find a way through this situation. What I need you to do is maybe shut down, or back out into the yard. Can you do either of those things for me?'

The thing hummed.

'Yeah, whatever. Do you understand? Understand? Can you please shut down or just back away outside?'

The thing took a sudden, purposeful step towards Owen.

'Crap!' Owen cried. His handgun came out from under his jacket. He emptied the clip on automatic. Sparks flashed and blinked across the thing's chest as multiple high-velocity rounds struck it. And disintegrated.

Owen eyes widened. 'Oh, shit,' he said.

The thing looked at him. There was a pulse of dull yellow where its eyes should have been.

They got out of the SUV, looking around.

'Which house is it?' James asked.

Twenty yards away, the front door of a house vaporised in a sheet of light and wooden fragments. The blast took out the doorframe too, blew the garden gate off its hinges and stove in the side of a parked car, which promptly exploded in a belching, expanding cloud of flame.

Pieces of glass and debris rained down. Car and house alarms all down the street began ringing and whooping.

'I'm going to say that one,' said Jack.

TWENTY-ONE

Acrid smoke billowed through the hallway and the sitting room.

'Owen?' Toshiko cried. 'Owen?'

The smoke caught at her throat and she began to cough.

'Owen?'

Davey was fumbling about behind her, dazed and blinking. The picture of the Scottish Highlands had fallen off the chimney breast and shattered on the hearth.

Toshiko peered out into the hallway. The blast had snapped all the banisters on the stairs. The carpet was scorched, and the old wallpaper was bubbling and peeling.

'Owen?'

No reply.

She thought about drawing her side-arm, but realised that it was pointless. Owen had proved that much, in what had probably been the last moment of his life.

She dropped down and crawled forward, peeking out into the hallway. The front door had entirely gone, and a cold draught was stirring in through the smoke.

She looked the other way. At the end of the hall, the kitchen door was splintered open. There was no sign of the thing.

She got up. Something stirred at the foot of the stairs, and she pulled her gun anyway.

It was Owen. He was curled up in a ball.

'Owen?'

'What?' he answered, over-loudly.

'Owen, be quiet.'

'Bloody well deafened me,' he said.

'Shush. How are you alive?'

'What?'

'How are you still alive?'

'I ducked. Onto the stairs. Jesus Christ, that thing plays for keeps. Where is it?'

'I don't know,' replied Toshiko.

Davey limped out into the hallway. He looked around. 'Oh no,' he murmured. 'Oh no.'

'Mr Morgan? Sir?' Toshiko called. 'Go back in the room, Mr Morgan. Please, sir. We need you to be safe.'

Davey Morgan stayed where he was. He bent down and picked something up. The hall table had been smashed. The picture that had been standing on it had fallen and broken. Davey brushed off the glass fragments and smoothed the photo inside the frame.

'Oh, Christ, I'm sorry. It's all right, love. It's all right.'

'Davey! Sir!'

Davey turned to face her. 'Look what happened to my house!' he cried. 'Look what it did to my bloody house!'

Toshiko went over to him and tried to calm him down. The photograph was black and white, and showed a smiling, slightly self-conscious middle-aged woman in horn-rim specs.

'Davey, I have to get you clear,' Toshiko said. 'You have to go outside. Out the front.'

'Who's this now?' Davey demanded, ignoring her.

Jack hurried in through the hole where the front door had been. He narrowed his eyes and blinked at the smoke.

'Everyone still alive who should be?'

'Yes,' said Toshiko.

'What can you tell me?'

'I think it went out the back,' said Toshiko.

James and Gwen appeared behind Jack. Both had side-arms in their hands, raised in 'safe' grips.

'They won't do any bloody good,' said Owen loudly. He was on his feet, leaning against the wall and wiggling a finger in one ear.

'Why?' asked Gwen.

'Because it's bloody well bullet-proof,' said Owen. 'And if it looks at you, hint, be somewhere else.'

'What happened?' Jack called as he pushed past Toshiko and the old man and headed towards the kitchen.

'I tried to defuse the situation peacefully,' said Owen.

'This would be why the lower part of this house recently exploded?' asked James.

'Ultimately,' Owen nodded, his voice still just the wrong side of loud. 'It was a stand-off. A matter of the first one to flinch.'

'And?' asked Gwen.

'I flinched first,' said Owen. 'Sorry. I've always been a flincher.'

'Get these people out of my house!' Davey cried.

'Get the old guy out of my hazard radius,' said Jack. He stepped into the little back kitchen. It was dingy and worn. A single teacup and saucer on the drainer, a bowl of cat food on the floor, a ragged-looking jacket hanging from a peg. Jack drew his revolver, and edged towards the broken backdoor. Gwen came through from the hallway behind him.

'Any ideas yet?' she asked.

'That was a phasic weapon,' said Jack. 'Very distinctive energetic pattern. Very advanced.'

'So, yeah, then?'

'Let's say I've got a hunch.'

'Let's say your coat disguises it well.'

He looked at her. 'Making jokes? Really?'

They reached the door. The little backyard was empty. They advanced down the back path. The chorus of house and car alarms had not yet abated, and now police sirens added to the mix.

'We'll need to pull rank,' said Jack. 'We can't let the uniforms near this, though they might want to start getting the street evacuated. The streets on either side too, probably. In fact, Cathays.'

'Special access, right. I'll go talk to someone,' said Gwen. She went back into the kitchen, passing James and Owen on their way out. They joined Jack.

'See it?' asked Owen.

'Uh-uh. Not so far.'

'Well, it's kind of hard to miss.'

They went to the gate.

It was standing in the walled lane behind the houses. Just standing, slightly crooked, as if listening.

As the three of them stepped out of Davey's back gate and saw it, it turned, first its head, then its upper body, then its feet, repositioning them under the rotating torso.

'Oh, hell,' said Jack, a note of genuine disappointment in his voice.

The thing tilted its head slightly. The humming sound coming from it changed pitch.

Where the thing's eyes should have been, there was a pulse of dull yellow.

The three men threw themselves sideways into Davey's yard as a roaring cone of heat rushed down the narrow lane and demolished two outhouses and part of a wall.

Small lumps of brick and fine grit sprinkled down.

Owen rolled over and inched himself backwards until he was leaning against the yard wall. 'That's twice that's happened to me,' he said. 'I've decided not to risk a third try.'

James looked at Jack. 'You know what it is, don't you? You've got that look.'

'I'm pretty sure I know it. I've seen pictures.'

'Pictures?'

Jack crawled back to the gateway and took a quick look out. The thing was walking away down the back lane slowly.

Jack ducked back in. 'It's Melkene tech. A Serial G, I think. Yeah, Serial G. I'm sure of it.'

'Go on.'

'What can I tell you? The Melkene were a pretty advanced race. Particularly good at manufacturing artificials, or what Owen would call robots.'

'That thing's a robot?' asked Owen.

'It's a soldier,' said Jack. 'About five hundred years ago, the Melkene found themselves in a hot war with a rival species. They were losing. Their soldiers – all artificials – were too predictable. They lacked, how can I put it? Uh, the balls for serious warfare. Just point-and-shoot mechanicals, with no killer instinct, no passion.'

'So?' asked James, fairly sure he wasn't going to like the rest of the story.

'So they manufactured the Serial G. Removed all the logic inhibitors and algorithmic compassion restraints they had traditionally equipped their artificials with. The sort of fundamental safeguards any advanced civilisation with a conscience would have insisted on installing in their artificials. The Melkene were desperate. Their backs were against the wall. They gave the Serial G ungoverned sentience, a ruthless streak and absolutely no compunction whatsoever about committing atrocities. The build remit was: whatever it takes, no matter how cruel or abominable, these things must be capable of doing it, in the name of victory. Put simply, in order to win their war, the Melkene created your basic... regiment of psychotic, homicidal artificials.'

'They deliberately made mad killer robots?' Owen asked.

'Well, that's a huge oversimplification,' said Jack.

'But essentially on the money?' asked James.

Jack nodded. 'Yup. They deliberately made mad killer robots.'

The three of them sat there in silence for a moment.

'Sometimes,' said Owen, reflectively, 'you have to wonder why you ever turn up for work, don't you?'

'How did things go for the Melkene, Jack?' James asked.

'Oh, they won.'

'Well, that's nice for them.'

'Not so much. There was a huge outcry in the Galactic Community. Outrage at what the Melkene had done. In remorse, the Melkene decided to recall the Serial G units. The Melkene were extinct about, oh, six weeks later.'

'I've seen this film,' said Owen.

'God, I wish it *was* a film,' said Jack. 'Because of their ungoverned sentience, the Serial Gs were judged responsible for their actions. They were impeached on about 16,000 counts of war crime and genocide. They scattered and went to ground.'

'And one's walking about here?' asked James.

'Yes it is.'

'In Cathays, on a Thursday?'

'Seems so.'

'A genocidal robot war criminal?' asked James.

'That's also completely bullet-proof?' asked Owen.

Jack looked at them both. 'Repetition's good, but, guys, we've got all the facts together now, right?'

James nodded. 'Things are as bad as they look.'

'Oh, God, no,' said Jack. 'Things are much worse than they look, my friend.' He held up the heavy service revolver clenched in his hand. 'You know what this is?' he asked.

'Uh, no?' Owen replied.

'Absolutely useless, is what it is,' answered Jack, putting the gun away. He got up and hurried to the gate, head down. 'It's gone,' he reported. 'It's moving.'

'What do we do?' asked James.

'Not much,' said Jack. 'We follow it. See where it's headed. Try to keep it contained away from population centres. Think hard and pray for miracles.'

'It's probably heading back to my shed.'

They looked around. Davey Morgan stood outside his ruined backdoor, gazing at them. Toshiko hovered behind him.

'What did you say, sir?' asked Jack.

'Yank, are you?' asked Davey.

'Kinda,' admitted Jack.

'Got to know a lot of your sort, back then,' said Davey. 'Good old boys. Tough as old boots, they were.'

'Thanks,' said Jack. 'What were you saying about a shed?'

'Mr Morgan has been talking with the machine,' said Toshiko gently. 'They have an understanding, of sorts.'

'Old soldiers together,' said Davey.

'Is that right?' asked Jack, walking over.

'I tried to make Mr Morgan wait out front,' whispered Toshiko to Jack. 'He wouldn't be moved.'

'You could have smacked him silly and dragged him,' Jack whispered back.

'Yes, I could have, but I'm a nice person,' whispered Toshiko.

Davey Morgan looked at them both. 'It's not polite to whisper,' he said.

'No, it's not,' said Jack, turning to him. 'Mr Morgan, wasn't it?'

'Davey.'

'OK, Davey. I'm Cap'n Jack Harkness. Tell me about this shed.'

'It's up on my plot,' said Davey. 'On the allotments, I mean. I kept your smart weapon there after I dug it up. I think it likes it there.'

'Where is this shed exactly?' asked Jack.

'I'll show you,' Davey said. 'Hang on a mo.' He turned, and limped back into the kitchen.

'Does he realise there's some degree of urgency?' Jack asked Toshiko.

'He can help us, Jack,' Toshiko insisted.

Jack pursed his lips. He pulled out his phone and tried to dial. Dead.

'We're still inside that thing's jamming range,' he said. 'Serial Gs are fitted with a comprehensive suite of communication counter-measures.' He tossed his phone to Owen. 'Take that, and get walking. I don't care how far you have to go. As soon as you've got a signal, call Ianto and tell him to go to the Armoury, book out catalogue item nine-eight-one, and bring it here as fast as is humanly possibly. Got that?'

'Armoury. Nine-eight-one. Right,' said Owen, and hurried off through the house.

Davey re-emerged from the kitchen, a cap on his head. He was buttoning up a threadbare jacket. 'Off we go, then,' he said. 'I just had to get my digging jacket.'

'Well of course you did,' said Jack.

Davey Morgan led the way down the back lane behind the houses to the allotment path. Jack, James and Toshiko followed him. It was slow going. Davey had a pronounced limp that was obviously troubling him.

The sky had blackened. The sporadic rain had turned into a shower, and worse was undoubtedly coming. The wind had picked up. Choirs of alarms were singing across the backyards, punctuated by the whoop of a police klaxon.

'Gwen's dealing with the police,' Toshiko told Jack. 'She's keeping them back, clearing people from the houses here.'

Jack nodded.

'A lot of them don't want to go,' Toshiko added. 'A lot of them want to see what's going on.'

'They'll die then,' said Jack.

'I suppose they might,' said Toshiko. 'Let's hope the police are persuasive.'

'Yeah, let's hope.'

'Jack?' asked James.

'Yeah?'

'What's catalogue item nine-eight-one?'

Jack smiled. 'James, you so don't want to know.'

'Apparently, I do.'

Jack glanced at him. 'It's one of the Armoury items I don't let you play with.'

'And that's going to take this thing out?'

Jack shrugged. 'Couldn't honestly say, James, but I can guarantee it'll make a whole lot of noise.'

'Really?'

'Oh, yeah. There will be noise. There will be bright lights. There will be woe. There will be weeping and consternation. The streets of Cardiff will resound with the lamentation of estate agents.'

'This is Torchwood going to war, then?' asked Toshiko.

'No, this is Torchwood trying to prevent one,' said Jack.

'You people have never seen a real war,' said Davey.

'Sir?' Jack asked, looking at the old man.

'I said you've never known a real war. Not a real one. It never leaves you, war doesn't. Everything you saw or did, it all clings like a smell you can't ever wash off. Sixty years, sixty damn years, it hasn't ever washed off.'

Davey had stopped by an iron gate. It stood open on its bolts, as if it had been pushed aside.

Beyond the gate lay the allotments: portioned-out strips of ground, a patchwork of rectangular plots, some with sheds, some with rainwater tanks or tool chests, some neglected and overgrown. A hazy mist drifted over the winter beets and rhubarb leaves. The rain began to fall harder, pattering off the vegetation.

Jack walked into the allotments, and looked around.

'I could come to like a place like this,' he said. 'When I retire. Not so much with the rain, obviously.'

He looked at Davey. 'Your shed?'

'Up along there, Captain,' Davey said, with a gesture. Raindrops dripped from his raised sleeve.

'Tosh tells me you've spoken to this thing?'

'Tosh?'

'The nice Japanese girl there.'

'Oh, right. Yeah, we've spoken a little. I dug it up, after all. Kept it safe. We chatted. Reminisced, really, one old boy to another. War stories. Memories of life during wartime.'

Jack wiped rain off his face and looked at Davey. The old man's eyes were very sharp, very knowing.

'So, was it good to talk?' Jack asked him.

'Good?' replied Davey.

'I have no idea, no frame of reference, so I'm asking you. Was it good to talk?'

'I suppose,' said Davey. 'It was refreshing to meet someone who got it. To be truthful, Captain, I've never had anyone I could talk to about… about the service. Not Glynis. Not really. She never got it. God knows, I never wanted her to get it. It understood, though. I could tell it things. We shared things. Memories. It was nice for me.'

'Yeah?'

Davey nodded. Drops of rain ran off the end of his nose. 'Nice to be respected. To be acknowledged. Only a soldier understands what another soldier has been through. In the end, we're a lonely breed in that regard.'

'I guess you would be.'

'I just—'

'What?' Jack asked.

Davey shook his head. 'I just wished we could have kept it to that. It kept having these dreams, see? At night, its dreams leaked into mine. I tried, but I couldn't bear them. The things it had done. Laughed about. Awful things. I have my own bad dreams, Captain Harkness, and I'll carry them to my grave, where God can judge me, if he likes. I couldn't carry its dreams too. I wanted to. I tried. One old soldier to another.'

'It's OK,' said Jack.

'You're going to have to kill it, aren't you?' asked Davey.

'I think we are. I wish to hell I knew how,' said Jack. 'Davey, let's see this shed of yours.'

The rain beat down relentlessly. The shed was a silent, damp box. Its windows were broken and its door was half-open. Jack and James gazed at the decaying remains of the bodies spread and staked out in front of it. Toshiko looked away, swallowing hard.

'What do we do?' James asked Jack.

'I guess we… find out if it's inside,' said Jack. He took a step forward.

The shed juddered violently. It stopped shaking for a moment, and then juddered again.

'Get down,' said Jack.

The shed blew apart. It came to pieces in a flash of yellow light. The panelled walls burst out in all directions in a flurry of splintered boards. The pitch-treated roof ascended, in one burning piece, and crashed over into a plot two allotments away.

Swathed in flames, the Serial G turned and looked at them. It was standing on a scorched rectangle of ground that had been the floor of the shed. The downpour sizzled as it fell around it.

'Keep your heads down!' Jack yelled, on his belly in the soaking grass. James was face down with his arms over his head. Toshiko was trying to get the old man into the cover of a compost bunker.

'Tosh! Get him out of here!'

Toshiko replied something inaudible. Jack was well aware how impractical his last instruction to her had been.

The Serial G took a step forward off the burning patch of shed floor. Its long, thin legs extended slightly, taking it up to over ten feet tall. The huge steel hooks that formed its hand opened and closed with a noise like a luxury liner's anchor chain running out. It turned its head to the left, then to the right, and took another step. It hummed. Rain streamed off it.

It was coming towards them. With a curse, Jack got up and ran, head down, through the rain, between rows of cold frames and bean poles.

'Jack!' James yelled.

The Serial G turned its head to follow Jack's movement. There was a yellow pulse.

Jack had thrown himself headlong into a bed of wet brambles and elephant ear rhubarb leaves. He felt the scorch of the heat cone as it shaved the air above him. The blast exploded up a patch of ground in a great, muddy divot, and crushed a galvanised water tank with a kettle-drum bang. The water inside evaporated instantly in a screaming belch of steam.

The Serial G began to trudge towards the spot where it had seen Jack drop down. Jack heard its steps pulping vegetables and snapping canes. He heard the drum of raindrops. He couldn't get up. That would be suicide. He rolled instead, scrambling through the soaking undergrowth, twigs and nettles scratching his face.

The Serial G fired again, but its blast fell short, violently excavating a cabbage patch and turning a large cold frame into a blizzard of glass and wood chips.

Jack winced and tried not to cry out. One flying chunk of glass had stabbed into his upper left arm, and another had cut his cheek on the way past.

The Serial G took another two steps.

Jack sprang up, wincing at the tight pain from his upper arm, and started to run for better cover.

The Serial G turned immediately, its torso rotating. It raised its left arm to shoot it out and snatch Jack off his feet.

'Oi! Buggerlugs!' James yelled. He came up from behind a composter and emptied the clip of his side-arm at the metal figure.

His distraction worked. Too well.

The Serial G ignored Jack and turned to face him instead.

TWENTY-TWO

It all happened very fast.

James ducked back down behind the composter. The rain was hammering down. The Serial G pulsed its dull yellow glow and the brick composter pulverised. Toshiko glimpsed James's body cartwheeling backwards in the storm of flying brick fragments and flaming hanks of compost mulch.

She yelled his name. He was dead. He was so surely dead—

She saw him get up, unsteady, dazed, his hair matted and his shirt torn. He looked around, as if trying to remember who he was, where he was.

She watched him see the Serial G. It took a stride towards him. Pieces of burning mulch were still fluttering down to the ground in the rain.

James turned to run.

The Serial G snapped out its left arm in another lashing, hyper-extension. It failed to grab James cleanly, but the steel hooks crashed into his shoulder and the side of his head like a punch, and spun him wildly around, his skull smacked around to the left. He fell hard and crooked.

The limb retracted as rapidly as it had extended.

The Serial G took two more long steps forward through the rain and tilted its head down—

—and rocked backwards suddenly. It rocked again, arms swinging, its legs forced back several steps, as if it was suddenly trying to walk head-on into a force seventeen wind.

It shuddered as though it had been struck. It recoiled another step.

There was a dull yellow pulse where its eyes should have been.

A flash and a thunderclap of splitting air followed as the blast cone detonated less than two metres in front of it. The beam of energy simply splashed apart as if encountering some barrier in mid air directly ahead. The backwash of the blast caused the Serial G to sway on its heels yet again.

From her vantage point behind the eggshell-blue potting shed, Toshiko stared in wonder and fear, not really understanding what she was seeing. She wiped rain out of her eyes.

'It doesn't like that,' said Davey quietly. 'Oh, it doesn't like that at all.'

'What?' she asked distractedly, unable to tear her gaze away.

The space where the Serial G's eyes should have been glowed dull yellow again, and again, and then again. Three blasts in quick succession. Each one detonated in turn right in front of it. The pressure crack of tortured air was so fierce, Toshiko had to clap her hands over her ears. She felt each quake of discharge in her diaphragm.

For a nanosecond, as the third pulse went off, she thought she glimpsed something haloed in the glare, a moving shape much smaller than the Serial G, illuminated for a moment in the light storm breaking around it.

'What the hell is that?' she whispered.

'Tough little devil, isn't he?' asked Davey.

'Who? Davey, what are you talking about?'

Davey got up and pointed. He pointed very specifically at nothing at all in front of the Serial G.

Jack rose to his feet, clutching his injured arm. It throbbed wickedly, but he barely noticed. His entire attention was on the Serial G and what the Serial G was doing.

Out there in the rain, it appeared to have gone mad, or at least a good deal madder than the Melkene had made it. It was thrashing its arms, stumbling back pace after pace, as if it was experiencing a fit or—

A dent, a clear, solid dent, suddenly appeared in its chest plating. The Serial G shuddered and swung its right arm like a wrecking ball. The arm came to a violent dead stop in mid air, as if blocked, as if held in place. Indentations began to appear in the smooth, oiled alloy of its broom-stick forearm. The steel hooks of its hand opened and closed spasmodically, chewing the air.

The arm was suddenly free again. It sailed back, straightening and righting.

'Oh my God...' Jack gasped as he began to realise what he had to be witnessing.

'Jack?'

He turned. Gwen had crept up behind him, hunched low. Her eyes were wide.

'Not a good place to be,' Jack said.

'I did all I could in the street. I could hear these noises. I couldn't just stay put—'

She paused. 'What the bloody hell is that?'

There was another thunderclap burst of phasic discharge. Gwen jumped.

'Get down,' Jack said, pulling her towards an old tin bath serving as a water butt. Rainfall speckled the surface of the bath's contents. 'The technical name for it is very bad news. It's real nasty. A twenty-seven. Scratch that, it's a one hundred and twenty-seven. It's way out of Torchwood's class. We're just bystanders.'

'Christ…'

'But look at it, Gwen. Look at it and tell me what you think it's doing.'

'Scaring the crap out of me is what.'

'No, look at it! What does it look like it's doing?'

'It's fighting,' whispered Toshiko. 'It's fighting something we can't see.'

'Speak for yourself, Miss,' said Davey. 'Oh, it doesn't like it. Not at all.'

'Mr Morgan? Davey? Please tell me right now what you think you can see.'

'That bloke, of course. That bloke there in grey, giving it what for.'

Move. Don't lie there. It's not safe.

James woke up. Pain flared through his shoulder and neck and jaw. His mouth was full of blood. He stirred. He was vaguely aware of a huge din close by, metal on metal, whoops of superheated air. The ground shook. Rain soaked him.

Move. Get up and move now. It's not safe.

'What?' he murmured. He raised his head slightly and blood ran down his chin from his mouth, and down his upper lip from his nose. He couldn't focus properly.

I will not ask you again. Get up and move.

The voice was gentle, and oddly unaccented. It lacked even the slightest trace of region or background.

Get up and move.

James blinked and shook his head. He felt the downpour on his scalp. He knew he was hurt, quite badly hurt. His vision cleared slightly.

He saw the Serial G.

It was facing him, less than twenty yards away. It was behaving oddly, swinging its arms, its legs braced. It was the most active and mobile James had seen it, almost urgent.

He got up very shakily, soaked to the skin. He'd lost a shoe somewhere, and his shirt was ripped. There was blood down the front of it. His own blood.

He started to move. He broke into a limping run, hobbling up towards the northern limits of the allotments, away from the Serial G. The allotments ended in a bank of thick bushes, then a wall, behind which were the backs of houses. If he could get as far as the wall…

He fell twice. He felt stricken and woozy. He spat out more blood and part of a tooth and ran on.

'James!' Gwen cried. 'It's James!'

'Get down!' Jack bellowed, and jerked her back into cover.

'He's hurt!'

'Yeah, I think he is. But he's running clear, look. He'll be OK.'

Gwen fought at Jack to get up.

'Stop it!' he snapped. 'James will not thank me if I let you get smoked by that thing.'

Gwen gave in and slumped down beside Jack. She watched James's distant, staggering form until it disappeared behind a thicket of untended elder.

'You really think that robot thing is fighting something?' she asked, wiping rain off the end of her nose.

'You got a better explanation for its behaviour?' Jack asked.

The Serial G swung its right manipulator limb at him. It was impressively fast, and agile for a construct. By comparison, the raindrops in the air were frozen and static.

Mr Dine was impressed. It had hurt him already. Tech level forty-one-plus. Cold-cast vitalium/terybdonum composite alloy chassis. Hazard (type 1) grade physical assault, hazard (type 1) phasic weapon array. Hyper-aggressive intercourse.

His shield barriers, both standard and custom, were taking a pounding. The phasic weapon had a bite to it, although it seemed to need a ten-second lag to cycle up and recharge for shooting during sustained discharge. Mr Dine had speed on his side.

He ducked the sweeping limb, and hit the Serial G with another kinetic ram, his palm extended. The construct staggered backwards, and blitzed Mr Dine's shield barriers with a phasic burn at ninety per cent of power capacity.

Mr Dine leapt backwards, lifted slightly by the resounding impact. Coiling, he threw himself forward again under the grasping, groping claws of the manipulator limbs, and closed for contact.

Palms open, he delivered two more kinetic rams, squirting power from the cuff outlets of his battledress system. The construct vibrated with the double impact, taking the full force in its torso.

Mr Dine exploited his momentary advantage. He balled his left hand into fist form, invested primary power down his shoulder into his left arm, and punched.

A blow like that could split granite or fracture steel. It struck the composite alloy faring of the construct's torso and made a significant dent.

The impact threw the Serial G backwards. It lost its footing entirely in the rain, flag-pole legs kicking helplessly, and crashed down onto its back.

Mr Dine didn't hesitate. He fused his right hand into a blade form, like the end of an adze, and pounced to drive it down into the thing's heart for a kill.

The Serial G was not done. Though it was down and floundering on its back in the rain, its grotesquely elongated limbs flailing, it was not done.

It lashed its right arm around like a bull-whip, and caught Mr Dine in mid air with a noise like two racing locomotives meeting head on.

'Look out!' Davey shouted, and threw himself into Toshiko. The pair of them tumbled over into the wet grass.

An instant later, the eggshell-blue potting shed they had been standing next to was comprehensively demolished, as if a cruise missile had struck it from the front. Pieces of tile and wooden lapping winnowed out from the impact.

Toshiko raised her head. Raindrops struck her. The Serial G was on its back like an upturned beetle, its limbs waving. With a hiss, its limbs retracted, impossibly, into its torso housing, vanishing entirely for a second. Then its legs re-extended, lifting the sculptural body back upright. It rose straight up to a height of nine feet, and then its arms extruded from the sides of the torso, sliding out of nowhere smoothly and fluidly until its vast hook hands dangled below its hips again.

It let out a hum, and the hum changed pitch. It turned its head and looked through the rain, across the ravaged allotment plots, directly at Toshiko.

No, not at her, she realised. At the wreckage of the potting shed.

It hummed again.

'Had enough, have you?' Davey asked, struggling to his feet. 'Gave you a beating, didn't he?'

A wavering hum.

'Regroup? No? Just stop it now, eh? Just stop it now,' Davey said.

The Serial G turned its head away and began to stride up the allotments towards the back wall.

'No!' Davey cried. 'Come back here!'

It ignored him.

'I think it's a bit scared now, to be honest,' said Davey to Toshiko. 'Rattled, you know? It wasn't expecting that. It intends to run, go to ground.'

'It said that?'

Davey nodded. 'It needs time to repair.'

He limped over to the ruins of the potting shed and pulled back some of the remaining side panels so he could look in. The steady rain pattered off the wood and the grass.

'All right there?' Toshiko heard him say. She clambered up and hurried to join him. The potting shed was just a tangle of debris, slats of wood, old duck boards, scraps of ply. Davey pulled himself in, wobbling precariously.

'It's OK, just lie still,' he said.

She couldn't see what he was talking to.

Something rose up out of the wreckage. Something like a man, or the shadow of a man. A matt-grey ghost with a strange, thorny outline. Pieces of debris fell off it as it stood up.

'Davey,' she warned.

'It's all right,' he said, hushing at her with a wave of his hand. He kept his gaze on the figure.

'Just stay put. It's gone now. Just stay put,' Davey said. 'That's a nasty scrape you've taken.' He pointed.

The shadow looked down. It put its left hand against its side where a dark, ink-like liquid was seeping out. The hand came away, fingers soaked and dripping with the gleaming black fluid.

'You should—' Davey began.

The shadow simply wasn't there any more.

'Oh,' said Davey. Unsteady on the tumbled kindling, he looked around at Toshiko. 'It's gone,' he said.

'It's moving!' Jack whispered.

The Serial G was plodding away up the allotments in the beating rain.

'That's the way James went,' said Gwen. She leapt up and began to run after it.

'For God's sake, woman!' Jack barked, and ran after her.

He'd reached the end wall. It was made of brick and seven feet high. There was no gate, no doorway.

James fell against the wall and slid down it. His breathing was ragged. His whole upper body hurt, especially his shoulder and his jaw. He spat out some more blood. It was hard to focus, to think. His head felt like it was coming off. His mind felt like it was boiling.

His hands were shaking.

James looked up. He heard a distinctive hissing, pneumatic tread. A hum.

The Serial G parted the elder bushes twenty feet from him in a spray of raindrops and stepped into view. James pushed himself backwards, willing himself into the unyielding wall. He held his breath.

The Serial G paused, then cocked its head and looked in his direction.

On the other side of the wall, James started to run. Another back lane, an alley, narrow and dank, filled with wheelie bins and soaked pieces of household junk. The lane ran along behind the walled backyards of another terrace.

It was quite painful to run. James faltered, and came to a halt. He leaned against the allotment wall, panting hard. He wiped blood from his nostrils. The rain dribbled down his face.

A sudden thought entered his head, unbidden, a realisation. How had he cleared this wall? How had he cleared this seven-foot wall?

How—

Twenty-five feet behind him, the wall in question exploded in a fury of phasic energy. Bricks flew and scattered, making the clip-clop sounds of horseshoes on the alleyway paving.

The Serial G stepped through the three-metre-wide hole it had made in the wall. The crumbling edges of the brick work glowed and smoked.

James started running again. The Serial G behind him snapped out a limb on elastic metal to grab him, and missed. Steel hooks the size of milk bottles clanked shut on empty air. The Serial G took off after him, taking huge strides on legs as long and thin as scaffolding poles.

James risked a look back. A serious error. He slammed headlong into a wheelie bin and came down with it, sliding along the paving, garbage spilling out around and over him.

He looked back. The Serial G bore down.

Mr Dine ignored the pain. He accessed reserve investment and cleared the wall in the rain. He landed in the alley behind the construct and leapt at its back.

The Serial G halted and writhed, trying to shake off the adversary clamped around its neck and torso. Its manipulator limbs snaked backwards, attempting to grasp Mr Dine and shred him.

Mr Dine plunged a blade fist into the base of its neck. The alloy there dented deeply.

The construct's hum turned into a whine. It thrashed back and forth, slamming itself into the wet, alleyway walls, trying to wrench off its attacker. Bricks chipped and crumbled in bursts of dust as if hit by gunfire.

It succeeded in grabbing Mr Dine with the hooks of its right claw. It ripped the First Senior off its back and threw him sideways. Mr Dine punched through the back wall of a yard and then the kitchen wall of a house. He came to rest in the ruins of a kitchen table. His violent passage had torn the stainless-steel sink and drainer away from its cabinet mount, and water gushed, under pressure, from the broken pipes. The PVC replacement window, frame and all, fell out of its hole.

Mr Dine rolled over and got up. Black fluid spattered the quarry tile-effect vinyl flooring. He made a tactical assessment, scanning.

James got up and started to run again. There was an archway between houses, a walk-through, to his left. He darted down it, heading for the street.

The Serial G followed him.

Mr Dine read, quite clearly, that the construct was moving laterally to his left flank, ten yards away.

He turned, raised his arms in a protective cross in front of his face, and started to run. He exploded through the glass-panelled kitchen door, sprinted along the beige carpet of the hall and punched the front door clean out of its frame as he powered through it. He cleared the front garden wall, and landed on all fours like a cat on the roof of a parked car. The car's alarm began to peal as his impact dented the roof.

The local police had emptied the street about fifteen minutes earlier. At the far end, locals residents and policemen turned at the tape line when they heard the impacts and the alarm. They stared, mystified, down the street, through the rain.

James ran out of the walk-through into the road, soaked. He fell down and rolled in the puddles. The cloud cover was low and dark. Some of the street-lamps had come on.

Rainwater dripping off it, the Serial G strode out into the street behind him. It had retracted its legs considerably to duck under the walk-through. Now its legs extended again. It rose up, fourteen feet tall, its arms stretching out in proportion to its lower limbs.

Crouched and tensed on the roof of the car, Mr Dine waited for a second. Rainwater streaked down his grey, thorny body, diluting the inky black streaming from his side.

He took a breath.

He jumped.

The car he'd been crouching on bounced up and down on its shocks as he left it. He slammed into the construct and brought it over.

The huge metal figure toppled sideways under the force of the intercept, and demolished the ground-floor wall of a neighbouring house.

The impact threw Mr Dine clear. He rolled, and landed on his feet on a leatherette sofa. Unseated by the collapsing wall, a large television toppled off its stand in a flurry of sparks. A cracked aquarium began to gush its contents out onto the carpet. Dying, fragile, multicoloured fish flopped and wriggled as they were evacuated out onto the sopping pile.

In the street, James got up, leaning for support against a parked car, hearing the parping alarm of another car nearby.

The Serial G struggled and attempted to right itself.

'No. Not this time,' said Mr Dine. He leapt off the sofa and came down on top of it, a blade fist extended.

The tips of his reinforced fingers punched into the construct's chest and the alloy shattered like pie-crust. Mr Dine reached into the glowing interior, grabbed the construct's pumping, sentient CPU, and ripped it out.

The Serial G went into flatline arrest. The tiny reactor that powered it began to spin out wildly and overheat as system death overtook it.

Realising what was about to occur, Mr Dine turned to run.

The reactor superheated and winked out of existence. The Serial G exploded with it. So did the house, and the houses either side. Mr Dine was hurled like a limp rag across the street by the bow-wave of the detonation. At the end of the street, residents and police officers alike were knocked flat.

Jack and Gwen ran out into the street.

Pieces of up-flung debris were still coming down to rest. A gap where three houses had once stood blazed in the middle of the terrace row, churning thick, soot-black smoke into the sky. At the end of the street, people were shouting and screaming. Burning wreckage littered the road, sizzling in the rain. Everything was lit by the combusting ruins of the houses.

Jack lowered his revolver.

'Shit,' he said.

Gwen saw James, curled up in the middle of the road. She ran to him.

'It's all right, it's all right,' she sobbed, cradling him. Blood ran out of his slack mouth.

Jack walked across the street. Something with a vaguely human shape had landed on the roof of a parked Vauxhall Astra. The roof was crumpled and the windows burst out.

'I want to help you,' said Jack. 'Can I help you?'

Mr Dine slowly raised his head. He heard the voice.

'Please,' said Jack.

Mr Dine sat up. His investment was ebbing away. He was starting to crash, and the crash would be a bad one. He had been seriously damaged.

He rose and slid down off the buckled car roof. On his feet, he rose and looked at Jack Harkness.

'Please,' Jack said. 'I can help you.'

He held out his hand in the rain.

Mr Dine ignored it.

'Please,' Jack repeated.

Mr Dine turned and began to walk away. The damage overwhelmed him for a second, and he staggered, falling against the car. Jack shot out his hands to support him.

Mr Dine looked at Jack.

'Contact is not permitted,' he said. 'Contact is not… advisable.'

'I'm a broad-minded soul,' replied Jack.

'Contact is not permitted,' Mr Dine repeated. Then he was gone.

Jack Harkness was left looking at the inky black stains on his hands that the steady rain was already washing away.

In the allotments, Toshiko was slowly leading Davey Morgan back down towards the path. A cat mewed quietly and Davey scooped it up.

'There you are,' he said. 'You must be starving.'

Then, a moment before the blast lit up the row of houses behind them, Davey shuddered.

'Oh,' he said to her sadly, 'it's gone.'

TWENTY-THREE

Jack sat in the Boardroom. He idly checked the cleanly dressed injury to his arm, and then buttoned on a fresh shirt and waited.

One by one, Owen, Gwen and Toshiko wandered in and sat down. Toshiko simply sat and closed her eyes. Owen rolled back in his chair and put his feet up, as if he intended to snooze. Gwen flopped down, and sank her head over in her hands.

No one said anything for quite a while.

'Go on, somebody,' said Jack at length. 'I got nothing.'

There was no immediate response.

'Catalogue item nine-eight-one is pretty fancy,' said Owen eventually, making an effort to say something.

'What?'

'Nine-eight-one,' said Owen. 'Bit sexy, that. I didn't know we had anything like that in the Armoury.'

'If you'd known it was there, I'd have worried,' said Jack.

'I'm just a bit disappointed I didn't get to play with it. By the time Ianto arrived with it, it was all over.'

Jack muttered something.

'Sorry?' asked Owen.

Jack shrugged. 'I said... everyone's probably quite pleased you didn't get to play with it.'

Owen sniffed and nodded. He sighed. 'Everyone's probably quite right about that.'

'You put it away again, right?'

'Of course.'

'In the Armoury?'

'Yes, Jack.'

'Did you put it away or did Ianto put it away?'

'He put it away,' said Owen. 'Give me some credit.'

'Sorry,' said Jack.

There was another long silence.

'Anything else?' asked Jack.

'Davey Morgan's going to be staying in secure accommodation until his house is repaired,' said Toshiko. 'I've moved funds out of the Institute's accounts to cover the work he needs.'

Jack raised his eyebrows. 'We don't do that kind of thing,' he said.

'We do today,' said Toshiko flatly. There was a firmness in her tone that Jack decided he was too tired to take issue with.

'How's James?' he asked instead.

'I've got him sedated,' said Owen. 'I opened up one of the care rooms downstairs so he could be comfortable.'

'He looks awful,' said Gwen quietly.

'Will he be OK?' Jack asked.

'I think so,' Owen replied. 'He's been battered about, but I think so.'

'Shouldn't he be moved to…' Gwen fell silent.

'To a what?' Owen asked. 'A proper hospital?'

'That's not what I meant,' she said.

'I know what you meant,' said Owen. 'I am actually good at what I do, you know?'

'Owen—' she began.

'No arguing tonight, please,' said Jack, holding up a hand.

'Look,' said Owen. 'There are two reasons James is better off here. One, we've got better kit and technical medical support than any hospital I know of. Two… well, he's not actually hurt that badly.'

The other three looked at him. Owen shrugged. 'I know, he's a mess. And you told me what he went through. But it's basically just bruising and cuts and stuff. The blow to the head and shoulder were the worst of it, and even they were comparatively minor. Our beloved Captain Analogy was bloody, bloody lucky.'

'Are you sure?' asked Gwen.

'I scanned him thoroughly,' said Owen. 'Some muscle tearing and a slight crack to the cheek bone, but no head trauma to speak of. At any rate, not the sort of head trauma you'd expect after being punched out by a mad killer robot.'

'Just keep him under observation,' said Jack. He rose to his feet. 'Just now, Owen said it was all over. It isn't.'

He looked at them. Their faces were solemn, waiting for him to continue. His head bowed slightly, thoughtfully. 'When I realised what we were up against in Cathays,' said Jack, 'there was one clear upside to it all, as far as I could see. God knows, a Serial G is a big deal. As we chased around after it, I remember thinking, "At least this is it. At least we know what the warning was all about now."'

Jack took the black tile out of his trouser pocket and held it up. It was still flashing.

'If this doohickey is supposed to alert us to an approaching threat, or to an imminent war, the Serial G wasn't it.'

Jack chuckled humourlessly to himself. He tossed the tile down onto the conference table. 'I was so sure. When I saw that heap of junk stomping around, I was so damn sure.'

He looked around at them again. 'So, we're left wondering… What is it? What is it *really*? Was it, maybe that strange grey thing that managed to be both invisible *and* kill a Serial G in the same afternoon?'

'It didn't seem like a threat,' Toshiko said. 'It was on our side.'

'We don't know that,' said Jack. 'All we know is that it wasn't on the Serial G's side. That's not the same thing at all.'

Gwen got up. 'I'm going to look around Cosley Hall.'

'We've been through this, Gwen,' Jack said. 'There's no point.'

'I think there's a point,' Gwen replied.

'I've done it. I've been there,' said Jack. 'There are no clues.'

'That secret doohickey was doing nothing for years,' said Gwen, pointing at the tile on the table. 'Now look at it. What makes you so sure something hasn't suddenly changed at this Hall place too?'

Jack hesitated.

'Just because there was nothing to find last time you were there, doesn't mean there's nothing to find now. That's logic, see?' she said.

'She has a point,' said Toshiko.

'She's not going to Cosley Hall,' said Jack.

'Why not?'

'Because it's ten thirty at night and the place will be closed. She can go in the morning.'

Gwen stood for a second longer and then sat back down. 'That,' she admitted, 'is also logic.'

A bridge, a river, a palace. Shades whispering along the tops of the high walls.

Below the old, fossil bridge, the boiling river torrent thunders along its deep, stone-cut channel. The river is a mile wide. The sides of the stone channel have been polished like glass by the action of the river, year after year. Violet moss, soft as velvet, fringes the channel and coats the underside of the bridge.

Starlight glows on the silver-green bricks of the high walls and towers. The palace seems as insubstantial as smoke, or like a translucent husk of brittle, scaled skin sloughed off by some vanished reptile. Pinpricks of fire stipple the fur-black expanse of the sky.

It's cold. The air is clear and hard as crystal.

The shades are restless. They murmur and scratch, making soft, dry noises like a breeze stirring through desiccated leaves.

They see him on the bridge. He has passed through the gate, along the causeway, and onto the ancient bridge approach. The night wind stirs the old ribbons and garlands hung from the bridge's arches.

He doesn't want to run, although he knows he must, as much as he knows that it is ultimately pointless. The palace is a gravity well, its pull too great for him to resist. Nothing ever escapes from its orbit.

One foot, then another. His pace picks up. He's running, as he always knew he had to. He smells the air, the musky scent of the dried flowers in the old garlands. He hears the echo of his own footsteps along the wide span of the bridge.

The clear note of a siren sounds from somewhere far behind. The shades on the high walls begin to move, scuttling and scratching. It takes them no time at all to close the distance. They are fast, like birds whirling in a flock, whipping darting shapes.

Still running, he looks over his shoulder. They have reached the bridge. They are on the bridge. They are rushing towards him.

One leaps—

***

James opened his eyes.

'What the hell was that, then?' Gwen asked.

James had some trouble identifying where he was. It wasn't his bedroom, or his flat. It was a small room, with a single bed. Two lamps, set to a low level, provided a modest night-light glow. A bank of functional, clinical machines, flickering with a few display lights, filled the wall behind the bedhead.

Gwen was sitting on a chair beside him.

One of the care rooms, that was it. One of the Hub's care rooms that they only used occasionally, for overnight guests or long-term invalids. Tosh had been in one for a week after Operation Goldenrod.

Which was he, he wondered, guest or invalid?

He moved, and the pains in his shoulder and face decided him.

'Take it easy,' Gwen said. 'Did you dream again?'

'Mmm,' he said. His mouth was dry.

'Another dream for the man who doesn't dream?'

He cleared his throat. 'How about,' he swallowed, 'a drink? The man who doesn't dream has a mouth that's not been swept.'

Gwen handed him a beaker.

'Better,' he said.

'Remember anything about this dream, then?' she asked, placing the beaker back on the night stand.

He breathed deeply. 'Um… a bridge,' he said finally. 'Over a river.'

'Where was it?'

'In my dream.'

'Ha ha. I mean, was it a real bridge or what?'

'I think it was a real bridge. Yes, I'm sure it…' his voice tailed off and he shook his head slightly. 'No, it can't have been. It was too old and too ridiculously long to have been a real bridge.'

'Anything else?'

'I was being chased, I think.'

'By what?'

'The usual nightmare monsters that you can't quite see.'

'And how would you know,' she asked, 'if you never dream?'

'I've heard people talk about dreams often enough,' James said. He looked up at her.

'What time is it?' he asked.

'Two o'clock in the morning.'

197

'You should be in bed. You need sleep.'

'I was dozing. I wanted to stay here.'

'That's nice. You didn't have to.'

'Maybe I did.'

'Is everything all right?'

'Oh, yeah,' she replied. 'As all right as everything usually is in Torchwood. One thing, though.'

'What?'

'I was wondering if you could do me a favour?'

'What would that be?' he asked.

'In future, could you try not to get yourself half-killed by giant robots at all? It's not good for my nerves.'

'OK,' he smiled. 'Come here.'

He hugged her, and she curled up beside him on the edge of the narrow bed.

They lay there for a while. At last, once he'd thought about it long enough, he said, 'Gwen?'

But she'd fallen asleep.

Shiznay padded downstairs in the dark, her dressing gown pulled around her. She was half-asleep, but the noise was keeping her awake. Someone had left the kitchen vents on again.

The others were asleep in the flat over the restaurant, and the restaurant itself was dark: a forest of chair legs upturned on tables, lit by the amber streetlamp outside the front windows.

It was cold too. There was a draught.

Shiznay plodded into the kitchen. The cool air contained a mix of cooked spices, onions and cleaning fluid. In the twilight, the stainless-steel counters were bare and gleaming. Silhouette pans hung from ceiling rails.

The extractor vents were purring, a low-level chatter occasionally embellished by a clacking whirr.

She walked across the kitchen, found the cut-out switch by touch alone, and flipped it down. The vents went quiet with a dying murmur. She slid the mesh hatches shut.

That draught again, against her face.

Shiznay looked around. She saw that the backdoor was slightly open.

Tutting, she went over and bolted it. Her father would be furious with whoever had closed up. Leaving the fans on was one thing, but not locking up properly? Anyone could get in and—

Shiznay froze. Her spine crawled. Standing in that darkened kitchen, all alone, and imagining the consequences of an unlocked door, she'd just managed to completely creep herself out. She smiled to herself ruefully and turned to go.

Something made a tiny noise.

She froze again, and her spine crawled for real.

It had been just a tiny noise, a mouse noise. She listened for it, willing it to come again, hearing nothing but the bump of her own pulse in her ears.

Nothing. No, not nothing. A noise again. *There.*

As silently as she could, she took down the heaviest pan she could find and held it like a tennis racket. She thought about the rack of catering knives on the far wall, but it was too far away, and besides, scared or not, she didn't fancy stabbing anyone. Not even burglar-rapist-escaped looney.

Smacking him over the head, on the other hand, was something she thought she might adequately manage.

She listened for the noise to come again. When it did, she realised it was coming from behind her, from the walk-in pantry. The door to the pantry was open a little way too.

Shiznay wondered if she should call out. She was pretty sure that, by the time anyone woke up and got down stairs, she'd have had to deal with things alone anyway.

Hefting up the pan for a good first service, she crept towards the pantry door. She placed her hand on the handle. *One, two…*

She swung the door open. At first, she could see nothing. It was impenetrably dark, a shadowy cave filled with sacks of vegetables and stacks of cans in catering packs.

Then she saw the figure, gasped, and swung her improvised weapon up. She hesitated.

'Oh my goodness…' she whispered.

Mr Dine was sitting on the floor, his back against the wall. What remained of his clothes were ragged and shredded. His head leaned forward limply, his hands draped at his sides.

'What are you doing here? What are you doing in here?' she hissed, stepping forward.

He stirred, and slowly turned his head up to regard her.

'How did you get in? You shouldn't be here! You really shouldn't be here!'

'You… said…' he whispered.

'What?'

It was hard to hear him, his voice was so distant. Was he drunk? Out of his head? Had he been mugged, or something? Shiznay lowered the pan.

'You… said…' he repeated.

'What do you mean?'

'You said, "Come back when you want,"' Mr Dine whispered.

'Well, I…' Shiznay paused. She thought hard. 'Look, I didn't mean this. I didn't mean… My father would go off on one if he knew you'd broken in and…' She crouched down next to him. 'Mr Dine?'

He didn't reply.

'Are you all right?'

He opened his eyes and nodded at the pan she was holding. 'What is that for?'

'Cracking you over the head. You don't just go around breaking into places.' Shiznay stopped and laughed suddenly. Given his prior form, that was exactly the kind of peculiar thing Mr Dine would do.

'Are you all right?' she asked again. 'What happened to you?'

'I crashed,' he said, soporifically.

'You said that before. Is that… is that like a drug thing?'

'No, no.'

'What happened to your clothes? Were you roughed up?'

'I suppose you could say that.'

'I should call the police,' she said.

'No.'

'Did you see who did it?'

'Shiznay—'

'The police will help you. You can't stay here.' Her mind whirled. If she rang the police, her father would know. He'd see how Mr Dine had broken in. There would be all sorts of trouble.

But she couldn't just turf the man out into the street, not the state he was in, even if she did ring in an anonymous 999.

'I'll have to call the police,' she insisted.

'No. They can't help me. Please do not call them. I just need to rest. To recover.'

She peered at him closer. 'Oh goodness!' she blurted, realising what she

200

was seeing. 'Oh good lord, they stabbed you! They stabbed you, didn't they?'

Despite the half-light, she could distinctly see the dark fluid oozing out of a gash in his ribs. There was a pool of it on the floor.

'It's not from a knife,' he said. 'I received a contact injury. It's healing. Let me take time to heal.'

'You need to go to Casualty. You need stitches at least. That's not just going to heal on its own.'

He suddenly looked at her quite fiercely. His eyes blazed intently. 'Yes, it is,' he said. 'I promise you, it is. I just need somewhere safe to lie and rest. Somewhere safe. I thought you could…'

'You can't stay here,' she said.

He sighed and nodded. He began to move himself, as though intending to get up. 'I understand. I will go.'

'Where?'

'I'll find somewhere.'

She put a hand out and restrained him gently. 'I meant… you can't stay here. In here. My father will be up at six, and there'll be food prep. People will come in here and find you. You can't stay in here.'

'Where, then?'

'Can you move? If I help you, can you move really quietly? Really, really quietly?'

'I think so.'

It took a moment to hoist him up. He was heavy and his skin was hot, almost feverish. Bracing him, she shuffled them out of the pantry and propped him against a counter.

'Stand there, just a second.'

Mr Dine swayed, but remained upright, holding onto the edge of the counter.

Shiznay went back into the pantry, dropped a sheet of old newspaper over the puddle of blood, and heaved two sacks of onions and sack of potatoes over to cover the paper. She picked up the pan, stepped out of the larder and closed the door. Then she hung the pan back up where she'd found it.

'All right,' she whispered, coming back to him. 'Here we go. Really quietly, OK?'

TWENTY-FOUR

He smelled coffee. Not just any coffee. Ianto's coffee.

He woke up.

He felt stiff and sore. His head throbbed. He looked around, but he was alone. At some point in the night, Gwen had gone.

Slowly, gingerly, James sat up. He worked his shoulder slightly, then leaned over and turned up one of the lamps. He saw his watch lying on the cabinet and picked it up. Nearly ten a.m. Quite a sleep.

With care, testing out his aches and pains, he swung his legs around and got out of bed. There was a hospital dressing gown on the back of the door.

'Oh, no!' cried Owen. 'Oooh no, no, no, no, no!'

He leapt up from his work station the moment he saw James shuffling into the main space of the Hub.

'What are you doing?' he asked, reaching James.

'I woke up,' said James.

'Lovely. Go back to bed.'

'I don't want to.'

'Listen, mate, when a doctor – like me – puts a patient – like you – in bed, staying there is part of the deal.'

'I'm OK.'

'We're getting you back into bed,' said Owen. 'That's first. Then I'll run a bunch of standard tests. Then, and only then, will I say if you're OK.'

'Can I have coffee?' James asked. He saw Ianto up by the coffee machine, busy. He waved. Ianto waved back.

'No, you can't,' said Owen, and began to steer James back towards the door.

James could see Jack in his office. The door was closed, and he was on the telephone, deep in conversation.

'What's Jack doing?'

'He's got a bee in his bonnet,' said Owen. 'That whole secret early warning thingy whatsit. He's making some calls.'

'To who?'

'Oh, like he's going to tell me,' snapped Owen.

'But at a guess?'

'The Pentagon, NASA, Project Blue Book, NATO, UNIT, International Rescue, Starfleet, and the Fortress of Solitude,' replied Owen, 'but that's me just speculating wildly.'

'Where's Gwen?' James asked.

'She's gone out with Tosh. She told me to say hi. There was a kiss too, but I'm not prepared to pass that on.'

'Where's she gone out to?'

Colonel Joseph Peignton Cosley was as forbidding as his home. Fifty-ish, jowelly, with a Kitchener moustache that suited his choice of army attire, he glared at Gwen, his hand on the pommel of his cavalry sabre, as if expecting her to kick off some trouble any minute.

'That's him in 1890,' said Toshiko, reading off the plaque.

Gwen folded her arms and continued to stare at the large, gilt-framed painting.

'He looks a bit of a…'

'A what?' asked Toshiko.

'Twat,' Gwen said. 'Not the kind of bloke you expect to know secret things about the fate of the world. More like the sort of bloke who'd know how to horsewhip his manservant or shove a bayonet into some African person.'

'"Horsewhip his manservant"?' asked Toshiko.

Gwen glanced at her. 'I know. Even as I said it, I knew it was going to sound dodgy.'

'At least Owen isn't here,' said Toshiko. 'Otherwise he'd be adding that to his little book of squalid euphemisms.'

The long, panelled hallway was gloomy and quiet. Other dingy paintings hung on the walls above items of stately, roped-off furniture. Heavy morning drizzle beat against the grand windows. From a nearby room, they could just make out the sound of a Cadw guide leading a tour.

Toshiko was leafing through the guidebook she'd bought. She'd opted for the fat, expensive guide instead of the thin illustrated pamphlet.

'Well,' she said, 'whatever he looks like, he's the man. Maybe he had hidden depths? Maybe the artist didn't do him justice?'

'Maybe he didn't know what it was he had either, which was why he gave it to Torchwood?'

They walked on. Toshiko nodded to a smaller painting.

'That's Mrs Colonel.'

'Oh!' said Gwen. 'Poor love. Do you think they'd have got a smile out of her if her husband hadn't spent so much time horsewhipping his manservant?'

Toshiko snorted.

'English, was he?' asked Gwen.

'Of course,' said Toshiko. 'His family had owned land up here for several generations. Old money, gentry. It seems he invested wisely in coal and shipping, army career not withstanding. Hang on...' she leafed through the guide. 'Yeah, an older house stood on this site. He had it demolished in 1868 to build this place in all its Victorian melodrama.'

'That's like an architectural style, is it?'

'Absolutely.'

Cosley Hall lay some fifteen minutes west of the city in parkland beyond Wenvoe. They had arrived just after nine thirty, and driven in through the imposing gates and up the long, planned drive to a house hiding beyond a screen of trees. Prior to her purchase of the guidebook, Toshiko had supplied an improvised guide commentary. The gates, she announced had been 'specially imported from the Carpathians' and the outbuildings to the west of the main house had been 'a stabling block for the Cosley family's pedigree pack of killer dachshunds'. The house and grounds were now in the care of Cadw, having been left to the Nation by the last of the Cosley line, who had died in 1957 of a 'surfeit of toff'.

'Don't make me laugh, I'm not in a laughing mood,' said Gwen, laughing as she got out of the car.

Much funnier was the fact that, once it had been purchased, the guidebook as good as corroborated Toshiko's invention. The gates might not have actually been Carpathian, and the dachsunds might actually have been beagles, but other than that she'd been close to the truth. The last of the Cosley line, William Peignton Cosley, had left the hall in a bequest to the Crown, following his death from a stroke in 1964.

Entry to the house and grounds was free, though a donation was appreciated. They'd asked the Cadw guide on the till – a young, blonde, studenty girl with a stud in her nose – if there were any papers or written records from the Colonel's era. The girl said she didn't know of any on display or available for inspection. There were quite a few books in the library, but most of them dated from the 1920s and 1930s, when the last Cosley, William, had built up a collection of geological works.

Gwen and Toshiko wandered around the hall for an hour or two. Whenever they were out of sight of other visitors, or the guides and the tour parties, Gwen surreptitiously took a portable scanner out of her coat pocket and swept it around, to zero effect.

They stopped eventually in the dining room, and gazed at a dinner table set with crystal and silver for forty guests who would never actually arrive. The voice of a guide drifted in from down the corridor behind them. A door closed somewhere.

'I feel a bit of a plank, actually,' said Gwen. 'Jack said this would be a bust and he was right. Of course. I don't know what I thought we could do here. Imagine the skill with which he'll have gone over the place already.'

'It was worth a try,' said Toshiko. 'Your logic was spotless.'

They traced their way back out of the baronial Victorian dwelling, pausing one last time in front of Colonel Joseph Peignton Cosley.

Gwen fixed the portrait right in the eyes. 'What did you know? What were you told? Where did it come from? Who gave it to you? What the bugger did you think it was?'

'Why are you talking to a painting?' Toshiko smiled.

'God knows. Made me feel better. Come on.'

They were walking back through the reception area, past the postcards, and the books on kings and queens, and the novelty pencil sharpeners, when the studenty blonde girl with the nose stud called out to them from the till.

'Oh, there you are,' she said, 'I thought you'd already gone. I asked Mr Beavan about you, about the questions you were asking, I mean. Hang on a jot.'

The girl picked up a walkie-talkie. 'Mr Beavan? Yeah, no, they're still here. In reception. OK, lovely.'

She put the walkie-talkie down again. 'He'll just be along,' she said.

Mr Beavan appeared about five minutes later. He was a small, neat, grey-haired man with pinched cheeks and large bags under his eyes that gave him a sort of treeshrew-like appearance. He was wearing a Cadw guide pullover.

He was, he said, head of staff at Cosley Hall, and had been since 1987. He knew a thing or two about the place.

'Ellie tells me you were asking about the family records. Papers, diaries, that sort of thing, was it?'

'Especially concerning the Colonel,' Toshiko replied.

'Interested in old Joe are you? He was quite a fellow. India, the Far East, South Africa. He was under Baden-Powell for the Relief of Mafeking.'

'We'd heard rumours,' said Gwen.

'What can you tell us about him?' Toshiko put in swiftly.

'Very much a principled man,' Mr Beavan said, seriously. 'Upright and convinced of his role as a defender of the realm and a protector of the people. He was astonishingly generous to the local community and the people who worked on his estate lands. I think he rather fancied himself as a local lord, ruling his demesne. Charmingly old-fashioned notion of the good old feudal system. Rose-tinted specs, I think, as was often the case in the late-Victorian age. Romantic dreams of a classical Britain that had never actually existed. He was very fond of Pre-Raphaelite paintings, funnily enough. Arthurian subjects.'

'That's interesting,' Gwen lied.

'Old Joe wasn't the first in his family to feel that way,' said Mr Beavan, warming to his theme. 'His father and his grandfather both thought of themselves as border princes. As in the old days, along the Welsh Marches. Noble soldiers guarding the threshold between adjoining lands. The Colonel was very much taken with that notion.'

'A bloke like him, then, usually leaves journals and diaries, doesn't he?' asked Gwen.

'Well, we know a huge amount about his life and career. British Army records are fairly thorough. And his family business interests are well documented. Chamber of Commerce, the municipal archives.'

'But personal stuff?'

'Well, that's why I pricked up my ears when I heard you'd been asking. There always had been suggestions that Colonel Joe kept quite extensive diaries, throughout his life, but we'd never found them. Then, quite by chance, about six years ago, one of the team turned up a bill of service in an old ledger of accounts, dated 1904. The bill related to a haulier, who had been employed to transport, um, 'sundry personal items' I think it said, all the way over to Long Marsh, just outside Manchester. It was very exciting.'

Gwen and Toshiko glanced at one another. 'I can imagine,' said Gwen delicately.

Mr Beavan smiled. 'Ah, well, you see, the Colonel died in 1904. Cosley Hall was taken on by his son Ernest, and his widow, Francie, upped sticks and moved away. She went to live out her last remaining years with her own family, the Cassons, who owned Long Marsh. A little research suggests that she took many of her late husband's most personal and private effects with her. Journals, for example.'

'So,' said Gwen, 'Colonel Cosley's stuff is at this Long Marsh place, then?'

'Sadly, no,' said Mr Beavan with another smile. 'I wish it was that simple. If it was, I'd have popped over there myself long since to take a look. No, Long Marsh was shut up in about 1930. The Cassons lost a fortune, in the shipbuilding trade, I think it was. The family was ruined, anyway. Long Marsh swiftly fell into decay, got pulled down, and I believe there's a cinema there now. Most of their possessions were sold against debt, but the contents of the library, and all the family papers, were gifted to Manchester Museum, where they remain to this day.'

'On display?' asked Toshiko.

'No, no. Not at all. Uncatalogued in museum storage. I've known students and a couple of would-be biographers get a licence to trawl the catacombs. Thankless task. But the last one who did was Brian Brady, who's working on a full biography. He pops in quite often, though he lives up in Manchester somewhere himself. He told me he'd found quite a lot of fascinating material. If you'd like his number...'

'Oh well,' said Toshiko, as they crunched back across the gravel to the SUV. 'it was worth a try.'

Gwen pulled her phone and dialled the number Mr Beavan had given her.

'You're not serious?' asked Toshiko.

'Hang on,' said Gwen, holding up her hand. She shook her head and lowered the phone. 'No, I just got an answerphone.'

They got into the SUV. 'You'd seriously go all the way to Manchester after some old diaries?' asked Toshiko.

'No,' said Gwen. 'That would be daft. I just wish it wasn't the only lead we had. I hate going back to Jack empty-handed, especially when he's told me I'll be coming back empty-handed.'

Toshiko started the engine. 'You do know that proving Jack wrong is not the primary objective of our work?'

'Bugger. Isn't it?' said Gwen.

James looked up as Owen walked back into the care room.

'Well? Am I ever going to play the violin again?'

'Like Maxim frigging Vengerov, mate,' said Owen. 'Your unqualified diagnosis that you were OK was pretty much spot on. I'm not picking up anything this morning that gives me cause for concern.'

'So I can get dressed and leave this room?'

'Yup. Provided you take it easy. Really easy.'

'OK.'

Owen turned to leave.

'Hey,' said James.

'What?'

'How thorough are those tests?'

'What do you mean?' Owen frowned.

'How thorough are the tests you ran on me? On anyone in this situation?'

'Scale of one to ten?'

'Yeah.'

'Six, seven,' said Owen with a shrug. 'I mean it's a pretty good, cover-the-bases work-up, bloods and CAT, looking at the obvious. A thorough assessment.'

'What would it pick up?'

'What do you want it to pick up?' Owen asked. He looked at James quizzically. 'What is this? You're freaking me out.'

James opened his mouth to reply then laughed and closed it again. He looked down at the floor, then back up at Owen.

'What?' asked Owen, in half-jokey frustration, shaking his hands in the air.

James pursed his lips. 'Could you... could you run some more tests on me? More critical ones? More thorough ones?'

'How much more thorough?' asked Owen.

'Scale of one to ten?'

Owen nodded.

'What do you think?' James asked.

Owen raised his eyebrows and whistled. 'Shit. Why?'

James let out a long breath before replying, as if he was trying to make sure he was doing the right thing.

'I think…' he began. 'Christ, I can't believe it's you I'm confiding in.'

'Doctor-patient privilege,' said Owen.

'Yeah. Even so.'

Owen pursed his lips and pointed a finger in the direction of the door. 'You want me to get Jack, then?'

'No.' James stood up. He paced for a moment. Then he sat down on the chair again. 'No, not Jack. Not yet. I need you to help me with this, Owen. If it all comes up clear, Jack need never know. Nor Gwen. Just be our secret. You will then be permitted, from time to time, to take the piss out of me for being an idiot, and no one will ever know why.'

Owen frowned. He closed the room door, picked up another chair from the corner and carried it across to face James. 'OK. You're talking some fairly bonkers talk now. What's going on?'

'I'm scared,' said James.

'Of what?' Owen asked him.

'Myself,' he said.

In the middle of the afternoon, after the lunchtime rush (though it wasn't much of a rush at the Mughal Dynasty buffet lunch), Shiznay managed to sneak away as soon as she'd cleared the last of the dishes. People were busy elsewhere, with other things. Her mother had gone shopping to the garment market. Her father, as was his custom, was taking a slow hour to read the day's paper before gearing up for the evening shift. He did this sitting alone in the restaurant with the radio on.

Shiznay snuck upstairs. She could hear the little transistor set buzzing away.

The Mughal Dynasty had once been two large Edwardian semis, and all the rooms in the upper floors retained most of their original fixtures and fittings, including door handles and locks. Every door had a mortise lock. Her brother Kamil's arguments with his mother over issues of privacy had led to him making regular use of his key. It was never a surprise to find Kamil's door locked, especially when he was away.

Her brother was away for the whole weekend. He'd left the previous evening to visit his friends in Birmingham.

Her brother didn't know Shiznay had discovered, about a year before, a spare key that fitted his room.

Checking there was absolutely no one around, Shiznay unlocked the door and went in.

Pale afternoon light slanted in through half-drawn curtains. Kamil's room was a mess as usual, a jumble of clothes and CDs and PlayStation games. There were some pin-up pictures of pneumatic women stuck on the wall. Naked pneumatic women, in general, one of the main reasons Kamil denied his mother access.

Mr Dine lay where she had put him, sprawled across Kamil's unmade bed. She'd wash the sheets later. Kamil probably wouldn't notice anyway.

Mr Dine stirred and looked up at her. He looked just as bad as he had done the previous night, though at least his stab wound seemed to have stopped leaking.

'It's all right,' she whispered. 'I just came to check on you. I brought you some stuff.'

She held up the bottle of mineral water she'd taken from the cooler downstairs, some fresh fruit and a tub of ice cream.

TWENTY-FIVE

There was a stiff breeze coming in off the Bay, but the rain had cleared. The sun had come out, weak and watery, but a sun nonetheless, and the sky was big and full of voluminous white clouds.

It was just the middle of the afternoon, with an hour or two of daylight left. The Friday-night traffic had started already, murmuring in the Cardiff streets behind him.

Dressed, showered and shaved, James walked down to the end of the Pierhead boardwalks and stood at the rail, looking out towards the Norwegian Church and the chemical works beyond the Queen Alexandra Dock. A water taxi chugged by, leaving a tail of foam behind it.

He'd spent a long time shaving and showering in the Hub's bathroom, a long time staring at himself in the mirror. Both of his eyes had remained resolutely brown.

'Taking the air?'

James looked around. Owen was approaching along the empty quayside. He had his coat on, his hands stuffed in his pockets.

'Clearing my head,' James replied.

'Thought I'd come and find you. I finished processing the tests.'

'That was fast.'

'I got the impression you didn't want me to hang around.'

'Come on then. How long have I got, Doctor?'

Owen leant his back against the railing. 'Well, to answer your first concern, you're not sick. Not even a little bit. Nothing untoward except for the bumps and bruises you've collected this week.'

'Nothing at all? Not even a suggestion?'

'You're in amazingly rude health, mate. I've run a sweep for just about every clinical condition I can think of: disease, infection, degenerative syndromes, you name it. You're a fine, healthy human being. Healthier than me, I shouldn't wonder.'

'Yeah? No shadows on my head CT? No lurking enigmas in my major organs?'

'Nothing at all.'

James looked out at the sea. 'OK, then.'

'To address your second concern,' said Owen, 'I can't find anything… out of place either. No foreign objects. No implants. No buried tech that's got in under your skin. I'm as sure as it's possible to be that you haven't in any way been… what shall we say? Infiltrated? Interfered with? Corrupted?'

'You make it sound dumb that I asked. Isn't that a very real danger in our line of work?'

Owen shrugged. 'I suppose. But don't forget the Hub's set up to monitor that kind of thing and sound all the bells and whistles if it finds something.'

'It doesn't matter how clever we are,' said James. 'We're not going to recognise everything.'

'Back to that, are we?' Owen pouted. 'Look, I did the work. Hand on heart, you're clean. There's nothing that would explain why you think you jumped over a seven-foot wall or tossed a supermarket trolley the length of a checkout.'

He glanced at James slightly warily. 'Well,' he added.

'What?'

'You're clean physically. And the cognitive tests were thorough, but I can't dismiss all psychological possibilities.'

'It's in my head, you mean?'

Owen nodded. 'Lot of stress involved in what we do. Hell of a lot of stress this week. Every single thing you've told me about happened bang in the middle of a high-stress situation. The Serial G right on top of you. That idiot you chased the length of Pontcanna. The mind does things under stress, James. Afterwards, you might think, "What the hell was that?" But it wasn't anything at all. Stress pisses about with perception, and with memory. And don't forget the Amok subjected us to severe mental… buggeration. That on its own left us tired and vulnerable to all kinds of lapses and mind tricks.'

'So it's just me, then?'

Owen laughed. 'You'll be fine. Bit of rest, weekend off, glass of wine, the love of a good woman.'

'Speaking of which,' he added, and strolled off, passing Gwen coming the other way.

'Thanks, Owen,' James called.

Owen waved a dismissive hand as he walked away.

'Thanks for what?' Gwen asked, looking over her shoulder at Owen's receding figure.

'Just keeping an eye on me,' said James. 'He's all right, really.'

She turned and looked up into his face, as if studying it.

'What?' he asked her.

'Just looking for a bit without a bruise on to aim a kiss at.'

He pointed to his mouth.

'That'll do,' she said.

They walked along the Quay, arm in arm.

'So Jack said to take an early mark, provided we left our phones on,' Gwen said.

'POETS?'

'Indeed. What do you want to do?'

James shook his head. 'Not much. Go home, relax. Maybe get a film.'

'OK.'

They walked on a little further.

'I thought I'd ring Rhys,' she said.

'Oh?'

'I thought I might arrange to meet him. Tomorrow, maybe, or Sunday. Have that talk.'

'The big one?'

'Yep, the big one. I've left it long enough. Is that all right?'

'It's all right with me,' he said.

Owen walked back into the Hub and sat down at his work station. Toshiko called out a goodbye as she headed off.

Jack came out of his office and walked down the concrete steps to Owen's level.

'What d'you tell him?' Jack asked.

Owen looked around, hard-faced. 'I told him the truth.'

'That all?'

'I didn't tell him that you knew. Or that you had already suspected something yourself. He'd have thought I'd squealed on him, and he'd never have trusted me again.'

Jack sat down on Toshiko's wheelie stool and rolled himself backwards and forwards looking at Owen. 'He'd have forgiven you,' Jack said. 'He'd have soon realised that you can't get away with conducting the raft of tests you did today without me noticing the medical bay was running overtime.'

Owen huffed.

'Come on, Owen, you should have brought it to me anyway,' said Jack. 'It's a security issue.'

'No, it was a favour for a mate. He was scared. I was able to put his mind at rest. There's nothing wrong with him. He's not sick, he's not compromised, and he's not a bloody shape-shifting alien invader.'

Jack stood up. 'It's a security issue whichever way you want to dress it up. There's something going on. It may be just stress, or something psychological like you say. Or it may be something different. Something that we can't read or taste or scan for.'

'We're talking about James,' said Owen.

'We are.'

'Our own Captain Analogy.'

'Yeah. And that's why I'm taking it End of the World seriously.'

Owen rapped his fingers on the edge of his station. 'Just say,' he said, 'just say there is something up with him. Something bad. Should we be letting him go home with Gwen like that?'

'Gwen'll be fine.'

'I thought you said this was a security issue?'

'Gwen's a big girl,' said Jack. 'If something comes up, she'll let us know.'

Friday night was typically busy from six until eight thirty. Then the lull came, like the eye of a storm, before the pubs turned out later.

As soon as things quietened down, Shiznay took a break, and told Dilip, the cover waiter, she'd be upstairs for five minutes.

'Call me if my father needs me,' she said. Her father was busy in the kitchen, supervising the phone orders and yelling at the moped drivers.

She went upstairs with the foil takeout punnets of salad, rice and lamb pasanda, and a bottle of lager.

Her mother and her aunts were in the living room, chatting loudly and watching the television. They were laughing at the antics of a quiz show host.

She scurried down to Kamil's room, and let herself in.

Mr Dine lay on the bed, apparently exactly where she'd left him. She put the food and the beer bottle down and turned to see if she could wake him.

Another man was standing in front of the window, beside the wardrobe. She hadn't seen him when she had first entered the room. He was so deep in the shadows he seemed to be made out of them.

At the sight of him, she felt terror wash through her, an awful, vicing effervescence of fear and shock. She made a noise in her throat and backed away sharply, knocking into Kamil's hi-fi stand.

The man in the shadows stepped towards her swiftly, and reached out his hand, as if to touch her face or choke her. His expression was utterly blank. There was no rage, or anger, or malice in it, no smirk of lust, or grin of cruelty.

Before he could touch her, Mr Dine stopped him. He was suddenly just standing there, between the two of them, one hand raised to block the other man's extending grasp.

'No,' he said.

The intruder blinked. He was wearing what seemed to be a plain grey T-shirt and dark jeans. He was lean, and of a similar height and build to Mr Dine. His hair was dark and close-cropped.

Shiznay's eyes were very wide. Her voice seemed to have vanished entirely.

The intruder tried to move his hand. Mr Dine held it tightly and refused to allow it to stray.

'No,' he repeated.

They stared at each other for a moment, then Mr Dine let go. The intruder withdrew his hand and took a step backwards.

Mr Dine turned and looked at Shiznay. She shook.

'W-who is… who is…?'

Mr Dine looked into her eyes. Immediately, she felt a little better. He raised a slender finger and put it to his lips. 'Shiznay, go down stairs. Return to work. Do not be afraid. You will not remember this.' His voice was level and heavy.

She nodded, and went out, shutting and locking the door to Kamil's room behind her.

She took a few steps down the corridor, and then stopped, frowning. She heard her mother and her aunts laughing raucously.

'Shiznay?'

She shook herself. Her father was calling to her up the stairs.

'Shiznay!'

'Yes, Father?'

'What are you doing up there, girl?'

'I don't know,' she said.

'What?'

'I said… I'm just coming, Father.'

In the dark, cluttered bedroom, in the amber glow of the street-lamps shining in through the rumpled curtain, Mr Dine turned back to face the intruder. A car went by outside, and white stripes travelled across the ceiling's shadows like the luminous, sweeping hands of a clock.

'Why have you come?' asked Mr Dine.

'Necessity,' said the intruder.

'There is no necessity.'

'Your opinion is noted. It does not matter. I have been sent.'

'By order?'

'By the highest order.'

Mr Dine paused. 'When were you inserted?'

'At nightfall.'

'Am I to consider myself relieved?'

The intruder shook his head. 'Supported. Unless you have cause to be relieved. Do you wish to stand down? You have sustained damage.'

Mr Dine looked down at his ribs. The deep wound had become an ugly weal of purple bruising, smeared with black residue. 'It is healing. I have had worse. You have had worse.'

The intruder nodded.

'In war, yes. Supported by my kin. Not alone. Not in the prosecution of such a singular duty.'

'This is my duty still,' said Mr Dine. 'It was given to me, the highest honour, and I will discharge it.'

'That is to be assessed,' said the intruder. 'Are you able to invest?'

'Of course.'

'Then do so,' said Mr Lowe.

'Pause it, I really need to wee.'

'No, no,' said James, 'the next bit is really funny.'

'That's the problem,' said Gwen, getting up off the sofa. 'I'm laughing so bloody hard, I'm going to wet myself. Pause it.'

James reached for the remote. The image on the TV froze. She put the half-empty bowl of kettle chips on the side and went out.

James sat back, and took a sip of his wine. The warm fuzz of alcohol was taking the throb out of his cheek and shoulder. He wondered if he should have asked Owen if it was all right to drink. He thought there was very little chance of Owen ever saying it wasn't all right to drink.

'I can't believe I've never seen this before,' Gwen called from the loo.

'I can't believe you've never seen this before either. It's one of my favourite movies. This, *Tootsie, Ferris Bueller* and *Mad Max II*.'

'*Mad Max?*' she called.

'*Mad Max II*,' he corrected.

'Was that *Beyond Thunderdome*?'

'It was before *Thunderdome*. Are you actually sitting on the loo with the door open talking to me?'

'Sorry.'

James got up and stretched. Outside, youthful voices were singing ebulliently on their way between pubs. It was ten thirty. He went to the window, and pulled back the curtain, peering out. Two boys were racing down the centre of the road, holding traffic cones on their heads like witches' hats. Five others ran along after them, laughing. He was about to drop the curtain back and turn away when he saw the men. Two men, loitering in the shadows by the phone box. What were they up to?

Just standing. They seemed to be looking up at him, at his flat. Two men standing in the shadows—

No, they *were* shadows. A minicab spurted by, and its headlights washed the roadside. The 'two men' turned into the flat, sidelong shadows they were, and then vanished. Once the cab had gone, the men were back, staring up, but now James knew they were just dark shapes created by the hedge and the railings.

He laughed at himself, and turned away.

Gwen came back in and bounced over the sofa back into her seat. 'Come on,' she said, patting the seat cushion beside her. 'This is such a laugh. I can't believe Sally Field and Glenn Robbins made a film together and I didn't know about it. When was it made?'

'1988,' said James, moving back to join her. 'Actually, I only went to see it originally because of my enduring love for Glenn Robbins in *Eternity Base*.'

'Which one was she in that?'

He looked at her in horror. Her face was straight for a moment.

She burst out laughing. 'I do know! I'm kidding!'

'Good. I thought we were about to have our first domestic then.'

'She was the cyborg, wasn't she?'

He glared at her and then began to tickle her mercilessly. She squealed and hit him with a cushion.

'Don't make me get the first season out and force you to watch it!'

'Stop it! Stop it! Commander Cully! Commander Helen Cully! Faynights!'

'What now?' he stopped with the tickling.

'Faynights,' she said, lowering her cushion. She was still smiling, but there was a slightly sad look in her eyes. 'Doesn't matter.'

'You OK?'

'Yeah. Anything left in that bottle?'

'Seeing as you insisted on buying a litre of Chardonnay, yes.'

'Top me up,' she said, holding out her glass and snuggling against him.

James obliged. She reached for the remote. It had slipped down between the seat cushions.

'What's this called again?' she asked.

'*Sisters in Law*,' he said. 'Because they're sisters—'

'—and they're both lawyers, right, right. Can I wind it back a bit, because I was laughing so much at the thing with the dog, I thought crisps were going to come flying out of my nose.'

'Give it to me,' he said, reaching to take the remote.

Both their mobiles rang at once. Hers was on the side, his on the dining table beside his keys. They split off the sofa and reached them simultaneously, glancing at the displays.

'Jack,' said Gwen.

James nodded. 'You take it.'

Gwen put the phone to her ear. 'Yeah?'

'Gwen? Is James with you?'

'Yeah, what's up?'

'I wanted to call everyone. No need to come in, but I wanted you to know.'

'Know what, Jack?' Gwen asked.

'My little secret doohickey,' said Jack. 'The pattern on it changed about an hour ago. The lights are flashing up a different sequence.'

'What does that mean?' Gwen asked.

'Well, seeing as we have no idea what the original pattern meant, I can safely say I have no clue,' said Jack. 'However, it can't be good. Just a guess, but say a change in Def Con?'

'You sure you don't want us to come in?'

'There's no point yet. I'll call you if anything changes.'

He hung up.

Gwen lowered her phone.

'Fighter Command?' James asked.

'No,' she replied. 'But the tile thing has started flashing something different. He wanted us to know.'

'OK,' James nodded. He dropped back onto the sofa. 'That thing's really got him worried, hasn't it?'

'Aren't you worried?'

'I'm worried Jack is worried. Come on, let's watch the film. You haven't seen the witness selection bit yet.'

'Hang on,' she replied. She pressed a key to search her phone's memory, and then pressed redial.

It rang. Rang. Rang.

'Hello?'

'Oh, hello. Mr Brady? Mr Brian Brady?'

'Yes. Who is this?'

'I'm so sorry to be calling so late,' said Gwen. 'My Name is Gwen Cooper, and I'm calling from… from Cardiff CID. Have you got a sec?'

Five minutes later, she came back and rejoined James on the sofa.

'What was that about?' he asked.

'Nothing.'

'Come on.'

'I've got a lead, haven't I?'

'What, like a dog?'

She cuffed him. 'A proper lead. I'm going out tomorrow. A little jaunt.'

'Why?'

'There's a chance I can help Jack out. Some things I might be able to learn.'

'You going to tell me what?'

'No, it's a secret. I want to impress.'

James nodded.

'By the way, did you ever… did you ever call Rhys?'

She snuggled up against him. 'Yup. I'm seeing him Sunday for lunch.'

'OK. You OK with that?'

She nodded. 'Play the bloody movie.'

She laughed. They both laughed. They howled.

After the movie was over, with News 24 playing mute on the TV, they began to kiss.

Ninety minutes later, with Gwen sleeping in a naked, loose-limbed sprawl that dominated the bed, James got up. He went into the bathroom and splashed water on his face.

In the mirror, he had eyes of different colours, one blue, one brown.

He blinked.

No, both brown. Too much Chardonnay.

He went into the living room and turned the TV off. He picked up the empty crisp bowl and took it into the kitchen, then scooped up the wine bottle and the two glasses. There was a splash left in the bottle.

Oh, what the hell?

He poured it out into his glass, put hers in the sink, and slid the bottle into the recycle bin.

Sipping from his glass, he walked back into the lounge and turned off the uplighters and side lamps. He was wearing her dressing gown. It was soft, and it would be OK so long as Owen never saw him in it.

He peeked out of the window.

The shadows were still there.

They weren't shadows.

James swallowed. He was being silly. He was a little bit drunk and a little bit strung out. They were the shadows he'd seen before.

He knocked back the last of the wine, then looked back out.

Not shadows. Men. No, definitely shadows. Who stood still that long, who stared up that long?

He pulled off Gwen's robe and found his jeans and his shirt. He put on his shoes without socks, and had the good sense to pocket his keys.

He slipped out of the flat, squeezing the door shut after him.

His downstairs neighbours, the Aussies, were in. He could hear them having loud sex as he slunk down the dim staircase. Their mountain bikes cluttered the hall.

He edged past the bikes in the hallway blackness, stepping on menu leaflets and junk mail that all three flat owners had discarded on the floor.

He opened the front door.

It was cold outside. Cold as marble. An October night, almost Halloween.

Yeah, great idea to think of that right at this second, James decided.

He stepped outside. The sky was a silent black bowl pinpricked with dots of fire.

His breath steamed the air. He wished he had brought a coat.

He walked down the path into the street. There was a distant noise of late traffic. The amber smog of Cardiff stained the low sky in front of him with light pollution. Two streets away, someone was yelling and laughing.

He strode directly across the road, tacking between parked cars, their bonnets and roofs just displaying the first etching of frost. He headed towards the phone box.

He headed towards the shadows of the two men. They were still there. Silent, unmoving, even as the night wind licked the trees and all other shadows rocked and nodded.

A step closer now. They still didn't move. It had been his imagination, his stupid imagination. Just shadows. Just shadows.

He closed on them.

'Hello?' he said.

There was no answer. Black and violet shadow patterns stirred as the trees hissed and creaked.

'Who the hell are you? What do you want?'

He stepped forwards. The shadows had gone. He jumped. Where had they—

All in his mind.

He felt decidedly stupid. He turned.

Two grey shapes stood in front of him.

'Jesus!' he said, recoiling. Anger swelled. 'Who the hell are you?' He lunged forward.

The grey shapes vanished.

James spun around. They were behind him again. Just shadows.

'What the hell are you? What do you want with me?'

He lunged again. The shadows melted.

He spun. Behind him again.

'What do you want?'

We are here only to protect the Principal.

'What?'

Your actions and behaviour are contrary to the Principal's best interests.

'I don't understand what you're saying.'

He looked around. A trio of boozed-up lads were ambling down the street on the opposite side of the road.

'All right?' one of them shouted.

'Yeah, yeah, I'm fine,' James called back.

He looked back at the pair of shadows. They'd gone again. He wheeled. They were right behind him. He grabbed at them.

They darted away.

'Shit!' James cried. He grabbed again, without thinking, not where the shadows were, but at where his gut told him they might be.

He realised he had taken hold of something.

A matt-grey forearm, studded with thorns.

James looked up from the arm. The grey thing he was holding onto tried to pull away.

'No, you don't,' James said, tightening his grip.

It struggled, but it couldn't break free.

'What are you?' James demanded, gazing into its grey face. 'Are you what Jack saw? Are you?'

Let go.

'Not a chance.'

Let go.

'Not until you tell me what you are.'

You will not remember this.

'I'll… what?' asked James.

The alarm buzzer woke him at eight. He thumped it off. It was Saturday. Bloody Saturday. He cursed himself for not resetting the alarm the night before. He hoped it hadn't disturbed Gwen.

He woke again at nine, then at ten thirty. Daylight was streaming in through the window. James roused and looked around. He was alone in bed.

He got up, grumpy and bewildered, and expected to find Gwen in the shower. She wasn't there either.

He found the Post-it on the counter, attached to a packet of croissants.

Gone off on my jaunt early. See you later. XX Gwen.

James sighed and headed back to bed.

TWENTY-SIX

She got the eight fifty out of Cardiff Central, Platform 1.

It was a dull morning, with a flat sky that teasingly promised to clear and warm up. Gwen was a little tired, but she soldiered on, invigorated by a sense of purpose.

She got herself a window seat and settled in. Almost three and a half hours to Manchester Piccadilly. She'd bought a coffee and a breakfast roll from a Baguette-away on the concourse, and a paper and some magazines from the news-stand. She sat back to read the headlines. Someone shouted something outside, and coach doors double-slammed.

After a few minutes, the train started to move, just a silent, sliding motion. A faint vibration made her steady her coffee cup.

The speaker crackled some kind of 'welcome, here's the buffet' announcement that she didn't properly listen to. The carriage was half-full, and no one seemed likely to invade her space.

The speed picked up. Suburban east Cardiff toiled by like a laboriously moved stage backdrop. The sun came out for about ten minutes. She had a go at the quick crossword.

Bored with that, she sat back and put on her MP3 player. Random shuffle. She looked around the carriage, amusing herself by watching the other passengers: a middle-aged man in a suit, reading a broadsheet; two young student travellers with bright cagoules and Gore-Tex backpacks that kept impeding people on their way down the aisle; a young mother with a small boy, who was playing with some toys as she passed him grapes from a Tupperware box; a nice-looking young bloke, who seemed intent on snoozing; a trendy type with fashionable specs working on a laptop; a nondescript guy reading a novel. A young woman who thought a lot of herself, texting on a fancy clam-shell phone; another middle-aged man who looked like a teacher or an academic, working through a sheaf of documents with a pen; two matronly women in expensive twin-sets, travelling together, chatting animatedly.

Her MP3 randomly selected 'Coming Up For Air'. She looked out of the window at the trees flashing by and thought about what she'd say to Rhys.

When she'd had enough of that, she picked up one of the magazines she'd bought.

James wasn't entirely sure what Gwen had meant by 'later', so he assumed the evening. A plan to welcome her with a really pull-out-the-stops, home-cooked meal formed in his mind. He liked cooking, and he figured he'd get a lot of boyfriend points with a gesture like that.

He left the flat and set off on foot, intending to pick up some bits and pieces at the upmarket deli and grocers he liked to use. It was a good walk – he usually drove – but the sun was coming out, he was in no rush, and he felt he needed the exercise and the air.

His head was a little muddy. He'd lolled around in bed far too long, and polishing off a whole bottle the night before had been a mistake, nothing paracetamol wouldn't cure.

Jack, Ianto and Owen were arranged in a little, conspiratorial huddle in the work station area of the Hub when Toshiko arrived. They all looked at her and nodded hello. Owen looked especially sour. He yawned.

'What's going on?' she asked, taking off her coat.

'Sorry to drag you in, Tosh,' said Jack, not sounding sorry at all. 'A little situation has come up.'

'Situation?' she asked.

'A confluence of events,' said Jack. 'Pull up a chair. I've already run through this with Owen and Ianto.'

'Where are Gwen and James?' Toshiko asked, sitting down.

'I haven't called them,' said Jack. 'Not yet. You'll see why.'

Toshiko glanced at Owen. 'What's going on?' she asked.

'Just listen to Jack,' said Owen, darkly.

'OK,' said Jack. He held up the black tile. 'This has been doing weird things all night. The pattern's changed a couple of times. You got to figure that we're on some kind of countdown now.'

'But still nothing on any of our systems?' asked Toshiko.

'Nothing at all.'

'Nothing we can see,' said Owen, pointedly. Toshiko didn't fully understand the reference.

Jack put the tile down. 'I was kicking my heels here, trying to come up with something and failing miserably. I got hung up on the idea that maybe one of the events that's occurred recently, maybe in the last week or two, might hold a clue. After all, there's been plenty of wild stuff going down. I went through everything I could think of, every angle, every loose end.'

'And?' asked Toshiko.

'I found this,' said Jack.

'We don't know that it's connected to your doohickey in any way,' Owen objected.

'True, we don't,' Jack replied, tapping some keys on the nearby work station, and angling the flat screen so that Toshiko could see it, 'but even if it's not, this is a doozy. It'll roll your socks right up and down.' He looked at Toshiko. 'Figuratively.'

Fuzzy black and white footage appeared on the screen, jerking frame by frame. Jack skipped through the time code with a blurting whizz or two of the picture.

'What am I seeing?'

'A little data-capture I carried out last night. This is the mini-mart in Pontcanna on Thursday. Security-cam footage taken at the time James and I cornered your con man.'

Toshiko leaned forward. 'What exactly am I looking at?'

'You're looking out across the checkout lanes towards the store front,' said Jack, freezing frame and pointing, 'from above and to the right of the lanes. These are just shoppers here, OK. Checkout girl, checkout girl, checkout girl… OK. Let's punch it.'

The footage began to play in real time. There was no sound.

'There's our guy. He's trying to get out. The tubby guy there with the shopping cart has blocked the lane. And there's James. He's running up, he's spotted the guy. The guy sees him. Decides to use the tubby guy's cart as a weapon and… bingo.'

'Whoa!' said Toshiko. 'Run that back. Did I see that right?'

Jack stepped the footage back and replayed. 'Our guy rams with the cart and... pow!'

'That's not possible,' said Toshiko.

'And yet,' said Jack.

'How?' she asked, looking up from the frozen screen image at Jack.

'I've always envied Captain Analogy's upper body strength,' Jack said.

'Stop making fun,' said Toshiko.

'Maybe the trolley wasn't as heavily loaded as it looks on the footage,' said Owen, 'just empty boxes.'

Jack shook his head. 'Nobody, and I mean nobody, slings a shopping cart the entire length of a store, not even an empty one, and especially not by gripping it at the top. You could shove it a fair way, tip it over, sure, and if you got under it, you could probably lift it and toss it a few yards, but not what we just saw.'

'PCP, something like that,' said Toshiko.

Owen shook his head. 'He was clean as a whistle on the labs, and don't you think we'd have noticed if our mate was off his chuff on hard drugs? So off his chuff, I'm saying, that he's experiencing freakazoid physiological effects?'

'I don't know what to say,' said Toshiko.

'Don't say anything,' said Jack. 'I got something else to show you.'

The snack trolley made its way down the aisle.

Gwen sat up and looked for some change. The rocking of the train was making her sleepy, and there was still more than half the journey to go. As she reached over, one of the magazines slipped off her lap.

She bent over to pick it up. She wanted to take it with her. There was a whole feature on Glenn Robbins and her career after *Eternity Base* that James would want to read. She folded the magazine open on the right page to remind herself.

The trolley was taking ages to arrive. It was having trouble negotiating its way past the students' backpacks. They were getting up to move them, apologising.

Come on, I need bad train coffee, Gwen thought.

She noticed the small boy with his mother again and smiled. He was playing with a bright, plastic Andy Pinkus toy.

She thought about James. That put a bigger smile on her face. It was kind of sweet. She'd only been away a few hours, and she missed him, really missed him.

On cue, the MP3 offered up another track by Torn Curtain.

'Coffee, tea, madam?' the snack girl asked.

'Sir?'

James realised he was being spoken to. He frowned. On the other side of the seafood chiller counter, the assistant was holding a taped-up plastic bag towards him.

'Your fish, sir.'

'What?'

'I'm sorry, do you want this, sir?'

'Yeah, thanks.' He took the heavy little pack and put it in his basket. Where had his mind been? What had he been thinking about? He'd just completely zoned out in the middle of the shop.

He thought the walk might have helped his head, but it was worse. He had a pain behind his eyes, and his ears felt as if they were slightly blocked up. Everything had a boxy, hollow sound to it.

He wandered on through the shop, ignoring the expensive, pre-packed dinners with their enticing photos. Veg, that's what he needed.

Why was that man looking at him?

Oh, he wasn't.

He'd seemed familiar though. Where had he seen him before?

James drifted into the fruit and veg section. What did he need? He couldn't remember what he was intending to cook. He had to turn the package over in his basket to read the label.

Sea bass. Right, sea bass. He needed tarragon, shallots, garlic, some new potatoes, some mangetout.

He pulled a plastic bag off the roll, and went over to the trays of garlic bulbs to select a couple. They looked good. The skins were the colour of vellum. They were some special quality strain of garlic, according to the label.

Someone reached in past him into the tray to pick up some garlic. James looked down at the invading hand. That was just rude. People could wait just a moment, couldn't they?

There was no one beside him. The hand was his hand. He stared down at it. It didn't look right at all. He didn't recognise it.

James shook himself. He closed his eyes and opened them again. The hand

228

was still there. It didn't look like his, but it was. The fingers wiggled. It made a fist. He could feel its attachment to him.

'This is stupid,' he said out loud.

It was stupid. It was his hand, all right. Absolutely. There was nothing funny about it. It looked perfectly normal.

James realised he was breathing quite rapidly. The pain behind his eyes had grown a little sharper. He grabbed two bulbs of garlic, bagged them quickly, and dropped them into his basket. What else did he need? Apples. Apples? Apples. He picked up a packet of conference pears and put them in his basket with the garlic and the fish.

Why was that man looking at him?

Where had he seen that man before?

Ianto opened the box.

'What's that?' asked Toshiko. She was very unsettled.

Ianto took the object out of the box.

'It's the side-arm Owen was carrying a week ago Thursday,' said Jack, 'the night we went after the Amok.'

'It looks broken,' said Toshiko. The weapon was buckled, as if it had been twisted in a vice.

'You may recall,' said Jack, 'in all the hullabaloo, Owen ended up pointing it at James.'

'To be fair, I wasn't quite myself,' said Owen.

'No one saw what happened after that, but James managed to disarm Owen, grab the Amok, and get it contained.'

'OK,' said Toshiko. That agreed with her memory of events.

'The gun got damaged in the struggle,' said Jack.

'It's beyond repair,' said Ianto. 'I put it in the Armoury. I was intending to break it down and dispose of it.'

'When I showed Ianto the mini-mart footage of James's cart-tossing world record, he went to fetch it. It had been bugging him. Look at it close, Tosh. Real close.'

She took the broken weapon from Ianto and turned it over to examine it. 'It's been sheared around. Twisted. What could do that?'

'What do those grooves suggest?' asked Jack. 'What do they look like to you?'

'Well, fingermarks,' said Toshiko, 'but that's just—'

Jack took the gun from her. He punched something else up on screen. 'They're fingermarks, all right. Fingers pressed into the steel so deep, they actually left prints in the metal. We got a match. Want to guess who with?'

'Oh God, please don't say James,' Toshiko answered.

Despite the coffee, Gwen had nodded off for a bit. She woke up, and had to remind herself why she was on a train. She was going to Manchester, to see some bloke. That was it.

She felt like crap.

The doze hadn't left her with a headache exactly, but she felt genuinely odd. It was a nagging, empty sensation, as if she'd lost something.

She looked around. *Had* she lost something? Had she mislaid something before she'd dropped off? A pen, her MP3, her magazines, her wallet, maybe that was it.

No. None of those things.

Then why did she feel quite so hollow? It felt for all the world like a sudden, plunging dip in blood sugar. She had a sort of craving, a yearning to get some unknown, unidentifiable substance back into her system. The simple lack of it was making her suffer withdrawal.

She was forty-five minutes out of Manchester Piccadilly. She decided to get a cookie or some chocolate from the buffet, maybe a tea as well.

She got up. She felt light-headed and empty-sick. The train was too hot, the two chattering women in the twin-sets too loud, and the girl on the clam-shell too obnoxious.

The small boy, travelling with his mum, looked up from his toys at Gwen as she edged by.

'All right?' she fake-smiled at him.

She certainly wasn't.

Why was that man looking at him? That oh-so-familiar man?

I'm just being paranoid, James thought. *He's just got one of those faces, and I'm in one of those moods.*

He started heading to the Please Pay Here.

There was the man again. No, it was a different man. This one was dark haired, not blond, and was wearing jeans and a dark T-shirt instead of a suit. But he also looked uncannily familiar.

It's just going to be one of those days, James told himself. *Just face it.*

The stab behind his eyes was back. Sounds all around him seemed boxier than ever. He looked down into his basket, to check he was done. It was full of stuff. He wasn't entirely sure why he'd put most of it in his basket. Tippex? A globe artichoke? Cat treats? *Really?*

He looked up in slight panic, wondering if anyone in the Saturday crowd could tell he was having a quiet breakdown in the middle of the shop. He saw the dark-haired man in the black jeans.

The man made eye contact with him.

James turned and headed for the exit. He was walking quite fast, on the very edge of actually trotting.

'Excuse me? Sir?' a shop assistant called out.

He realised the basket of unpaid-for goods was still swinging off his arm. He threw it aside and started to run in earnest. There was some commotion behind him at the disturbance. His basket landed on the floor, and spilled out his sea bass and his packet of geranium seeds and his block of marzipan and his hair-clips and his conference pears and all the other things he had collected.

'So, what are we saying?' asked Toshiko.

'James is not James,' said Jack. 'James is in danger. We're in danger. Something's happened to the real James. This James is an impostor. This is the real James, but something seriously crazy is happening to him. This has something to do with the alarm. This has nothing to do with the alarm.' He looked at the other three. 'Take your pick. Any or all of the above.'

'I checked James out,' Owen insisted. 'Full work-up. There was nothing—'

'Nothing we can see,' Jack corrected.

'All right, all right,' Owen replied, conceding.

'What do we do about it?' Toshiko asked.

Nobody spoke for a moment.

'Whatever we can,' said Jack. 'Whatever we damn well can. And let's hope part of that whatever is helping our friend out.'

'Do we know where he is?' asked Owen.

'I could try his phone,' offered Ianto.

'Don't,' Jack said. 'Try Gwen instead.'

A cookie hadn't helped. She was feeling worse. The wretched sense of loss gnawed at her. She felt like bursting into tears.

But over what? It was hard to reconcile anything in her recent memory with these pangs that seemed to register on a scale with grief or bereavement. In fact, the more she tried, the more she realised her recent memory seemed downright patchy. What had she done yesterday? The day before? The robot thing in the allotments, in Cathays. Yeah. That had been pretty full-on. Maybe this was what post-traumatic shock felt like.

If she was actually ill, that would help to explain the way she felt. It would explain the emotional fragility, the sense of loss, the emptiness.

There was a void inside her, a big dark hole. Its presence gave her an appetite, a searing need to fill it up. She was hungry and thirsty, she was craving, but no amount of food or drink would do.

The train was just beginning its roll into Manchester Piccadilly. She knew why she'd made the trip – to visit this bloke – but it all seemed so pointless now she was arriving. She couldn't reason out why she'd ever thought this trip worthwhile. She had no intention of doing anything except getting off this train and on the first one back to Cardiff. Screw this Brady guy. Sorry, but screw him.

She'd put her MP3 back in, but it kept playing her random tracks she didn't know; annoying indie pop that she didn't like at all. It sounded like Rhys's stuff. Had he put them on there?

It made her really want to call him. She wanted to talk to Rhys more than just about anything she could think of. It was a gut feeling, as if talking to him would provide a fix that would soothe her cravings. Something, some dull feeling of restraint, stopped her from hitting his number on her phone list.

The music went on: more stuff she didn't like or know. She pulled out her earphones, and stuffed the MP3 into her bag. Outside, grey platforms crawled past. She could see the mighty span of the station roof. The train rocked to a halt. There was a rifle salute of opening doors.

People were getting up, gathering their things.

She breathed hard, trying not to cry. She got up. She left her rubbish, her coffee cups, her food wrappers, her paper. She had some magazines too. One was folded back on a glossy article about what Jolene Blalock had been up to since *Enterprise* wound up. She'd saved that for Rhys, she remembered. She rolled the magazine up and put it in her bag. She dumped the rest.

She got up, and joined the queue filing down the aisle. The women in twin-sets were still chattering. The young woman who thought a lot of herself was loudly telling her clam-shell she was just getting off the train.

The small boy and his mum were just in front of her. She stepped back to let them into the queue. The mum smiled a thank you. The boy toddled along, clutching his Spongebob Squarepants toy.

Gwen got off the train and walked out of the bustling disembarkation tide to the quiet side of the platform. She stood, breathing hard, hurting. The air was cold and tangy with fumes. Whistles and voices and door-bangs and the patter of footsteps barely filled the echoing vault. A Tannoy announcement rang out into space.

Unable to stop herself, she started to cry. Tears streamed down her face. She shuddered with each sob. The sense of loss was as overwhelming as it was incomprehensible.

Her phone rang. It rang for a while before she was able to answer it.

'Gwen?'

'Jack?'

'Gwen, are you OK?'

'Yeah. I… Yeah.'

'Where are you?'

'Manchester Piccadilly,' she replied.

'OK. Why?'

'I… It's complicated.'

'Gwen,' Jack's voice said. 'This is important. I need to talk to you about James.'

She swallowed. She sniffed. She thought about that.

She said, 'Who?'

TWENTY-SEVEN

He left the food hall and ran along the upper landing of the shopping centre. It was busy. Hard sunlight shone down through the atrium's glass roof onto hundreds of jostling people.

His mind was busy too. His heart was pounding. He—

He slowed down. He was being stupid.

James came to a halt, and slowly turned around, scanning the crowd. No one gave him so much as a passing look. Too many minds were focused on their Saturday shop, too many attentions were wrapped up in conversations with partners or friends or whining kids.

Sounds, too many sounds, all boxy and hollow. It was like being underwater in a busy public baths, and hearing the swell of voices in the air transmitted by the water alone.

His palms were tacky with sweat. He looked at his hands, holding them out in front of him. For one, quick, stomach-swooping moment, they weren't his hands at all. They belonged to someone else.

Big Wooof. Big, *big* Wooof. Alienated and scared by parts of his own body, James reeled. Owen had been wrong. Some insane kind of transmutation was happening to him, right there, in broad daylight, in front of hundreds of people. Or Owen had been right, and he was simply going mad.

Someone was looking at him. James felt it, like a sixth sense, a hot tingle. He looked up, searching the crowd as it poured around him.

He saw the man, the lean blond man in the black suit. The man was standing twenty feet away, the crowd flowing around him too. The man was staring right at James.

James knew he'd met him before somewhere. Where, where, *where?*

Why is he looking at me?

James turned his head a few degrees to the right, very slowly. Ten yards to the blond man's left, another figure was making a silent, still island in the stream of bodies. The dark-haired man in the black jeans.

He was staring at James too.

James froze. He had every intention of running, but his legs wouldn't move and his body refused to turn. It was as if they had some hold on him, some hypnotic hold, just like that bloody replacement window con man *hadn't*. This was how Jack and Gwen and all the poor suckers he touched must have felt: charmed and immobile.

This was what it was like to be a prey item locked in a predator's gaze.

The blond man turned his head and looked through the crowd at the dark-haired man. The dark-haired man turned his head and looked back. Simultaneously, they started to walk towards James. They took strong, purposeful strides. They moved closer together until they were coming on, side by side, in step.

Two figures. Side by side.

Two shadows beside a phone box, in the middle of the night.

James remembered. The memory returned in a hot, dizzying hit, as if he'd been whacked between the eyes with a mallet. He bolted.

Oh, now people noticed him. They cried out and complained loudly as he shoved his way past them. Who did he think he was? Where did he think he was going? Couldn't he show some bloody manners?

His spinning mind supplied answers as he ran. To the first two questions, he had no idea. To the third, no he bloody couldn't.

He looked back. The men were coming after him. He slammed through the crowd to the head of a descending escalator, and pushed his way down it. A woman bellowed as he kicked over the shopping bags she'd set on the step beside her. A man cursed him as he elbowed past. A young guy riding beside his girlfriend tumbled down two steps and clung to the handrail as James barged him to one side.

He leapt off the escalator onto the middle level of the atrium. Above him, the two men were weaving down after him, single-file, switching back and forth to avoid people. They had to wait while the bellowing woman gathered up her spilled purchases with the help of other shoppers. Forced to a halt, the two men kept their eyes on James as they slid down the moving steps.

James started running immediately he was off the escalator. He crashed into an elderly man and knocked him flat. He stumbled as the elderly man fell, but didn't stop. More people began to shout at him. He ran on.

The two men reached the bottom of the escalator, and started to sprint after him.

James crossed the landing space, looking left and right. He needed another down escalator to reach street level. He turned, and collided head-on with a young husband and wife. They had two kids with them, and the youngest tripped as he tangled with James's legs. Bumping down hard, the kid started to cry immediately.

'You stupid bastard!' the wife yelled.

'Look where you're going, shithead,' the husband roared. He was thick-set and hefty, a bloke used to responding with his fists. He swung an angry punch at James.

Instinctively, James raised a hand, just a warding hand.

The thuggish husband grunted and sailed backwards through the air. He actually left the ground. He flew ten yards and struck a retail barrow set up in the middle of the landing to sell Russian dolls and autographed photos of footballers. The barrow went over beneath him in a huge and noisy clatter. A general commotion began.

James ran to the escalator. People were getting out of his way.

The lower escalator was a long sweep. As soon as he got onto it, James found his progress blocked by shoppers. Some of them tried to shrink and cower away from him. Some of them cried out in alarm.

Penned in, James looked back up the sliding steps. The two men appeared at the top of the escalator and began to rush down after him, dodging around a few solo riders, who flinched from them. The two men were gaining.

James gripped the moving rail. He looked over at the drop, at the faces looking up to see what the fuss was about. The dark-haired man was four steps behind him, reaching out a hand.

James vaulted the moving rail and dropped.

Dozens of people screamed.

Jack put down the cordless slowly. He paused for a moment.

'Jack?' asked Toshiko, rising from her seat. 'Jack, what's the matter?'

'Was that Gwen?' Owen asked.

'Jack?'

Jack turned to face them. 'You know,' he began quietly, 'you know how this all seemed terribly, you know, wonky?'

Owen nodded. Toshiko just stared.

'Well, you won't believe what Gwen just said to me,' said Jack.

He was flying, arms out, falling. Someone was screaming in a really piercing way.

He landed. He landed with legs coiled like springs to cushion the impact. He didn't even fall or stumble. As soon as he was down, he sprang forwards and started running again.

A pathway opened in the crowd in front of him, Terrified, horrified faces recoiled out of his way.

More screams rang out in his wake. He didn't need to look back to know that the blond man and the dark-haired man had followed his example and thrown themselves off the escalator.

They would be coming. Fast now, fast, and making no sound.

He could see the entrance of the shopping centre ahead. Oblivious crowds washed in and out, only just beginning to ripple as they realised something was up. The entrance itself was two pairs of automatic glass doors framed by side panels of floor-length glass.

There were too many people, too many people in his path. Some were too slow getting out of his way; others were too scared or confused. One young guy simply ducked down and James sailed over him.

There was no time to stop, no time to even slow down. The main doorways were too thick with people.

James raised his hands in front of his face in a protective cross. He accelerated. He came through one of the side panels in a splash of shattering glass. Shattering *strengthened* glass. Fragments flew in all directions, and the main weight of the glass panel collapsed like a sheet of dislodged ice, cascading across the pavement in a glittering, crashing torrent.

Yet more screams and hysterics. Shoppers fled in panic. James didn't stop. The road ahead was two strides away, heavy with crawling traffic.

He didn't break stride. He took off. *Bang*! off the roof of a minicab. *Bang*! off the bonnet of a Mini. Three powerful skips took him across to the far side of the road.

Behind him, Mr Dine exited the shopping centre through the hole in the glass panel James had made.

Mr Lowe came out a second later through the main doors, slamming pedestrians aside like a charging bull. People tumbled out of his way, some struck so hard they would require medical attention. One girl actually cartwheeled on her way to colliding with a heavy rubbish bin.

Though Mr Dine had exited the shopping centre first, Mr Lowe's ruthless drive put him in the lead. He flew out across the traffic, crunching in the roof of an Audi and then vaulting over the high back of a minibus. His gymnastics, his sheer grace, would have scored him maximum points at any Olympics. No one really saw it because he had become just a blur by then.

He landed on the far pavement, his impact cracking the expensive zigzag paving stones.

Mr Dine landed beside him. There was a terrible commotion of voices and shouting and car horns all around them. They each scanned the crowd. They looked at one another.

There was no sign of James.

Mr Dine looked at the scrum of injured people outside the Mall entrance.

'That was unnecessary,' he said.

'It was appropriate. Only the Principal matters,' Mr Lowe replied.

Thirty yards east of them, the passengers of a bendy-bus erupted in alarm. A man was clinging to the outside of the moving vehicle, looking in at them through the window. The driver began to slow the bus as he heard the ripple of panic behind him.

James gazed in at the alarmed passengers. So much agitation, so much fear. As the bus slowed, he let go of the hand- and toe-holds he had dug in its metal skin.

He landed on his feet and used the bus's momentum to propel his onward flight.

They were behind him still, both of them. He could taste it.

He crossed the road again, weaving through the moving traffic, and ran down an underpass. He slowed. He was barely panting.

He took out his mobile.

'How could she not know?' Owen demanded.

Jack shrugged.

'How could she not? How?'

'Just take it easy,' Jack suggested.

'I will not. I bloody well will not!'

'Then go and sit over there where I can't hear you,' said Jack.

'I'm having trouble understanding this too,' said Toshiko.

'Join the club,' Jack snapped.

'Something hot,' Ianto called. They crossed to the station he was monitoring.

'Show me,' Jack said.

'Some kind of incident at the Capitol Mall,' Ianto said. 'Reports of property damage, injuries. Some kind of foot pursuit. Some guys apparently leapt off a moving escalator.'

Jack studied the screen. 'Not much to go on. Could just be—'

His phone rang.

'This is Jack.'

'Jack, it's James.'

Jack hesitated before answering. He pointed to Ianto and then at his phone. Ianto nodded and started to tap at the keyboard.

'Jack, are you there?'

'Yeah, James. We were worried about you. Where a—'

'Jack, listen to me. Something's going on. Something wrong.'

'James, what do you—'

'Just listen. I haven't got much time to talk. They're after me.'

'Who's after you, James?'

'The men. For Christ's sake, Jack, help me. I'm going crazy here. Talk to Owen. Owen can tell you about it. Tell him I said it was OK to tell you.'

'James,' said Jack carefully. 'I think I already know. Owen didn't need to tell me.'

There was a long silence.

'Oh,' said James. 'OK. That's good, then. I trust you, Jack. I trust you.'

'Glad to hear it. What kind of trouble are we talking? Scale of one to ten?'

'Twenty-seven, you idiot! Please!'

The line muffled for a moment. There were some indistinct noises.

'James? James, are you there?'

'Jack, they're coming! They're—'

'CALL ENDED' read the screen of Jack's phone.

'Did you get it?' Jack asked. 'Please tell me you got it.'

Ianto nodded. 'GPS is just punching it up. Phone location…' He looked at Jack. 'Phone location two hundred and thirty-three yards south of that Mall.'

'I'll start the car,' said Owen.

The dead centre of Cardiff: gleaming shops and boutique arcades, and bold new developments overlapping with the last relics of the City's poorer past. Saturday afternoon, a weak sun smiling, the town crawling with the retail-hungry and the credit card debt-addicted.

The black SUV ploughed through the inner-city traffic, anonymous as a storm cloud.

They pulled up on double yellow lines and got out. Jack, Toshiko and Owen.

'Ianto?' Jack asked into his Bluetooth.

'Hearing you.'

'Fix?'

'You're right on it.'

Jack looked around at the other two. 'Boiled egg,' he said.

Side by side, they began to run.

James looked up and down the tiled cavity of the underpass. He stuffed his phone back into his pocket. No signal.

Traffic thumped by overhead. He took a step towards the east end of the underpass.

The man in dark jeans appeared, walking slowly down the slope towards him. James switched back. The blond man in the suit came down the steps to the west.

James tried to back away from both advancing figures, a feat he quickly realised was technically impossible.

He held out his palms in either direction.

'That's far enough!' he barked. His voice echoed along the little tunnel.

They slowed down, but continued to advance.

'I mean it!' James cried.

They halted.

'I want you to leave me alone. Leave me alone!'

That is not possible, ever.

'What?'

The safety of the Principal is our paramount concern.

'Which of you said that? Who said that?'

The dark-haired man took a step closer.

'Whoa! No you don't!' James exclaimed.

The dark-haired man stopped.

We are here only to protect the Principal.

'Yeah, so you said.'

Your actions and behaviour are contrary to the Principal's best interests.

'Great. Maybe I can help with that.'

The blond man smiled. 'That is unlikely. You have been compromised.'

'I've been what?'

'You have been compromised,' said the dark-haired man. 'Your investment has been damaged and, as a result, your self-protection protocols have been compromised.'

'I really don't understand,' said James, keeping his hands raised, aimed at both of them.

'That is the point,' said the blond man. 'You don't understand. By now, you should, but you clearly don't. We see this. This proves your investment has compromised you.'

'Lower your hands,' said the dark-haired man.

'Just explain… please. Explain what you mean,' James said, keeping his hands up.

The blond man sighed. 'Explanation should not be necessary. The jeopardy upload should have re-installed your base consciousness by now. This also proves that your self-protection protocols have been compromised. You should know yourself and understand this situation. You should not be resisting. You should be ready and willing for extraction.'

'Well, I'm not,' said James, 'whatever that means.'

'You are—' the dark-haired man began.

'You, shut up,' warned James. 'I'm listening to you both. I want to understand, but you're going to have to start making sense really soon. Speak plainly. Explain it in terms I can grasp.'

'Plainly?' asked the dark-haired man.

'Information evidently must be seated in terms that can be understood using this milieu's frames of reference,' said the blond man. 'Like the fact that chocolate ice cream… is animal fats and flavourings, pretty much.'

The dark-haired man looked uncertain. 'None of this is important. Only the duty is important. The Principal must be protected and recovered.'

He moved forwards.

'Back off!' cried James.

The dark-haired man did just that. With a *groof!* of punched-out air, he flew back down the underpass and fell down, rolling hard.

The blond man sprang at James. James tried to ward him off, but the blond man clutched him tightly.

James swung around and slammed the blond man into the wall. Tiles shattered and flew off their cement settings.

The blond man dug his fingers in tighter, and James whirled him in the opposite direction. Another wall, another impact. Yet more cracked and fragmented tiles.

Don't do this. Don't do it. This is a mistake. You will come to see that. This is an ugly thing that stains my duty and tarnishes my—

'Shut up!' James cried. He wheeled around and threw the blond man into the ceiling. The blond man crunched into one of the recessed lights and shattered it.

He fell onto the floor, landing on his hands and knees in a rain of clear plastic debris.

The dark-haired man was running at James. James reached out and his fist connected. The dark-haired man turned three, boneless somersaults on his way back down the underpass.

James turned and made his escape. He took the underpass steps three at a time. He heard sounds behind him.

He ran off down the street, and jinked left into a residential side-street, a quiet, exclusive mews.

He glanced behind him.

They were coming after him. They had changed. They had revealed their true forms.

They were grey shades, thorny shadows from the high walls in his dream, leaping and scurrying, like whispers, like wraiths. They were barbed, and armed for killing.

They ran faster than he could. They were made that way. They ran faster, leaping, bounding, closing the distance. They made no sound. Not even footsteps.

Still running, he looked over his shoulder. The shades were there.

One pounced—

TWENTY-EIGHT

Jack's Webley went off, deafeningly loud in the narrow mews.

He was flanked by Toshiko and Owen. Both of them had side-arms aimed, circling, hunting for targets. Jack held up the black tile. Its surface danced with lights.

'Know what this is? Anyone? Anyone?' Jack called out.

James sank to the ground at their feet, panting.

'Jack?' he gasped. 'Jack? They're right behind me'

'It's OK.' Jack told him. Jack kept the tile held up high.

'Come on. Are you a coward? I'm just a guy with an old gun and few friends. You afraid of that? I don't think so. I've seen you. I've seen you take down a Serial G with your bare hands. You're a proper killing machine. Nothing like me, I'm a pussycat. You could take me, pop, just like that. So stop being coy. Damn well show yourself.'

'Oh crap,' Owen breathed.

Smoky grey shapes prowled forwards into the mews from the shadows. A pair of them. They were there and they weren't there, like subliminal messages or peripheral images. Grey thorns rippled and swirled, fading in and out of real-time.

'OK,' said Toshiko, swallowing, 'two of them?'

'Doesn't matter,' Jack replied quietly. 'One would be enough to kill us. Two, what's the difference? We can only be so dead.'

'I love it when you're jolly,' said Toshiko.

Jack waggled the tile. 'You're busy,' he called out to the grey shapes. 'I realise that. Busy and intent on your purpose. That's fine. We won't get in your way. Hell, we couldn't if we wanted to. Just tell me something. Do you know what this is?'

Yes, Jack Harkness.

Jack winced. The words had passed through him like a knife. He forced up a smile. 'Great. So, are you going to tell me about it?'

The two grey things in the limits of the shadows swished and bristled their thorny backs.

'Here's an idea,' said Jack. 'Look me in the eye. Look me in the eye, you sons of bitches.'

The grey things growled. One moved forward, its thorny greyness pouring off it like folds of dirty smoke.

It re-formed as its invested self melted away. It became a lean, blond man wearing a black suit. It stepped towards Jack.

'You got a name?' Jack asked.

'Yes,' said Mr Dine.

TWENTY-NINE

'This wide open enough for you?' Jack asked.

He and the individual called Mr Dine were walking down Mermaid Quay towards the Bay. It was getting late and growing dark. The sky was smudging over. There was a threat of rain on the wind.

Jack gestured to a bench facing the railings and the sea.

Mr Dine nodded and they sat down. Mr Dine kept glancing back down the Quay. Mr Lowe was following them at a distance, a sliver of shadow.

'Your pal, he doesn't like this, does he?' Jack asked.

'No,' said Mr Dine. 'Mr Lowe has only recently been inserted here. He does not understand the nuances of this place or your society.'

'And you do?'

'Not terribly well,' admitted Mr Dine. 'Better than my colleague, I think.'

Jack nodded.

They looked at the sea.

'Where are you from?' Mr Dine asked.

'Not from round here,' Jack replied.

'I realised that.'

'You?'

'I'm from precisely around here, Captain,' replied Mr Dine.

'Because of the Rift, right?'

Mr Dine thought for a moment. 'Rift? Is that what you call it?'

Jack nodded.

'That's nice. That's a better name than ours.'

'What do you call it, then?'

'The word we use literally translates as "the Stumble" or the "the Misstep". We usually refer to it as "the Border".'

'OK. The Border's been here a long time.'

'For as long as we can remember. The First Senior is dedicated to guarding it.'

'First Senior?' asked Jack.

'Us.'

'Uh-huh. Torchwood is dedicated to guarding it too, from this side.'

'I know. That is why the Principal was inserted amongst you. You are the most interesting and compelling thing on this part of the border.'

'Yeah, what does inserted mean?'

'We have intercourse with you. Sometimes aggressive intercourse.'

'I'm sure you do. Not tonight though, baby. I'm not in the mood.'

Mr Dine considered Jack's remark and laughed. 'That is a sexual joke. It contains intentional ambiguity that makes it funnier.'

'Hey, I'm here all week,' said Jack, 'don't forget your waitress.'

Mr Dine frowned. 'Do you mean Shiznay?'

'I don't know who Shiznay is,' said Jack.

Mr Dine smiled and shook his head. 'In that case, you have lost me. You have made a cultural reference that is outside my investment data-archive. I'm sure it was funny, though.'

'Not really. So tell me about James,' Jack said.

Gwen walked into the Hub. Her face was pale and drawn. She had been crying a lot for quite a while.

'Where is he?' she asked. 'I want to see him.'

'Just hold on,' said Jack.

'No, Jack. I bloody won't just hold on. I want to see him. I need to.'

Behind Jack, Toshiko and Owen sat at their stations, watching Gwen. They both looked shaken too.

'Gwen,' said Jack.

'I forgot him, Jack,' she said quietly. 'I just forgot him. Everything about him and about us just went out of my mind and left a horrible gap. It's as if he was never really there.'

'That's kind of the point, I think,' said Jack.

'How could I just forget him?' she moaned.

'As I understand it, there's a certain range involved. The camouflage effect, the ability to blend in, it only works up to a certain distance. A hundred or so miles. A hundred miles from wherever James is. You went out of range, Gwen.'

'And he just slipped my mind? That's mad.'

'But you know it's true, right?' asked Jack.

Gwen nodded. 'I know that, once I'd forgotten him, it broke the spell. As I came back, the memories, the feelings, they all returned too, but they weren't the same. I could see them for what they were. I could see they were lies.' She looked at Jack, fiercely. 'I don't like lying.'

'If it's worth anything, he didn't know he was lying,' said Jack.

'What is he?' Gwen asked.

Jack smiled sadly. 'That's the worst thing, you know? The worst thing of all. He's James. He is James. Except there is no James Mayer.'

James rose off a chair and stood facing them as Jack and Gwen entered the Boardroom.

He went to hold Gwen, but she backed away sharply.

'Gwen?' James asked.

'We have to talk, James,' Jack said. 'We have to talk about stuff, and it's not going to be an easy talk. But I want you to hear it from me.'

'I don't… I don't get any of this…' James said.

'Well, you will. You don't get it because you've been hurt. Damaged, I suppose I should say. The bit of you that should switch on in an emergency, and tell you all the secrets you need to know, well, that's broken.'

James stared at them. Gwen swallowed when she saw his eyes. One brown, one blue.

'You make me sound like a machine,' said James.

'You are, kinda,' said Jack.

'He's not,' said Gwen emphatically.

'OK, he's flesh and blood. That's a real human body you've got there, James. Accept no imitations. I meant machine as in something that was built.'

James shook his head. He looked desperately at Gwen. She couldn't meet his eyes.

'Let's sit,' said Jack.

James sat down slowly. They took chairs on the other side of the table.

Jack cleared his throat. 'This is how I understand it. I had it explained to me very patiently, and I still have trouble getting my head around it. Here goes…'

He looked at Gwen and then at James. 'Cardiff isn't the only place that rubs against the Rift. There are other places out there, other places, other worlds. We all share a common border. In one of those places, they've known about this Border for ever. The people there understand the Border as a fact of life. They see it as their duty to watch it, to police it, to patrol the things and people that go back and forth.'

'The way Torchwood does,' said James.

'On a much bigger scale,' said Jack. 'The guy in charge, he's a Border Prince. It's his duty and his calling, and they live long lives and take their duties very seriously. They hand the responsibility down, father to son. The sons – and daughters too, I guess – the heirs anyway, they grow up learning the skills they need to take on the duty when their turns come. It's a long, formal training, an apprenticeship. As part of it, they're sent out, from time to time, to live in other places and immerse themselves in the other places that share the common border.'

'Like a cultural exchange?' scoffed James.

'I'm not joking,' said Jack. 'They are given a form that perfectly matches the locals, and they're given the ability – the innate ability – to blend in seamlessly. While they're abroad, they don't know what they are. I guess that's so they don't give anything away. Only when they're called home, do they remember who they really are.'

James shook his head. 'You really fell for this, Jack? I thought you were the sceptical type. This is just nonsense.'

'I don't...' Gwen began. 'I don't think it is. It makes me want to throw up to think about it, but it's real.'

James looked at her. He looked frightened.

'What are you saying? Jack, what are you telling me? You think that's what I am? Are you telling me you think that's what I am? One of these things? Come on!'

'You're a real person,' replied Jack, 'a real human being, right down to every last atom of you. Perfect in every detail. There'd be no point in the exercise if you weren't.'

'No,' murmured James.

'But James Mayer is just an identity, built for you to wear.'

'Shut up!' said James.

'There is no real James Mayer.'

'Shut up!'

'You know how hard this is for us?' Jack snapped. 'We know you! You're part of us! Right in the heart of everything we are! You're the best friend we never actually had, and it's going to kill us to lose you!'

James swallowed. 'Lose me? What do you mean?'

'You have to go home, James. You have to go be yourself again.'

'This is just a pack of lies,' James exploded. He got up, shoving his chair back. 'You've been duped!'

'Yeah, we have,' said Jack. 'You too. Sit down.'

James glowered at them for a second. Slowly, he returned to his seat.

'This is what they told me. You can't stay any more. The spell's broken. They sent a guy here with you, a minder to look after you, to watch your back. You're the heir to the throne, after all. It's the minder's job to keep you safe, and pull you right out if things go wrong. If you're hurt, or you get sick, he's there to take you home.'

'And you got hurt,' said Gwen.

James stared at them.

'In the event of injury or damage, there are supposed to be dormant protocols that wake up inside the Principal – that's what they call it – protocols that cut in and help the Principal to understand what he is so he can prepare for extraction. These include all kinds of physiological upgrades, combat skills, super powers.'

James looked down at his hands. They were shaking.

'All that kind of got screwed up this time,' said Jack. 'They didn't cut in properly. That's why this all seems like a heap of crap to you.'

'No kidding,' said James.

'So, that's how it is,' said Jack.

'And what?' asked James. 'I just leave? Or do they take me?'

'I think it's best if you go willingly,' said Jack. 'They don't want to hurt you.'

'And you'd let them?' asked James, bitterly. 'I thought we were friends?'

'We are,' said Jack. 'Sometimes, this is what friends do for each other.'

'No,' said James, shaking his head. 'I can't accept this.'

'I know it's hard.'

'I don't believe any of this.'

'Of course. That's how it works, but what you believe in is the false part, the part that isn't real.'

'This is real,' James insisted. 'This is… my world. This is what I know and all I want—'

'The world's not quite what we think it is,' said Jack.

'No,' James repeated.

'James—'

'No!' he snarled. He was on his feet again. Gwen flinched. Jack rose quietly.

'James…'

'You may be able to just sell me out,' James said, 'but I don't have to go along with it. Even if I'm the only bloody person who can see what's really true here—'

'James, please,' said Gwen.

James gazed at her. 'I adore you, Gwen. We were going to… How can you betray me too?'

'I'm not,' she said. Tears welled in her eyes. 'It's not like that. Nothing's the way we thought it was.'

James blinked his mismatched eyes. The door of the Boardroom swung on its hinges.

'Shit!' Jack cried. 'He's running! Tosh! Close the perimeter!'

They ran out of the Boardroom and down the stairs towards the work stations. Toshiko was at her keyboard.

'Did you see him?' Jack yelled.

'Not a thing!' Owen yelled back.

'We're too late!' Toshiko declared. 'Hub breach. He's already out. He's on the Quay. I've got him on monitor.'

Jack headed for the exit, Gwen right behind him.

'Try and keep him fixed,' Jack yelled over his shoulder.

THIRTY

It was getting dark outside. Rain was setting in from the west. The lights in the bars and restaurants were glowing along the Quay.

Jack and Gwen ran through the rain along the boarded walk.

'Tosh?' Jack called.

'I've lost him… hang on…'

'Tosh!'

'OK! I've got him again. He's doubled back. He's heading around towards Harry Ramsden's.'

Gwen had already switched that way. Jack followed her. The boards were wet and skiddy under their soles.

James got as far as the Graving Docks, running out into the sleeting wind. The sky was a black cliff, an empty gulf of night rushing down.

The shades were there, whispers of smoke on the dockside, flanking him.

'James!' Jack yelled as he ran up.

'Don't touch him! Don't hurt him!' Gwen shouted. She could see the grey shapes quite clearly.

One rushed at James.

'You bastards! No!' Gwen howled.

James saw it coming.

Frantic, he turned in towards it. There was a crack, and the shade hurtled away, flopping and writhing convulsively on the dock walk. Thorny limbs thrashed.

Mr Dine saw Mr Lowe go down. He knew the First Senior would be on his feet again in a moment. Mr Lowe would be angry and keen to accomplish his duty without hesitation. His pride had been dented. He would be ruthless, perhaps even teach the Principal a lesson in respect.

Mr Dine would not allow that. He stepped forwards. His investment blew off him like steam. He walked up to the Principal.

Jack and Gwen were ten yards away, sprinting to reach James.

James looked at the lean, blond man in the black suit standing before him in the evening rain. The man had the tiny trace of a sympathetic smile on his face.

'Time to go,' he said.

'This is where I live,' said James. 'This is the world I know. Please.'

'It is time to go,' said Mr Dine.

He held up his hand. Just a slight gesture.

There was a crack of bone, sharp above the sound of the wind and rain.

James folded up and fell.

Gwen screamed. Jack held onto her.

She sank to her knees, sobbing wildly.

Jack approached Mr Dine. He looked down at James's crumpled body. Mr Lowe melted into view behind Mr Dine.

'Are you taking him now?' Jack asked.

'We have taken him,' said Mr Dine. He glanced at the body. 'The Principal has no further use for this,' he said.

'What will I—' Jack began to say, but when he looked up, Mr Dine and Mr Lowe had disappeared.

Jack knelt down, and gathered James's body up in his arms.

THIRTY-ONE

Jack Harkness sat at his desk. His fingers played with the black tile on the glass desktop in front of him.

'The Lord of the Border had friends here once,' Jack said, 'friends he trusted. He gave them a way to look after his son, something that would warn them if the son was at risk.'

Jack tapped the tile. It was no longer flashing, no longer lit up. It was just a dead black square.

'What are we going to do?' asked Gwen softly. She rubbed her nose with a screwed-up tissue.

'Do?'

'How are we going to cope?' she asked.

Jack shrugged. 'The way we usually cope. There's a chance that everything will gradually fade out. All the artifice, all the make-believe.'

'All the lies,' she said.

'It'll all go, I think,' said Jack. 'It'll all melt away and we won't remember a thing.'

'How long will that take?' she asked, 'A day? A week? A year? My God, Jack, how many times might this have happened to us before?'

'I have no idea.'

She sniffed, and blinked tears. 'I don't know what scares me more – the fact that it might take a year, or the fact that we might forget him completely.'

Jack didn't answer. He got up. 'Come on, let's go and find Tosh and Owen. We need to be in one place for a while and just talk.'

'OK,' she said. 'I'll be there in a moment. I've got to phone Rhys first.'

'Sure. I understand.'

He rested a hand on her shoulder. 'It will be OK, Gwen. Trust me. It will be OK.'

She shook her head. 'No, Jack. It's the End of the World,' she said.

TORCHWOOD

ANOTHER LIFE
Peter Anghelides

ISBN 978 0 563 48653 4
UK £6.99 US$11.99/$14.99 CDN

Thick black clouds are blotting out the skies over Cardiff. As twenty-four inches of rain fall in twenty-four hours, the city centre's drainage system collapses. The capital's homeless are being murdered, their mutilated bodies left lying in the soaked streets around the Blaidd Drwg nuclear facility.

Tracked down by Torchwood, the killer calmly drops eight storeys to his death. But the killings don't stop. Their investigations lead Jack Harkness, Gwen Cooper and Toshiko Sato to a monster in a bathroom, a mystery at an army base and a hunt for stolen nuclear fuel rods. Meanwhile, Owen Harper goes missing from the Hub, when a game in *Second Reality* leads him to an old girlfriend…

Something is coming, forcing its way through the Rift, straight into Cardiff Bay.

Featuring Captain Jack Harkness as played by John Barrowman, with Gwen Cooper, Owen Harper, Toshiko Sato and Ianto Jones as played by Eve Myles, Burn Gorman, Naoki Mori and Gareth David-Lloyd, in the hit series created by Russell T Davies for BBC Television.

TORCHWOOD

SLOW DECAY
Andy Lane

ISBN 978 0 563 48655 8
UK £6.99 US$11.99/$14.99 CDN

When Torchwood track an energy surge to a Cardiff nightclub, the team finds the police are already at the scene. Five teenagers have died in a fight, and lying among the bodies is an unfamiliar device. Next morning, they discover the corpse of a Weevil, its face and neck eaten away, seemingly by human teeth. And on the streets of Cardiff, an ordinary woman with an extraordinary hunger is attacking people and eating her victims.

The job of a lifetime it might be, but working for Torchwood is putting big strains on Gwen's relationship with Rhys. While she decides to spice up their love life with the help of alien technology, Rhys decides it's time to sort himself out – better music, healthier food, lose some weight. Luckily, a friend has mentioned Doctor Scotus's weight-loss clinic…

Featuring Captain Jack Harkness as played by John Barrowman, with Gwen Cooper, Owen Harper, Toshiko Sato and Ianto Jones as played by Eve Myles, Burn Gorman, Naoki Mori and Gareth David-Lloyd, in the hit series created by Russell T Davies for BBC Television.